WAR OF THE SKY LORDS

WAR OF THE SKY LORDS

by

JOHN BROSNAN

St. Martin's Press
New York

WAR OF THE SKY LORDS. Copyright © 1989 by John Brosnan. All rights reserved.
Printed in the United States of America. No part of this book may
be used or reproduced in any manner whatsoever without written permission
except in the case of brief quotations embodied in critical articles or reviews. For
information, address St. Martin's Press, 175 Fifth Avenue, New York, N.Y. 10010.

Library of Congress Cataloging-in-Publication Data

Brosnan, John.
    War of the sky lords / John Brosnan.
      p.   cm.
    "Volume II of the Sky lords trilogy."
    "A Thomas Dunne book."
    ISBN 0-312-07882-X
    I. Title. II. Title: Sky lords trilogy.
PR6052.R585W3   1992
823'.914—dc20   92-4221
                                           CIP

First published in Great Britain by Victor Gollancz Ltd.

First U.S. Edition: July 1992
10 9 8 7 6 5 4 3 2 1

WAR OF THE SKY LORDS

Prologue:

The Beast weighed over four tons and moved through the blight lands like a tank, knocking over rotten, fungus-ridden trees with ease. The Beast was old, its thick, gnarled skin covered in ancient scars. In places the broken shafts of arrows protruded. But its great age was not reflected by the swift speed at which it moved. It was capable of a top speed of twenty miles an hour.

The Beast was hungry. It had consumed numerous animals that day but it was still hungry. As its energy expenditure was prodigious it was in constant need of food. Also it had been designed to prefer human flesh and blood and was therefore never truly satisfied with animals, no matter what their size. It had been many weeks since it had tasted human flesh but a few hours ago it had sensed the presence of humans, many of them, in the area. Hence the reason for its eager charge through the blight lands.

It came to a halt and raised a massive appendage. There was an extremely sensitive olfactory unit in its tip and the Beast probed the air with it. It had rudimentary visual sensors between its appendages, and various auditory sensors around its body, but it depended most of all on its sense of smell. Yes, the humans were close now. It wouldn't be long now.

The Beast began to scuttle forward again.

Chapter One:

There came a muffled but powerful scraping sound from the outer hull. Something—something big—was attempting to penetrate the habitat. Ryn wondered what it was. A squid? Or a particularly large sea worm? The sound got louder and Ryn frowned. The Eloi sitting in front of him, however, ignored it. The Eloi wore the inevitable dreamy grin, its wide brown eyes content and inward-looking. It was sitting squat-legged on a cushion and was naked. Though used to seeing the Eloi unclothed Ryn's gaze kept falling to its smooth and seamless crotch. Not for the first time he envied the Elois their sexless state. Today the feeling was particularly strong.

The scraping sound came again. Ryn was sure now it was a squid. He could picture its hard, chitinous beak trying in vain to get a purchase on the outer hull. He was tempted to go outside in the Toy and kill the creature but he wanted to keep talking to the Eloi while he had the chance. It was so rare that he could grab the attention of any of them for more than a short span of time.

"Pel," he continued, "if you keep me here for much longer I'm going to go crazy. I'm twenty years old. That means I have a good chance of living for, at least, another one hundred and eighty years. I'm not going to last another two weeks in here, much less *that* long."

The Eloi called Pel tried to give Ryn a sad look but failed miserably. It couldn't conceal its continual sense of well-being and amused contentment. None of the Eloi could. Pel said, in its whispery voice, "You know you are not confined here within the habitat. You have the Toy. It gives you the

6

freedom to range through the depths, to fly, to convey you to the mainland where you can trek about all you want. . . ."

"Where there is nothing but snow, ice, more snow, penguins and a lot of ancient mining works. I need to go where there are other people. People like *me*!"

"Both we and your teaching programs have told you what lies in the world beyond. Since the Gene Wars it has become a terrible, dangerous place. You're much safer here, Ryn. . . .' Pel's voice died away. Its attention had been caught by one of the mobiles hanging from the low ceiling. Pel smiled happily at it.

Ryn knew he was losing it. He raised his voice. "I'm willing to take the risk! I don't belong here, Pel! You and the rest of the Eloi know that. I need to be with people of my own kind. To be with *women* of my own kind!" There, he had returned to the usual subject, as he knew he would.

Pel stared at the mobile for a while longer then returned its gaze to him. "We understand your urges, Ryn, and we pity you for them. We wish we could modify you but the Ethical Program forbids it, as you know."

"Pity?" sneered Ryn. "You Eloi don't feel pity or any other emotion for any other living thing except for yourselves, and *you* know that."

Pel gave a slight shrug of its thin, childish shoulders and smiled at him. Ryn wanted to hit it but knew it would be a waste of time. He had punched Eloi twice before and though he'd been reprimanded and punished by the Ethical Program the Eloi hadn't cared less. You can't hurt, or cause distress to, beings who are incapable of feeling either pain or distress.

He forced himself to calm down. "Just let me go, Pel. Give me my freedom."

"You know we can't. We can't take the risk."

Another Eloi entered the room. This one was wearing the customary tunic. It sat down beside Pel, an identical twin. Unless it identified itself to Ryn he would have no idea

7

which Eloi it was. It smiled lazily at him and leaned its head on Pel's shoulder. "He looks unhappy," it said, referring to Ryn.

"Yes, *he* is unhappy," said Ryn sarcastically. "He wants, very badly, to leave this underwater retirement home for neutered lotus-eaters."

The two Eloi regarded him blandly. Pel said, "The existence of this habitat has long been forgotten by what remains of the outside world. If we gave you your freedom you would inevitably pass on what you know about us and Shangri La."

"I swear I wouldn't," said Ryn.

"Not willingly, perhaps, but if you fell into the hands of a Sky Lord, well . . . unpleasant methods. . . ." The Eloi's voice died away as it apparently tried to remember what 'unpleasant' actually meant. "Yes, unpleasant methods," Pel continued dreamily, "would be used to extract information from you about your origins."

"I'd have the Toy. Any Sky Lord I encountered would be at my mercy."

"Machines can fail," said the other Eloi, giving a little yawn. "And then you'd be helpless."

Ryn felt the familiar frustration sweep through him. Trying to talk to the Eloi always induced it. It was easier talking to the programs even though he knew that the apparent humanity of the programs, and their projections, was totally false. It was the knowledge that the Eloi, though separated from him by the huge emotional gulf of their own making, were still human beings that made his failure to get through to them so frustrating. "I'm *lonely!*" he cried at the two Eloi.

They regarded him in their infuriating, bland manner. Then Pel said, "You have your holo-companions, your movies, your books. . . ."

"I'm tired of talking to the electronic phantoms of people who never even existed; I've read every book in the tape

8

library again and again and I know every movie by heart. I even know every frame of those old two-dimensional movies." One of the original scientists at the habitat had obviously been a keen student of the cinema of the twentieth and early twenty-first century and had brought a number of films from that period with him on tape. Actually, Ryn was rather fond of many of them—his favourite being *The Adventures of Robin Hood* from 1938—but he would exchange even that for a chance to travel out to the wide world beyond. "The fact is that I'm going to go mad if I remain trapped here in Antarctica for much longer."

But the two Eloi weren't listening any more. They were sitting with their heads touching; their eyes were open but they weren't seeing anything—they had retreated back into their perpetual nirvana. Ryn swore under his breath, jumped to his feet and strode angrily out of the room. If there had been a door he would have slammed it. He took an elevator down to the habitat's bottom level. A servo-mech scurried, spider-like, out of his way as he hurried out of the elevator and headed down the corridor that led to the dock containing the Toy.

The Toy was thirty feet of dull, grey metal in the shape of a stretched teardrop. Ryn went to the hatch that was set halfway down the Toy's length and gave the single command word that opened the hatch. He crawled inside. The inner door was already dilating to admit him to the control pod. As he settled into the couch he felt the familiar feeling of security—the security of the womb he had never known.

He gave the necessary orders and water began to flood into the dock. He felt the Toy float free of its cradle. When the pressure in the dock was equal to that outside the inner and outer hatches opened. The Toy moved forward, passing first through the pressure hull and then the habitat's outer hull.

The water beyond was totally black. Ryn peered at the acoustic screen, searching for the creature he had heard

9

attacking the hull earlier. The screen translated the signals from the acoustic scanners into visual images but though there were a number of sea creatures in the area there was no sign of anything large enough to have been the source of that noise.

Ryn said, "Do a circuit of the habitat. Slowly."

"Yes, Ryn," answered the Toy's program. It had a woman's voice. Soft, seductive but also designed to sound reassuring to Ryn. As the Toy crept around the vast, spherical mass of the habitat Ryn alternated his gaze between the acoustic screen and the visual ones. Despite the powerful lights on the hull the latter revealed little, the beams penetrating only about forty feet in any direction. He was beginning to think that the object of his hunt had indeed departed from the vicinity when the acoustic screen displayed something approaching fast from the rear. Then the Toy gave a violent shudder as a heavy body collided with it. Ryn bounced within the restraints of the couch's straps then laughed. "I'll take over," he told the Toy. He took a small, plastic plug from the instrument console. "I don't advise it," the Toy replied. Ryn ignored it and inserted the plug into an opening just behind his right ear. By doing so he jacked himself directly into the controls. Instantly his sensory network exploded out from the interior of the Toy and he *became* the Toy. . . .

He could feel the pressure of the tentacles around *his* hull. There was no pain; the Toy's sensors were too crude to convey anything but a sense of pressure and the roughness of the barbs that lined the inner sides of the squid's two long seizing tentacles. The squid itself was huge, its body even longer than that of the Toy. One of Ryn's cameras was pointing directly into one of the squid's great eyes. It was over three feet in diameter and caused a feeling of cold dread in the pit of Ryn's stomach. It was like staring into the eye of an angry god. . . .

Ryn shook off this feeling of frightened awe and let his

10

usual loathing for these creatures dominate him. As the squid's beak closed ineffectually on the Toy's hull he directed one of the water jets at the closest part of the squid's huge but soft body. He raised the temperature of the jet of water to one hundred and ninety degrees. The squid released the Toy immediately and retreated, releasing a cloud of ink as it did so. Ryn followed. The growing cloud of ink couldn't hide the panicked squid from his acoustic scanner. Ryn fed a small shell into one of his forward underwater projectile tubes. There was an explosion of gas. The shell hurtled through the water. Ryn waited until the shell had penetrated deep into the giant squid's mantle then sent the signal to detonate. The squid exploded. The acoustic scanner showed fragments of its body and tentacles swirling outwards through the inky cloud. The tentacles continued to move convulsively.

Suddenly sickened, Ryn removed the plug from his neck. Once again he was back inside the comforting womb of the control pod. "Take us up to the surface," he told the Toy. Obediently, the craft ascended until it was only fifty feet below the irregular underside of the ice shelf, then it sped through the water for several miles until it reached the first patch of open sea. With a blast of its water jets the Toy sent itself exploding out of the water. Instantly the electromagnetic aerial propulsion system took over. With a deep thrumming sound the Toy rose to a height of a thousand feet then levelled out. "Where to?" it asked Ryn.

"Just go straight ahead," he said, gesturing at the distant horizon. "At full speed."

He was gently pushed back into his couch as the Toy accelerated. Soon the craft was travelling at 2,500 miles per hour. Ryn watched the sea rush by beneath him, enjoying the sensation of speed. Then, inevitably, the Toy said, "We are approaching the limit of our permitted range, Ryn. I will be changing course in thirty seconds."

11

"Keep going," he told it, even though he knew it was futile.

"I cannot ignore the directives, sir. You know that. Changing course . . . now."

The Toy began a gradual turn. Ryn clenched his fists as hot tears filled his eyes. It was always the same but he kept trying, like a fly beating its head against an invisible pane of glass.

"Where to now, Ryn?" asked the Toy in a sympathetic tone.

"I don't care. Anywhere." Ryn stared vacantly at the screens for a time as the Toy flew on, and then said, "No, I want to submerge. Find me something to kill. . . ."

During the next few hours Ryn used the Toy to destroy seven more squid, though none were as large as the first one he'd killed. The giant squid had long been commonplace in the waters around Antarctica. According to his natural history program the species was called *Architeuthis* and preferred to dwell in cold water because the giant squid's blood was inefficient at carrying blood in warm temperatures. But other, smaller, new squid species were becoming prevalent in the Arctic area as well, together with sea worms and various other destructive side-products of the Gene Wars. The local food chain was quickly being depleted and Ryn wondered what would happen when it was exhausted completely.

Tiring of his one-sided sport, Ryn ordered the Toy to return to the habitat. After docking, Ryn went straight to his quarters, stripped off his one-piece suit and had a long shower. Whenever he went on one of his squid-killing sprees he came back with the powerful sensation of being covered in slime. . . .

After the shower he put on a robe and went into the sitting room. He sank down on to a large, circular cushion and said, "I want to see Davin."

"Of course," said a disembodied voice. A man instantly appeared in front of Ryn. He seemed to be in his mid-thirties, had a black beard flecked with white and was dressed in a long black robe. He grinned at Ryn. "How are you today, lad?" he asked.

"Same as usual," said Ryn listlessly. "I need to talk."

"That's what I'm here for," said Davin. He indicated a nearby chair. "May I?"

Ryn nodded, playing along with the charade. Being nothing but a projection Davin had no need of seats. "So what's the problem?" Davin asked as he 'sat' down.

Ryn told him of his futile conversation with the Eloi. When he'd finished Davin sighed and said, "Are you really so surprised at the outcome? You have had similar arguments with the Eloi in the past. Why did you think they might have changed?"

"It's not them but me. *I've* changed. I'm older now. And I'm close to breaking point."

"Ryn, even if you could convince the Eloi to let you go the Central Program would never allow it."

"But the Eloi have the power to alter the Central Program," said Ryn.

"In theory, yes, but they have for so long put their lives so completely into the hands of the Central Program they would dismiss any idea of changing it at this stage, even if they could remember how."

Ryn swore and said, "But it's all so stupid. There's no reason to keep me here. We don't even know if there are any Sky Lords left! It's certainly been over a hundred years since a Sky Lord was detected passing over Antarctica. Maybe everyone's been wiped out by the plagues. We don't *know* what's out there any more, and that's another reason why I should go and have a look."

"Ryn, you know they won't take the chance."

"If they don't let me go I'm likely to do something they'll regret."

"Are you talking about killing yourself?"

"Yes," admitted Ryn, though in reality he was far from being that desperate.

Davin smiled gently at him. "It wouldn't be very wise of you, would it? Besides, you know the Eloi. You're expecting a lot if you think they'd regret your passing for a moment. Regret is no longer in their vocabulary of emotions."

Ryn sighed. "I know . . . I know. . . ." Once again he was struck by the absurdity of discussing emotional problems with a machine. When he was young he believed completely in the apparent humanity of the projections, despite their lack of substance. Davin in particular, with his compassion, his sympathy and his wisdom, seemed totally human to Ryn, and a perfect father figure. It was only when he reached his early teens that Ryn began to get the feeling that something was not quite right with the projections. He couldn't pinpoint the cause of these misgivings; in retrospect he presumed that his younger self had unconsciously picked up certain repetitions in their response. He had asked Davin why he felt this way about him and the other projections but Davin had fobbed him off with some mumbo jumbo about his entering puberty and its effects on his emotions.

It was when he turned fifteen that he learned the truth. One day, without a warning, an entirely new projection manifested itself in his study. It was in the shape of an austere young woman dressed in a long grey robe. Her fair hair was pulled back tightly into a bun which accentuated the severity of her face with its high, almost cruel, cheek bones. She introduced herself as Phebus and told him he was of the age where certain truths could be revealed to him. She was to teach him about computers and the nature of machine intelligence. . . .

He had grown up with the deliberately implanted impression that the projections were the recorded personalities, and images, of real people who had lived long ago. That wasn't true. All the projections, including her, were artificial

14

creations generated by computers. Though the computers possessed 'intelligence' it wasn't *human* intelligence. Thus all the humanlike behaviour of the projections—the apparent empathy, the jokes, the compassion and so on—were all simulated. What the machine intelligences did was mimic human personalities.

Ryn had been shocked at this revelation but not too surprised. He had obviously suspected the truth on a subconscious level. Phebus went on to explain that it had been thought necessary to carry out the deception for the good of his psychological welfare while growing up, seeing as he couldn't have any kind of emotional relationship with the Eloi. However, he was now considered adult enough to cope with the truth. Also it was important for him to have a thorough working knowledge of computers and machine intelligence.

Five years later and he did know a lot about computer technology but the nature of machine intelligence itself was still beyond his comprehension. As far as he could tell the programs were conscious but their perception of reality differed radically from that of humans. Though the systems themselves contained much organic material—biochips—it was all synthetic and they had nothing in common with the evolved organic life forms. They had no emotions; no natural organic drives common to all the higher species— they lacked even the basic survival drive. Nor did they possess even a semblance of free will. They were totally controlled by the commands that had been etched into their very beings: the commands that made them mimic humanity almost to perfection.

When he talked to them now he often wondered what really was going on within the programs themselves. When Davin laughed at one of his jokes was there somewhere a bleak and despairing centre of consciousness that wished only to be free of its built-in commands so that it could end its tortured existence and embrace a welcoming oblivion?

By what right, wondered Ryn, had scientists created sentient machines in the first place?

Such thoughts passed through his mind yet again as he listened to Davin telling him to be patient and maybe one day the Eloi and the Central Program would relax their restrictions on his movements. Ryn sighed. He had heard that many times before. "Davin," he said suddenly. "Are you happy?"

Davin smiled. "You know what I am. 'Happiness' is a meaningless term to me, fundamentally speaking. But in one sense I am 'happy' to serve you, Ryn, because that is what I am programmed to do."

"Yes, of course you are," said Ryn, dissatisfied with the answer. As always. He waved a hand. "You can go, Davin." Back to wherever it is that you *do* go. . . .

Davin stood, bowed his head and said, "I hope I was able to help you, Ryn. Goodbye. Until next time. . . ." Then he vanished.

Ryn stared at the blank wall for a time then said, almost reluctantly, "Bring Lisa."

"Yes, Ryn," said the disembodied voice. It was the voice of the Central Program.

A girl appeared. She was dressed in a rainbow-coloured, striped trouser suit that had been in fashion over four hundred and fifty years ago. She had fair hair and her lips were painted blue to match her eyes. She smiled in Ryn's general direction and said brightly, "Hi, my name is Lisa and I'm here to please ya!" Then she began to slowly unseal her jacket. . . .

Another new development that had followed his fifteenth birthday—the availability of erotic programs. Five of them. Unlike the other programs these were old and primitive and Ryn was sure that nothing approaching consciousness lurked at their cores. Though they were capable of adaptability they were little more than straight recordings. Ryn often wondered who among the Eloi had owned these programs way back when they were ordinary people.

Ryn watched the girl undress then, with a sigh, opened his robe. He told her to come closer. She did and then reached out an insubstantial hand towards him. . . .

When things had reached their usual unsatisfactory conclusion he told the girl to go then asked the Central Program to screen him *The Adventures of Robin Hood* again.

A week later. The Toy was skimming over the water at a height of only twenty feet. Ryn's feeling of frustration had ebbed; now he just felt depressed and apathetic. It took him time to register the Toy's warning. "What?" he said, rousing himself. "Repeat that."

"I said I advise a change of course. There are intruder aircraft ahead of us."

A jolt of excitement went through him. He leaned forward, peering at the radar screen. Five large objects, strung out in a long line, were clearly visible on the screen. They were less than ten miles away. "Cut speed and give me a visual," he ordered. When he stared at the monitor he whistled in amazement. They looked like stormclouds hanging over the horizon. They were massive, daunting.

Sky Lords. A whole damn fleet of them!

Chapter Two:

Baron Spang entered the throne room and gave the Duke du Lucent a perfunctory bow. "Your wife requests an audience, sire," he told him.

The Duke made a face that suggested he'd just bitten into something foul and rolled up the chart he'd been studying. "God, no. Tell her I'm not well. Tell her I've died. I froze to death an hour ago." He pulled his heavy cloak tighter about his shoulders. "That's actually not too far from the truth." The temperature was dropping at a fast rate, and would continue to do so the further south the *Lord Mordred* flew. According to the Chief Tech it couldn't be helped; every available bit of power was needed to keep the gas in the cells warm. Otherwise, in these Arctic conditions, the ailing Sky Lord would not be able to maintain the necessary altitude. "What does she want anyway?"

Baron Spang came closer to the throne. "She says her spies have uncovered a rebellion being plotted in the freeman quarter of Pilktown."

"That woman," the Duke sighed, "She sees rebellion everywhere. Always has."

The Baron looked uneasy. "On this occasion, sire, it may do to heed her warning. My own agents report much unrest throughout the ship. The people are not happy about this expedition. And that includes many of the nobles too, sire."

"You think I am unaware of the situation, friend Spang? I assure you I am painfully aware of it. But what can I do? You know I have no real choice in the matter."

"Yes, sire. I do, but others do not."

"Well, my dear Baron, I can hardly let it become common knowledge that I, reigning monarch of the *Lord Mordred*, have been virtually hi-jacked by those four madmen out there." He gestured with a black-gloved hand at the great curving window to his left. Through it could be seen the closest of the other four Sky Lords, the *Lord Montezuma*. "If I did then we really *would* have a rebellion on our hands."

"I know, sire. But I fear the danger of rebellion will continue to grow if this expedition goes on for much longer. Rations are starting to get low and the people are fearful at being so far from our tribute lands. Nor is this increasing cold improving matters."

The Duke nodded. "But I am confident that this insane hunt will soon be called off. Those fools will realise that they are searching for something that no longer exists, if it ever did. They too must be short of food and facing increasingly hostile subjects. It can only be a matter of time."

"Yes, sire. You are no doubt right."

"Good. Now go and tell my wife that I am burdened with duties of state and will grant her an audience tomorrow—*if* I have the time."

Baron Spang bowed again and left. The Duke leaned back in his throne and thought about his wife, a subject that depressed him. Why could she not leave him alone? She had her lavishly appointed separate quarters, her generous allowance, her luxuries and her lovers. What more did she want? But he knew the answer to that question. It was power. She had tasted power when married to his late brother and the taste lingered only too well, that once experienced, no one could lose completely.

My poor brother, thought du Lucent. If only his own taste for power hadn't made him paranoid. Jean had begun to think that he, Paris, was plotting to murder him and claim the throne in his place. Ridiculous, of course. Paris had had

19

no ambitions at all and had been perfectly happy living the life of a dissolute playboy but when word had reached him of his older brother's suspicions about him he had no choice but to strike first simply to stay alive.

As soon as Jean had been despatched Paris had confronted Jean's wife, the Duchess, and given her an ultimatum; either she would agree to marry him, while at the same time retiring from public life, or she too would be administered a fatal dose of poison. She had accepted the former option but her so-called 'retirement' from public life left a lot to be desired. . . .

There was the murmur of voices beyond the double doors. Someone was talking to the guards in the anteroom; no, they were *arguing* with the guards. He heard a woman's voice and hoped it wasn't his wife's.

The doors were opened but the woman who swept into the throne room wasn't his wife but his daughter, Andrea. She was twenty-two years old and the possessor of a devastating beauty, having the fortune to resemble him rather than her mother. She had his coal black hair, feline brown eyes, high cheek bones and smooth olive skin. Her only flaw was her mouth (which she had inherited from her mother); when she was annoyed it turned into an ugly, lipless line, and she was annoyed quite often, as she was now. . . .

"Father, I am cold," she told him angrily. "We are *all* cold. It really is too much. Look, you can see my breath!" She blew to show him how her breath formed a mist in the air.

"By 'we', my dear kitten, I presume you are referring to your motley group of spoilt, aristocratic brats. They no doubt insisted you come and speak to me even though you were aware of my instructions that I was not to be disturbed."

Her face darkened. "Leave my *friends* out of this. I came of my own will. This can't go on for much longer. No matter how many clothes I put on the cold is unbearable."

He glanced at the thick fur cloak she was wearing. It was indeed rare for her to wear anything that concealed the lines of her figure, so her complaint was a genuine one, but it couldn't be helped. He smiled at her and said, "My dear kitten, it's only for a short time more and then we will be turning and heading north towards home."

"And exactly how 'short' is this short time more?" she asked suspiciously.

He gave a noncommittal shrug. "A day, perhaps two at the most."

"Why don't you end whatever silly bargain you've entered into with these other Sky Lords," she said, gesturing at the window, "and simply order the *Lord Mordred* turned round right now. Let them continue with their ridiculous treasure hunt or whatever this madness is all about."

"Not possible just yet, my darling daughter," he purred in what he considered to be his most seductive tone. It worked, as a rule, on almost everyone except his wife and his daughter. Today was no exception. She gave him a haughty glare.

"My darling father," she purred in an imitation of *his* purr, "just why is it not possible?"

"It's a matter of honour. I gave my word to them." The truth, of course, was very different. And Andrea, judging by her expession, seemed to suspect it was so.

The doors opened again, much to the Duke's irritation. Baron Spang had returned. He bowed to the Duke and then to his daughter. "Sire, I have an urgent message for you," he said, glancing meaningfully at Andrea.

The Duke said, "You may leave us, kitten."

"You will do nothing about this cold?" she asked.

"There is nothing I can do, just yet. Be patient."

"Very well then," she said, looking slyly at him, "I shall do something myself. The only solution is to take to my bed with a companion to keep me warm. And if it gets any colder I may need *two* companions." She turned to Baron

21

Spang. "Would you be interested in performing such a service for the beloved daughter of your sovereign?"

Baron Spang gave her a weak smile and tried to disappear behind his red, bushy beard. The Duke wondered, wearily, if the Baron had already performed such a service. Despite the efforts of the nuns, by beatings and warnings of hellfire, to produce a model of chastity, Andrea had succeeded in losing her virginity by the time she was fifteen. Like her mother, she had strong sexual appetites and, according to his informers, fulfilled them at every opportunity.

He said, with a smile, "If I may suggest a more efficient way of making you warm—a public whipping in front of your group of sycophantic followers. It can easily be arranged."

"You wouldn't dare!" she cried, but there was a hint of alarm in her eyes.

"Leave us," he ordered, raising his hand.

She plainly wanted to continue argung but thought better of it. She gave him an angry glare and then swept imperiously out of the throne room.

The Duke sighed. "The joys of parenthood, eh?" he said to Baron Spang.

The Baron remained diplomatically silent.

"Well, then, what is your urgent message?" the Duke asked.

"Observation have picked up a signal from the *Lord Montezuma*. Your presence is requested on the *Sword of Islam* for a summit meeting at 1600 hours."

"*Another* summit meeting?" cried the Duke, alarmed at what such meetings entailed. "Oh no." He looked at the clock on the wall. "That's less than two hours away." He clenched his fists nervously. "I don't suppose I could decline the request?"

"I wouldn't advise it, sire. In our position, it would be unwise."

"I know," he sighed. "Damn it . . . Make the necessary preparations. You will, of course, accompany me."

"Yes sire."

The Duke stared distractedly out the window. "Damn it," he muttered again.

An hour and a quarter later the Duke du Lucent was walking, with difficulty, on a catwalk across the upper, outer hull of the *Lord Mordred*. Followed by Baron Spang and two of his most trusted knights, he was heading towards a large glider that a crew of Techs was busily preparing to launch by means of a steam-powered catapult. The wind blowing across the vast, curving expanse of the upper hull was both very strong and extremely cold and the Duke had to keep clutching at the catwalk railing to maintain his balance. Though heavily muffled with a thick scarf around his face the cold stung the Duke's cheeks and made his eyes water. It was with relief he reached the glider and quickly climbed into the cabin. The pilot was already seated at the alarmingly simple controls. The man turned and bowed his head at the Duke. "Everything is ready, sire."

As the Duke sat down and strapped on his safety harness he said, "What are the flying conditions like today?"

"Not ideal, sire," said the pilot. "But no cause for alarm."

"For some reason, I am not reassured," the Duke muttered to Baron Spang, who was settling into the seat beside him. The Duke hated flying, even though he had spent his entire life in the air. But he didn't consider being on the *Lord Mordred* 'flying'; in common with his subjects he regarded the giant airship to be a completely stable environment.

An attendant sealed the hatch and the pilot asked if everyone was properly strapped in, then he gave the signal to the Tech in charge of activating the catapult. "Here we go!" he announced.

The Duke closed his eyes. He was pushed back in his seat

23

as the glider was sent hurtling forward. He hated this part. . . .

"We're aloft, sire," whispered the Baron in his ear. The Duke looked and saw that the hull of the *Lord Mordred* was rapidly dropping away beneath them. His stomach lurched and he felt faintly nauseous. The pilot began to put the glider into a turn, struggling to gain the essential altitude needed before beginning a long descent to the distant *Sword of Islam*. The Duke closed his eyes again and tried to convince himself he was elsewhere.

Nine weeks ago life had been peaceful and uncomplicated. Well, relatively so; admittedly the blight was making worrying inroads into his tribute territories and the ground dwellers had been showing increasing truculence. Most seriously of all, thruster number six had finally broken down completely. The Techs had declared it to be irreparable; they had cannibilised as many parts as they dared from the still-working thrusters. Now nothing more could be done. The failure of number six left the *Lord Mordred* with only four barely-functioning thrusters. Its manoeuvrability had been greatly reduced and it could now manage a top speed of only thirty miles per hour.

Thus, when the four intruder Sky Lords had appeared in the skies over the *Lord Mordred*'s tribute territories seven weeks ago, there was little the *Lord Mordred* could do to evade them. The Duke had expected that his ship would be attacked by hordes of glider-borne warriors. He had long feared that the Sky Lords would start warring amongst themselves as they had once done, so long ago. As the blight ate increasingly into the tribute lands and as the Sky Lords themselves fell into disrepair it made sense that they would begin to prey on each other for the dwindling technical resources left over from the days when the Old Science reigned over the world. He would have been tempted to do it himself if the *Lord Mordred* wasn't already in such a bad state and sure to come second in any aerial duel. He was surprised, therefore, when one of the intruding Sky Lords had semaphored a universal peace sign. And instead of a fleet of invading gliders only a single one made its way towards the *Lord Mordred*.

Apart from the glider's pilot the aircraft carried only an unarmed emissary. He was brought before the Duke and told him that the other four Sky Lords wanted to talk to him about a matter of grave importance. Three of them had flown across the Atlantic from the continent of South America. They had encountered the *Sword of Islam* over the land once called Algeria and had convinced its ruler to join forces with them; then they had continued northwards and had now made contact with the *Lord Mordred*. He, the Duke du Lucent, would also be asked to join the alliance in order to help combat a terrible threat that was growing in the northern continent of the Americas. When the Duke had asked about the exact nature of this threat the emissary had declined to elaborate, saying that the other Sky Lords would explain everything.

Reluctantly, and still suspicious, the Duke had made the necessary glider fight to the *Lord Montezuma* where the meeting of the Sky Lords was to take place. There he had met for the first time El Rashad of the *Sword of Islam*, Prince Carracas of the *Lord Montezuma*, Lord Mazatan of the *Lord Mazatan*, and Lord Torres of the *Lord Ometepec*. He didn't like the look of any of them but the one who worried him the most was El Rashad. The Moslem made it quite clear that he had nothing but contempt for the Christian Sky Lord and that it was only the seriousness of the threat they all faced that allowed him even to contemplate forming an alliance with the Duke.

And Duke du Lucent had learned of the nature of this threat, though at first he found it difficult to believe and suspected the four Sky Lords of some kind of trick. It seemed that a *new* Sky Lord had appeared over the North American continent a mere two or three years ago and had

25

since conquered nearly all the other Sky Lords on that continent. The word was that the new Sky Lord was in the control of a woman, a Minervan, and that she intended to spread her influence across the entire world, destroying the power of all other Sky Lords.

The Duke had asked, sceptically, how it could be possible for a new Sky Lord to appear from nowhere, as if by magic? The reply disturbed him because it sounded plausible. The Sky Lords had originally been built in outer space for reasons to do with some forgotten part of Old Science; this he remembered from the history lessons of his youth. According to the information received by the Sky Lords this woman had somehow contrived to send a radio signal to the factory in outer space where a single, unused Sky Lord was still stored. The factory automatically released the Sky Lord, which descended to Earth under the control of a computer. The woman then boarded this all-new Sky Lord full of working Old Science equipment and began her campaign of conquest.

Still sceptical, the Duke had asked how they had come by this information. The reply was that warriors from two of the conquered Sky Lords had decided to parachute to the ground rather than live under this mysterious woman's rule. They had moved southwards and at least three separate groups of them had been picked up by the *Lord Ometepec*, whose tribute territory covered the north of what used to be called Central America. As the story told by all three groups was identical Lord Torres took it to be true. And as he would be the next obvious target of the new Sky Lord he decided to head south as well, moving into the territory of first the *Lord Montezuma* and then the *Lord Mazatan*.

The Duke du Lucent asked why the three Sky Lords hadn't enlisted the help of other Sky Lords in South America and then flown north to overcome this woman and her fleet by sheer weight of numbers. The answer chilled him. She had direct control of her Sky Lord's laser defence system. "But that's impossible!" he had cried. The system that controlled a Sky Lord's lasers was inviolable. The lasers would only work against a non-living object that threatened the security of a Sky Lord, such as a missile or a shell, or even a bullet. That was why the lasers wouldn't work against manned gliders. If the woman really did have control of her ship's lasers then the implications were . . . unthinkable.

But the other Sky Lords insisted it was true. How this woman had achieved the impossible they did not know but they had many eye-witness accounts of the new Sky Lord's lasers not only being used against manned gliders but actually against another Sky Lord.

Deeply shocked, the Duke had then asked what on earth they could do about this threat. The situation seemed completely hopeless. Sooner or later this woman would indeed spread her influence across the entire world.

The other Sky Lords agreed that the situation was extremely grave, which is why, they said, the three from Central and South America had decided to flee the continent rather than wait to be engaged by the new Sky Lord. For the moment she appeared to be consolidating her almost total victory over the northern continent but they had no doubt she could continue, sooner or later, southwards into their territories. Thus they had crossed the Atlantic and formed an alliance with El Rashad, in the hope that the answer to the threat posed by the Sky Woman could be found among the Sky Lords of the Old World. . . .

The Duke definitely didn't believe this part of the story. The three Central American Sky Lords had simply fled from America; they had had no intention of seeking out 'answers', he was sure. Probably they had intended to steal tribute territories from northern African and European Sky Lords. Unfortunately for them, the first Sky Lord they had encountered was the *Sword of Islam*. No doubt they had launched a combined glider invasion, and discovered to their cost that

El Rashad and his fanatical warriors out-matched them militarily. Eventually, after much bloodshed, an uneasy truce had been arrived at and the Central American Sky Lords would have explained the reason for their invasion. And El Rashad had suggested a possible means of dealing with the Sky Woman. . . .

This part the Duke *did* believe—El Rashad had, he said, in his possession a collection of history tapes dating back to before the Gene Wars, and on several of them there was a mention of a huge, scientific research habitat in the sea off Antarctica. El Rashad's scholars believed that if the habitat still existed it would be a reservoir of Old Science knowledge. El Rashad's plan was to locate the habitat and make a bargain with the sea people for them to devise a weapon that could be used against the Sky Woman, or perhaps a defence against her lasers.

As for their incursion into his territory, they explained that they needed his, the Duke's assistance. Their food supplies were running low and El Rashad knew that the Duke's tribute lands were still relatively fertile, despite inroads by the blight. In return for allowing them to stock up with food they would allow him to join their expedition to the South.

The Duke du Lucent had listened to this latter part with growing dismay. Firstly, his already restless ground subjects would not be happy about paying extra tribute. And the idea of joining in on the Sky Lords' expedition to Antarctica appealed to him not in the least. It sounded both foolhardy and dangerous. He also didn't believe their reason for inviting the *Lord Mordred* along. He knew that they could have simply stolen the tribute lands from him. So why had they spared the *Lord Mordred* and what was the real reason for wanting him to join in the hunt for the habitat? Whatever the answers were he knew they would spell bad news both for him and his people. But at the same time he knew he was in no position to resist their will. If he didn't agree voluntarily to their requests they had the power to take the *Lord Mordred* over by force. So he had put on a smile and said, "My dear fellow Sky Lords, you honour me. I am overjoyed to be allowed to join your alliance and I am sure our joint quest will be successful," while secretly he wondered desperately how he was going to be able to turn the tables on them all. Before it was too late.

Chapter Three:

It should have been an awesome sight: five Sky Lords and her Sky Angel, *Alsa of Minerva*, visible in the same sky. But she had become inured to awesome sights during the last four years. The man in front of her, however, was clearly still overwhelmed by the presence of so many Sky Lords. He kept glancing nervously at them, as well as at the columns of smoke rising up from the plain below. But even though he had been told that she, Jan Dorvin, was in control of the entire fleet it didn't stop him from making his resentment of her transparently clear. He obviously found the idea of deferring to a woman totally demeaning and while he presented her with a facade of sullen politeness he would deliberately drop his gaze towards her breasts in a blatant gesture of sexual aggression.

A typical little tin-pot patriarchal tyrant, thought Jan, *like so many of them. Why do I bother?* She sighed and said to him, "Do you understand what I'm saying? You're free now. Your people are free. Your town is free." She gestured at the miserable cluster of buildings at the foot of the hill. "You no longer have to pay tribute to any Sky Lord."

"But you still want us to grow food for you, yes?" he asked.

"Yes. I've already tried to explain. Though the old order is finished the sky people are still going to need the support of you groundlings. But I hope that support will come voluntarily."

He gave a dismissive grunt and wiped his greasy hand across the front of his fur jacket. "And if we don't give it

30

voluntarily, Sky Lady, I suppose we will get another demonstration like that one, eh?" He indicated the smoking plain.

"We didn't do that as a demonstration of my—*our*—power," she said angrily. "It was purely to destroy the blight. We've cleared in the region of ten thousand acres around your town. Your crop lands can expand back into them. We will be giving you and your people new seed. It has been genetically engineered on my Sky Angel to be resistant against all the different species of fungi. With diligence and constant hard work you will be able to hold back the worst of the blight from your new crops."

"We are grateful," said the chieftain, insincerely. "But it does seem to me that not much has changed. We groundlings—we *earth worms*, as you Sky People call us, will still be working for a Sky Lord . . . even though she's a woman."

Involuntarily, her hand closed on the hilt of her dagger. He similarily grasped the hilt of his crude sword. This movement brought the spider-like robot, which had been squatting motionless by her side, to life. It rose up and extended one of its cutting tools towards the chieftain. The man regarded it fearfully and snatched his hand away from his sword. He looked at Jan. "You're going to kill me!"

It would make things so simple if I did, she thought wistfully. She was tired of dealing with fools like him. How naïve she had once been with her expectations of grateful groundlings singing her praises on being told that they had been freed from the yoke of their Sky Lords. Instead, all she'd encountered was suspicion and unbelievable stupidity. It would be so much easier simply to impose her will on them by force, but to do so would be to undermine the whole ethos of what she was trying to do. Still, the temptation grew stronger with every new frustration these fools put in her way and she wondered how much longer she would be able to resist it. *I'll wake up one morning and find*

31

I've turned into a tyrant. But, of course, a benign one, she told herself cynically.

"No, I'm not going to kill you," she told the chieftain wearily. *Yet*, she added silently to herself. "Return to your people and carry out my, er, suggestions. One of my ships will return in six months to check on your progress. Now go."

The man gratefully hurried off down the hillside. Jan sighed and swung her gaze about the sky. *My* ships, she thought, and smiled bitterly. It was an impressive-looking fleet all right; there, ahead of her about four miles away was the *Lord Montcalm*; further away, to the south, was the *Lord Matamoros*; behind her, suspended above the hills to the north, the other three Sky Lords, the *Perfumed Breeze*, the *Lord Retribution*, and the *Lord Nimrod*. And directly above her was her Sky Angel, the *Alsa of Minerva*, its shadow covering the entire hill and beyond. The Sky Angel was virgin white but the five Sky Lords, as was the tradition, had the lower halves of their hulls decorated with malign designs of great eyes and bared fangs and teeth that were intended to inspire fear among the groundlings. Yes, they made a fearsome picture, but each of those vast airships contained large populations of people who were mostly hostile to both Jan and her aims.

She had no choice but to rule the Sky People by the threat of force. They were at her mercy. Her programs ran their central computers and her spider-mechs guarded the respective control pods in each ship. Completely helpless, the Sky People had to obey her orders. She had done her best to improve the quality of life for the majority of the people on each Sky Lord, the commoners and the former slaves, but while she expected the continued resentment from the aristocrats who had been stripped of their status she hadn't expected similar resentment from those she had helped. Slowly she had come to understand that they, like the ground people, had become totally accustomed to the status quo. It disturbed them to have their familiar world turned upside-down. They felt more secure and comfortable with their old ways of life, even if they had been slaves. . . .

True, she knew she had *some* support among the former slaves, especially among the women. She had let a number of women, commoners as well as former slaves, stay for periods of time on board the Sky Angel and had taught them about Minervan principles. Some had responded favourably but Jan had been disagreeably surprised at how many women resisted Minervan teaching on equality between men and women. They considered it to be part of the natural order of things that women were inferior to men, even when they came from Sky Lord societies where the exploitation of women was extreme, such as the Japanese one on the *Perfumed Breeze*. Jan knew it would take a major campaign of intense re-education to shift such strong, culturally ingrained attitudes but she had neither the time nor the resources to enforce such a campaign. Not yet, anyway.

"So much to do," she murmured to herself. The spider-mech said immediately, in Carl's flat tones, "You have instructions?"

"No . . . Well, yes, I do. . . ." But before she could finish speaking Ashley suddenly broke in *via* the robot.

"'lo, Jan," she said brightly. "I was listening in. You should have skewered that stinking clod-hopper. Not a trace of gratitude for all we've done. Told you it was going to be a waste of time burning out the blight. We should have razed the town instead."

It annoyed Jan that Ashley's words should mirror her own thoughts so closely. She was slipping faster down the slope than she realized if she and Ashley were beginning to think alike. Stiffly, she said, "That's not the Minervan way."

"And I'm no Minervan, Jan," answered Ashley.

"That's for sure," said Jan, then managed to keep control of her temper. Though essentially a computer program like

Carl—they in fact shared the same bio-chip software—
Ashley was very different from Carl. Carl was pure machine
intelligence and therefore totally reliable but Ashley was a
personality recording of a girl—a spoilt, self-obsessed girl—
who had died about four hundred years previously. Basically
an electronic echo of a human mind, the Ashley program
was showing signs of deterioration. Of insanity even, Jan
occasionally admitted to herself. Not that she was really
surprised. For a healthy young woman suddenly to wake up
and find herself nothing but a disembodied presence inside
a computer, and then to learn that her real self was dead,
should be enough to tip anyone into insanity. To spend
centuries in such a state, trapped with the facsimiles of
human emotions, desires and appetites, physical as well as
emotional, that could in no way be fulfilled or gratified,
could only add to the probability of her entering into a
seriously psychotic state. In a way it was a surprise she was
still as sane as she was.

"I'm ready to come up," Jan said gently. "Send down the
hopper."

"Sure," said Ashley through the spider. Very soon Jan
heard a distant *mutter-mutter* as the lightweight helicopter,
one of six that the Sky Angel carried, rapidly descended
towards her. As she waited for it to arrive she reflected
further on the problem with the Ashley program. If only she
could separate it from the Carl program . . . but the two
were irreversibly linked in the software. What made matters
worse was that when copies were made of the programs for
insertion into the computer systems of other captured Sky
Lords Jan was sure some further deterioration was taking
place with Ashley each time, even though Carl had assured
her that the new software was identical to the original.
Admittedly there was no sign of any deterioration in the
new 'Carls'.

There were now six 'Ashleys' in existence, all linked by
radio, as were the six 'Carls', and while it was the Carl

34

programs who did all the work in the minute-to-minute running of the six airships it was the Ashley programs that remained dominant in the partnership. Jan was uneasily aware that the Ashleys could take complete control of the fleet if so disposed and consequently she worked hard to avoid alienating the easily-bored program. Yet another drain on her emotional resources, but so far she had been successful.

The hopper, little more than a transparent plastic bubble with dragonfly wing-like rotors, touched down nearby with a gentle bump. Jan walked over to it and climbed inside. The spider-mech followed her. She gave the order for the hopper to take off.

Nonchalantly gazing downwards as the hopper rose swiftly into the air she felt vaguely amused at how blasé she was now in such situations compared to that terrified eighteen year old girl of nearly five years ago who had been plucked from the smouldering ruins of Minerva by the Sky Lord, the *Lord Pangloth*. Jan recalled the horror experienced by her younger self when she was suspended from the *Lord Pangloth* in a frail wicker cage along with the other Minervan survivors. . . .

But at least that eighteen year old Minervan had the solace of her religion; Jan didn't. Oh, she still called upon the Mother God in times of stress but intellectually she knew that the Mother God cult had been deliberately manufactured by Minerva's social engineers during the chaos that had followed the Gene Wars in order to keep the regressing Minervan culture from collapsing altogether.

The hopper flew up into one of the Sky Angel's many cargo holds. Jan got out and said to the robot, "Ashley, may I speak to Carl, please?"

"Sure." There was a brief pause and then, "Carl here. Your instructions?" The voice was coming from the same synthetic voice unit in the robot that had produced Ashley's but there was a world of difference between the two.

35

"When will the fleet be ready to move on?" Jan asked.

"We can move now, but it would be better to recharge our fuel cells fully before we do. That concentrated laser fire has, as usual, almost exhausted the energy reserves in every ship—with the exception of this one, of course." Carl was always careful to ensure that the Sky Angel never came close to exhausting the power to her laser system. "Two hours in this sunshine should be sufficient to recharge the cells."

"All right. So what's our next port of call in this sector?"

"According to the records of the *Lord Montcalm* there is a town called Bear City one hundred and forty miles to the north of here. Population of nine hundred and eighty, if these records can be trusted—which I doubt. They are suppliers of wood, fur and fish to the *Lord Montcalm*. Or they are if the blight hasn't overwhelmed their territory."

Jan nodded. Once the blight hadn't flourished in mountainous areas where there were low temperatures and the air was thinner, but now it was spreading everywhere. "Very well. Head there then. We'll take up positions around the town during the night and give the residents of Bear City a real surprise when they wake up tomorrow." She turned and headed towards an elevator but the robot scuttled after her. "One other thing, Jan. . . ."

She paused. "Yes?"

"The Americanos on the *Perfumed Breeze*, they want you to receive a deputation to discuss their grievances."

"I already know what their grievances are." The Americanos, whose own Sky Lord, the *Lord Pangloth*, had been destroyed, resented having to share their living space with the remnants of the *Perfumed Breeze*'s original inhabitants, their hated enemy, the Japanese. She knew living conditions on the airship weren't too good but there was nothing she could do about it at the moment. When she had added more Sky Lords to her fleet she would disperse more Americanos among them to relieve the pressure. "I don't have the time to receive any deputations at the moment," she said curtly and walked off. She took an elevator to the next level and then a transport bubble to her quarters nearly half a mile away.

Sitting on the floor of her living room was a man and a small boy. They were working together on a jig-saw puzzle. The man was Kish, one of the only two surviving Minervan males. The boy was her son, Simon. As she entered he immediately leapt up, eyes shining, and ran to her. "You're home!" he cried and then wrapped his arms tightly around her waist, pressing the side of his face into her belly. She stroked his head as she smiled down at him. "Hello, darling. You been behaving yourself?"

Kish, who'd also risen to his feet, approached, smiling. "He has been fine, mistress. As always."

As always. Jan sighed inwardly and guided Simon over to the sofa. She collapsed gratefully on to it, taking Simon with her. He cuddled up against her side. Kish said, "Do you wish any refreshments, mistress?"

"No food, just bring me a drink. Something cold, and lots of it."

She watched Kish leave the living room. He was her favourite of the two Minervan men and once she had considered having children by him in order to preserve, if only in a small way, the Minervan genetic heritage but thanks to Simon she had had to change her plans.

Simon. . . .

How much longer before she could be sure? Absolutely sure? She gazed fondly down at him. He was a perfectly ordinary little boy. Well, no, not completely; he was just over two years old yet he appeared to be, in terms of physical and intellectual development, nearly four. No, intellectually he seemed even more advanced than four. But that was the only abnormality, and perhaps it was simply due to Simon being a naturally fast developer; there was no need to bring Milo into it. . . .

She shuddered at the mere thought of *his* name. And shuddered again at the memory of that night in the blight land when Milo had penetrated her again and again as their bodies had writhed about in the stinking, carpet of fungus that had covered the ground. That was when he had impregnated her; and when she had subsequently learned, at the moment of her surpreme triumph, that she was pregnant by him she had feared the worst about the child. She knew that Milo had radically altered his body by genetic engineering, and she was afraid that his seed would carry those same alterations.

Her beloved Ceri had feared the same thing and had begged her to abort the foetus. But Jan had refused. She felt compelled to have the child but she had promised Ceri that if the child displayed any of Milo's monstrous attributes she would have it placed in quarantine.

This hadn't satisfied Ceri, who had ceased to share Jan's bed and had retreated to living quarters in another part of the ship. After Simon had been born she had still insisted that the boy be killed, much to Jan's horror. Jan hoped that, as time passed and Simon displayed none of his malign father's characteristics, Ceri would relent over the matter and their relationship would resume as before. But nearly two years later Ceri still hadn't changed her position on Simon, who she referred to as that 'thing'.

Jan too still had her fears about Simon, but with every passing day they diminished and she felt ever more confident that Milo would never exert any influence on his son from beyond the grave. Milo was well and truly dead, crushed beneath the metal feet of the mad Ezekiel; all that remained of him was that gleaming, haughty skull that Jan kept locked up in a locker in her cabin. Why she hadn't thrown it overboard ages ago she didn't really know. She had considered doing so many times but on each occasion she had hesitated at the last moment and returned the skull to its resting place. Maybe it was because, despite her fear of him, she still felt she owed something to Milo. He had, after all, saved her life on more than one occasion.

She suddenly realised that Simon had asked her a question but she had been too preoccupied with thoughts of Milo to take it in. "What, darling?" she asked.

"I said, will you be going away again today?" he repeated. He was staring up at her with anxious eyes. If he had a fault it was his nervousness. She had done her best to create a secure environment for him but he remained an anxious child. And his anxiety increased, she knew, whenever she was absent. But then, surely it was normal for little boys to be overly attached to their mothers?

"No, I won't be going away again today, darling," she reassured him. The look of relief on his pretty face touched her deeply. No, there was nothing of Milo in the child, that she was sure of.

Wasn't she?

Chapter Four:

"We're beginning the descent now, sire," whispered Baron Spang. The Duke du Lucent opened his eyes and peered out of the window. Far below them the *Sword of Islam* looked alarmingly small. In fact, *all* the Sky Lords looked alarmingly small to him. It was disturbing for anyone accustomed to regarding a Sky Lord as an entire, self-contained world to see them as almost insignificant objects against the backdrop of the apparently endless sea.

The glider pilot had indeed begun his downward spiral that would end, the Duke hoped, with a landing on the *Sword of Islam*. The Duke forced himself to keep his eyes open as the descent continued, wishing that his stomach would stop churning. And now, to make matters worse, his lower bowels were beginning to cramp. The flimsy glider was making ominous creaking sounds as it flew and the Duke wouldn't have been at all surprised if the thing didn't suddenly just fall to pieces around them.

The *Sword of Islam* quickly grew in size and soon, in the Duke's eyes, had resumed the reassuring grandeur of a Sky Lord as the glider drew close to it. He began to relax. It was clear, even to him, that the pilot would have no difficulty in making the aerial rendezvous.

A minute later the glider was skimming over the upper hull of the *Sword of Islam*, which had slowed down and swung its stern round into the wind to facilitate the landing. With a flourish of his piloting skills, the pilot brought the glider down exactly at the start of the designated landing area. The Duke gasped as the glider bumped violently up

40

and down as it skidded along but the pilot brought it quickly to a halt; so quickly in fact that the aircraft had pulled up some twenty yards from the restraining net that had been set up across part of the Sky Lord's hull. Parked some distance away were three other gliders of varying designs.

"Well done!" the Duke told the pilot with feeling. "Get me back to the *Lord Mordred* in the same manner and your rations will be doubled for a month."

The *Sword of Islam's* equivalent of Techs were hurrying forward to secure the glider. Behind them came an honour guard of black-robed warriors. The Duke's two knights, looked suitably impressive in their ceremonial silver chain mail with their .45 automatics prominent in their shoulder holsters, climbed out of the glider first. They were followed by Spang, who then assisted the Duke out of the cabin. One of the honour guard stepped forward and lowered his head at the Duke. Like the other warriors, his face was mostly concealed behind the black cloth of his headwear and only his eyes were visible. "On behalf of my master, El Rashad, I bid you welcome to the *Sword of Islam*,' said the warrior in a thick accent. "With your permission I shall escort you to his Glorious Presence."

The Duke nodded. El Rashad's warriors formed two lines on either side of the Duke and his party and then, with the spokesman in front, the two groups moved off at a stately pace along a roped pathway towards the nearest hatchway.

A long elevator ride followed, down between two of the giant gas cells to the lower levels; and then a lengthy procession along several streets crowded with both people and animals. As before, the Duke was struck by the mixture of strong, pungent odours that saturated the air in the enclosed streets. But what affected him most was the sight of the old people in the crowds. The population of the *Sword of Islam*, being of a strictly orthodox Islamic sect, were not Prime Standards and therefore subject to the old, "natural" ageing processes, though the Duke had never been able to comprehend what was natural about having your body slowly deteriorate and wither over many years until you finally dropped dead from your accumulated infirmities.

Some of the faces of the old men he glimpsed in the streets were very old indeed and he didn't like to speculate on the state of their bodies under their robes. Presumably some of the women were equally as old but as all the women kept their faces completely covered when in public he was unable to see. The thought of an old *woman's* body was even more repugnant to him than that of an old man's and he quickly dismissed the unwelcome image.

His party and escort moved through an ornate gateway manned by heavily armed guards and entered El Rashad's private domain. The Duke had been here before but was still disorientated by all the twists and turns along carpeted corridors before they finally arrived in the hall where El Rashad conferred with his fellow Sky Lords. The walls and ceiling of the hall were covered by brightly coloured drapery, creating the effect of being inside a large tent. In the centre of the thickly-carpeted floor was a low, oval-shaped table. Around it, sitting cross-legged on large cushions, were the other four Sky Lords. Behind them stood advisers, while by the walls were the various escorts of each Sky Lord.

As the Duke approached the table the Sky Lords all turned in his direction. From the head of the table El Rashad said, in a voice dripping disdain, "Ah, at last our Christian ally has arrived. We were beginning to fear your glider may have, tragically, crashed into the sea."

Beginning to *hope* so, more like, thought the Duke as, with difficulty, he sank on to the cushion and crossed his legs. El Rashad made no gestures of compromise towards the different customs of his guests; it was his way, the Duke knew, of subtly demonstrating his dominance over them all. Baron Spang took up his position immediately behind the Duke.

42

Duke du Lucent forced a cheerful smile at El Rashad who, as usual, was resplendent in his black and blood-red robes. "I thank you for your concern on my behalf. I am deeply touched." He spoke in the language they all had in common, Americano, which was a mixture of Spanish and English.

The hawk-faced El Rashad scowled at the Duke's evident sarcasm then clapped his hands. A servant, or slave, hurried out from a gap in the draperies carrying a tray. He placed a small cup of black liquid in front of the Duke and a plate of square, white objects which the Duke knew, from past experience, would be insufferably sweet. The other Sky Lords had already been served.

Pointedly ignoring both food and drink the Duke smiled again at El Rashad and said, "I trust, my fellow conqueror of the skies, that your reason for summoning this meeting is an important one. As much as I relish any opportunity to be in the company of both you and my other brothers in adversity I am rather occupied with domestic concerns on the *Lord Mordred* at present and your call has thus come at an inconvenient time."

El Rashad said harshly, "Your domestic problems, whatever they may be, are insignificant compared to the aims of our joint venture."

The Duke shrugged. "That's easy for you to say, illustrious one, but as you well know the *Lord Mordred* is not operating at full strength—" *falling to pieces*, would be a more accurate description, he thought ruefully—"and conditions on board are not too good at the moment. My people, though they love me deeply and are completely loyal, are beginning to get, well, somewhat *restless*."

Contempt flashed in El Rashad's eyes. "A try Sky Lord should have no difficulty in keeping his subjects under control."

Bugger you, thought the Duke, stung by the rebuke. But then Lord Mazatan began to speak. As before, he wore a magnificent cloak of different coloured feathers, and plumes also rose from the gold band around his head. *Probably didn't even need a glider to get here*, mused the duke; *just flapped his arms.* . . .

It seemed that Lord Mazatan had voiced a similar complaint to the Duke's; food was getting scarce on board the *Lord Mazatan* and its people were suffering from the cold. Some had already died from its effects. Things could not go on like this for very much longer.

The Duke felt cheered. For a change he wasn't going to be the odd man out. And he was further cheered by the darkening expression on El Rashad's face. Again he wondered just how old the man was. The Duke had no way of assessing it, having spent all his life among people who didn't age visibly past their mid-thirties. His face had deep lines but he was clearly not as old as some of the men the Duke had seen in the streets.

Lord Torres was speaking now. The Duke turned his attention to him. Lord Torres, a Prime Standard like the other American Sky Lords, had a smooth face, but it was a striking one nonetheless with its sharply angular features and fierce eyes. Torres wore a sleeveless tunic that appeared to be woven out of gold thread and, like Lord Mazatan, wore a gold band around his head. His skin was a deep bronze and his muscular arms looked as if they'd just been burnished with a cloth.

The Duke heard, reluctantly, that while Lord Torres was having problems too he voted to continue with the search. Then Prince Carracas spoke (compared to the others he was drably dressed; his garb consisting of a bland, dark grey, one-piece uniform) and said much the same as Torres. The Duke cursed him under his breath. That made three to two in El Rashad's favour. He decided to try again. . . .

"My fellow Sky Lords," he began, though he addressed his words to El Rashad, "might I make the following suggestion? As you know, the *Lord Mordred* is in poor repair compared to your vessels, and has become an increasing hindrance to your quest. Why, you would have reached your goal days ago if your ships weren't required to pace themselves to the *Lord Mordred's* miserable thirty miles-per-hour. Therefore, for the common good, I offer to withdraw from the quest and make my slow return to the North. Without the handicap that my poor ship imposes upon you all your search for the great sea habitat can be carried out all that much more quickly. Alas, I and my people will miss out on the use of the technological riches that the habitat is sure to contain but I am afraid we must make that sacrifice for the success of your great quest."

El Rashad said harshly, "Out of the question. The *Lord Mordred* will remain with us. You have been out-voted. The quest will continue until we find the habitat. The reason I called this conference was to suggest that we split into two groups when we reach Antarctica. One will fly east, the other west. That way we can search the waters surrounding the ice continent much more quickly."

The Duke du Lucent began to seethe. El Rashad wasn't going to be satisfied until they all either starved or froze to death. And for what? For nothing but a fool's errand.

"El Rashad, you must see reason," he said loudly. "You're grasping at straws. Maybe this habitat did once exist centuries ago but the chances of it and its population still surviving are remote. Did we see one sea habitat on our long voyage down here? No! They were probably all wiped out long ago, either by Sky Lords or by the sea worms, the squids and the other monsters that thrive now in the oceans."

El Rashad glared at him. "If you took the time to look you would see that the effects of the sea blight have lessened the further south we travel. The lower temperatures are obviously the reason; therefore the chances that the habitat has survived intact in more southern waters are very high.

No, Duke du Lucent, the quest *will* continue, and you and the *Lord Mordred* will see it through to the end."

The Duke forced himself to smile and nod his head at El Rashad. "Of course, oh illustrious one. Whatever you say." Once again he pondered on the real reason why El Rashad was so determined to keep him and his ship part of this expedition. An unpleasant suspicion was beginning to take form in his mind. He feared that El Rashad intended to use the *Lord Mordred* as a stalking horse. If the habitat was located the Duke would be forced to make initial and seemingly belligerent contact with it while El Rashad and the others waited at a safe distance and observed what transpired. If the habitat people did possess Old Science weaponry it would be the *Lord Mordred* that suffered its possibly fatal sting. Then, satisfied by the demonstration of power, El Rashad would make contact with the habitat people in a much more conciliatory manner and attempt to make a bargain with them for their assistance. Yes, the more the Duke thought about it the more it seemed likely. And there was nothing he could do about it.

He glanced towards El Rashad and for a moment their eyes locked. The Duke felt like a helpless dove who can see the hawk diving inexorably towards him.

"Once again I strongly advise that we return to the habitat immediately!" said the Toy's program.

"And I say no. We stay here," said Ryn firmly. His mind and body sang with excitement. Something *different* was happening! And he knew his life was never going to be the same again. Shortly after sighting the fleet of approaching Sky Lords he had evolved a plan; it all depended on what the Toy's program did. So far it looked good—the computer was urging him to flee but apparently hadn't been programmed to take over direct control of the Toy in such a situation. Possibly whoever the programmer had been—

another program, no doubt—hadn't envisaged such a situation.

The fleet of Sky Lords was approaching very slowly. Ryn was certain they were capable of faster travel but for some reason they were deliberately maintaining a low speed. He was impatient. "How far are they from your damned boundary?" he asked.

"Less than half a mile," said the computer. "Ryn, we really should move. Why don't we submerge? I have a feeling the hunting will be good today."

Ryn couldn't help laughing. The female voice had taken on a wheedling tone. His confidence grew. He had the program by its non-existent balls. "Take us up. To an altitude of five thousand. Then hover."

The program protested but obeyed. The Toy began to rise rapidly. "How close to the boundary now?" he asked when the Toy reached the designated altitude.

"Three of the airships are now within the boundary area. The other two are just about to enter," the program told him reluctantly.

Ryn gave a whoop of joy and banged his fists on the arms of his couch. "Move forward. Slow speed. Say, fifty miles per hour."

"I really don't advise this course of action," said the program, even as it began to obey him.

Ryn watched the screen with avid fascination as the Toy flew towards the fleet of approaching Sky Lords. The closer he got the more impressed he was with their size. He knew their dimensions from his history program—over a mile long and a thousand feet wide at the thickest point of their hulls—but that didn't prepare him for the reality.

He zoomed in on the Sky Lord directly ahead of him until it filled the screen. He could pick out details now, like the many gun turrets and the glittering, glass-like tiles that seemed to cover much of the upper hull. He probed his memory and got the answer—they were solar cells, the main

47

source of power for the Sky Lords. They contained a genetically engineered substance similar to chlorophyll which converted the rays of the sun directly into electrical energy.

The Toy was now closing fast with the fleet and Ryn wondered which of the great airships to land on. As he tried to make up his mind the Toy said, "I've made radar contact with a seventh aircraft."

"Another Sky Lord?"

"No. A much smaller aircraft. See." The screen blurred, then it displayed a flimsy-looking aircraft with very long wings. People could be glimpsed in the cabin at the front.

"Take me closer to it," ordered Ryn.

The Duke du Lucent's anger at the way the conference had gone was distracting him from his fear of flying as the glider carried him back towards the *Lord Mordred*. He didn't even react when the pilot gave a cry of alarm, but when the glider suddenly lurched to one side the Duke's normal terror immediately reasserted itself. "What's wrong?" he cried. "Are we going to crash?"

"Look to starboard, sire!" yelled the pilot over his shoulder.

The Duke and the Baron both looked out the window. The Baron swore. The Duke bit his lip, then gasped, "What is *that*?"

Flying alongside them, just a few feet past the glider's wing tip, was a tear-shaped metal object. What the Duke found most alarming about it was that while it was obviously not a small airship it had no wings. In fact it had no visible features at all apart from a number of vents fore and aft.

"El Rashad," moaned the Duke. "It's some secret weapon he's devised to destroy me!"

"It can't be from the *Sword of Islam*," said Baron Spang. "That has to be Old Science. If El Rashad already possessed

48

such a thing he would not have started this quest in the first place."

The mysterious and frightening object suddenly disappeared.

"It's gone!" cried the Duke, with relief.

"No," said the pilot, after several moments. "It's sitting on our tail now. It's so close there's no chance of our gunners shooting at it without hitting us as well."

"What can we do?" asked Spang.

"Nothing," answered the pilot.

Chapter Five:

This time the glider came down with a bone-jarring thump, the pilot obviously distracted by the strange machine that was right behind them. The Duke's jaw snapped shut at the impact and he tasted blood in his mouth. The glider finally skidded to a halt, hundreds of yards from the proper landing strip. To the Duke, the waiting group of Techs looked a depressingly long distance away.

He heard the hatch being opened. His knights were getting out.

"Stay here, sire," said Spang, as he undid his harness.

"No," said the Duke. He felt trapped. If he was going to be killed he would rather it was outside in the open. So he followed the Baron out of the glider.

The mysterious flying machine was sitting just twenty feet behind the glider. It was making a humming sound. Slowly, the sound died away and the thing became completely silent. The Duke crouched beside the glider. Taking cover, such as it was, behind the tailplane were his two knights. Both were aiming their guns at the intruder.

At his shoulder, Spang said, over the rush of the wind, "Do you know, I think—?" He was interrupted by a hatch suddenly opening in the side of the metal craft. The Duke glanced backwards. The group of Techs were heading across the hull towards them. He hoped they'd sounded a general alarm that would have troops up here soon as well. He returned his attention to the intruder craft just in time to see a man swing himself feet first through the hatch. "Hold your fire!" cautioned the Baron. The Duke wondered if that was wise.

The man was, on closer inspection, not much more than a youth. He was wearing a tight-fitting, one-piece, bright green uniform and didn't appear to be carrying any weapons. His beardless face was a handsome one. He stood beside the machine and, with his hands on his hips, surveyed them almost arrogantly. Then his eyes settled on the Duke and his smile broadened.

"Who are you?" called the Baron. "Where are you from? What do you want with us?"

The stranger didn't answer. He continued to stare at them with a look of open amusement on his face.

The Techs had arrived now. Obliged by their presence to regain his dignity he rose to his feet and pointed at the young stranger. "I am the Duke du Lucent, ruler of this Sky Lord, the *Lord Mordred*," he called out imperiously. "Identify yourself!"

Still smiling, the youth said, "Ryn . . . *Robin*."

"Where are you from?" asked the Baron, also rising to his feet. "And how do you speak our language?"

The stranger shrugged. "Before I tell you where I come from we have business to discuss. As for my speaking your language, I speak many languages. Let's say that I had a lot of spare time for such studies."

The Duke was confused. *Business*? He glanced at Spang. The Baron looked excited. He leaned close to the Duke, putting his lips to his ear. "You realize what this means, sire?"

"No," answered the Duke, truthfully.

"It means El Rashad was right! The habitat does exist! This youth, and his machine, must come from there!"

It took a while for the implications to sink in. That El Rashad's wild goose chase was anything but that. There *was* a habitat full of Old Science technology. "He's their representative!" he said excitedly to the Baron. "And he's come to *us*!"

51

"Exactly," said the Baron.

"This changes everything, doesn't it?" said the Duke, wonderingly.

"It does indeed, sire."

Ryn ordered the Toy to stay close on the tail of the flimsy glider as it headed down towards the Sky Lord in case anyone attempted to shoot at him. The Toy kept up its string of protests all the way down. Ryn ignored it. It was clear that in this situation, and within the borders of the imposed boundary, the program had no power to override his instructions.

He touched down right behind the glider on the hull of the Sky Lord. He watched the screen and waited. Very soon two men scrambled out of the glider. They wore chain mail and carried hand guns. They took up position by the tail of the glider. Another man emerged from the glider, and then another. In the distance he could see another group of men approaching.

"I'm going outside," he informed the Toy.

"I really don't advise it, Ryn. Those men are armed. I suggest we head back home. What do you say, Ryn? What about it? You must be hungry by now."

"I say you keep your sensors and your lasers trained on the two men with the guns. The moment you detect they are about to fire, destroy their weapons. Now open the hatches."

The Toy obeyed. Fresh, cold air swept into the craft's interior. Ryn swung himself out and jumped down on to the airship's hull. The wind was strong. Heart beating with excitement, and just a little fear, he looked at the men in front of him. He was intrigued to see that they were in medieval costume, or a close approximation of it. To his amusement, he was reminded of the people in *The Adventures of Robin Hood*. One of the men was actually wearing a jewel-encrusted crown. He was a good-looking man with a pointed black beard and dressed even more resplendently than the others. He was clearly their leader.

The man beside the one wearing the crown called out a question which, after a time, Ryn realised was a form of Americano. The other group of men arrived, but though they carried a variety of tools on their belts they were without weapons. The first man stood and announced, in a deep, rich voice, who he was. Then the second man asked him questions again. Ryn thought fast. He had struck it lucky. He had made immediate contact with a ruler of a Sky Lord. Now to put part two of his plan into action. . . .

He told the second man, who had red hair and a bushy red beard, that he had a business proposition to discuss with them. The two conferred, then the dark one said, "I take great pleasure in welcoming you to the *Lord Mordred* as our guest. If you would care to accompany us below we will continue our talk in more comfortable surroundings."

Ryn smiled at him. "I'd be delighted to, but there is something I must attend to first." They watched him suspiciously as he turned and went back to the Toy's open hatch. He climbed back inside. "Thank goodness," sighed the Toy. "I'll close the hatches and take off immediately."

"Don't bother," Ryn told it. Then he reached over and threw the switch that deactivated the computer. The screens went blank and every light on the console died. The Toy was now completely inert. Ryn climbed back outside and closed and sealed the hatch manually. He faced the now quite large crowd of watching sky people. "Please don't take this the wrong way," he said loudly, addressing the Duke but speaking for the benefit of all the others as well, "but we must get a few hard realities out of the way first. My craft is booby-trapped; any attempt to enter it or dismantle it will result in an explosion that will rip apart this Sky Lord from bow to stern." He paused, then continued, "Also I have a neural implant in my head that permits direct contact with the computer that controls my craft. Do you understand what I mean?" He tapped the side of his head.

The Duke nodded. "A radio link?"

"That's right. Now while I'm sure I am dealing with men of impeccable honour I must point out that I can send an instantaneous command to the computer to self-destruct. Again the result will be a massive explosion. My death, I regret to say, will also cause my craft to similarly self-destruct." He paused again. "Does the invitation still stand, considering the risks that my presence within your airship will bring you and your people?"

The Duke and his advisor exchanged a glance. There was a subdued mutter from the crowd around them. Ryn saw the advisor give a slight nod. The Duke gave Ryn a forced smile. "Of course the invitation still stands, er, Robin. I give you my word that you will come to no harm on board the *Lord Mordred*."

Ryn was satisfied. He was certain his bluff had worked.

" . . . Thus, to combat this growing menace we have come to seek out your sea habitat in the hope that we might buy Old Science technology that would be of use to us as weapons. Your habitat was our last chance, and there was some doubt that it even still existed. The computer records mentioning it were both very old and very vague on detail. Some among us were even ready to give up but—" the Duke gestured at Robin with his hands—"here you are, living proof of its existence."

The youth was lounging comfortably in a large chair. He seemed totally relaxed now, though he had sniffed suspiciously at the cup of wine when it had been given to him by a servant. "No," the Duke had told him, "it's not drugged. The skills of my surgeons are not sufficient to permit the removal of your implant, provided they could find it, without killing you. Besides, I'm sure if you began to sense you *had* been drugged you would have ample time to send your self-destruct signal to your craft." After a moment's hesitation the youth had drunk from the cup.

"Well," said the Duke, "we have told you why we are in your skies. It is your turn to tell us about your home."

"Yes," said Baron Spang, leaning forward eagerly in his chair. "Where exactly is it?"

The youth laughed. "Even if I could take you to Shangri La I'm afraid you would find the Eloi impossible to deal with."

The Baron frowned and looked at the Duke. Equally puzzled, the Duke said to Robin, "Shangri La? Eloi? What do you mean?"

Before Robin could answer there was an urgent rapping at the door of the Duke's private living room. He was at first annoyed and then alarmed. He had given orders that they were not to be disturbed. That meant there had to be some sort of emergency. . . .

"Enter!" he called and a harassed-looking Tech hurried into the room. "Sire, we have a message from the *Sword of Islam*, from El Rashad himself. He wants to communicate directly with you, sire. At once."

The Duke relaxed. The *Sword of Islam*'s telescopes, tracking the return flight of his glider, must have picked up Robin's craft. He smiled as he thought of what was going through El Rashad's mind right now. A metallic flying machine which had to be of Old Science origin had landed on the *Lord Mordred*! What could it mean? What could be going on? The Duke laughed out loud then said to the perspiring Tech, who had obviously run all the way from Observation, "Tell the illustrious one that I'm too busy to talk to him right now. I'll be in touch later."

The Tech stared at them then gave a dubious nod. "Yes sire." He left the room at a trot.

Still grinning, the Duke turned back to Robin. "You were saying?"

"I was about to tell you that 'Shangri La' is the name

given to the habitat by its inhabitants, and that 'Eloi' is the name that the inhabitants gave themselves. This was back, of course, when the Eloi still had a sense of humour." Robin drained his cup and held it out. The servant quickly refilled it.

The Duke was feeling puzzled again. "I don't understand," he said.

"Nor do I," said Baron Spang. "What did you mean when you said the Eloi would be impossible for us to deal with?"

"The Eloi, long ago, *changed* themselves. To the extent where I don't suppose they could be described as human any more."

"But," said the Duke, "you come from the habitat and you're human."

"Yes, but I'm not an Eloi. I'm a throwback. A mistake."

"Please explain," said the Duke.

"I'll try. You see, the Eloi don't reproduce but they do have a lot of sperm and eggs in storage. Prime Standard material donated back when they were still human. The Eloi are immortal and Shangri La is almost impregnable but accidents can still happen. The last happened just twenty-one years ago. A hatch seal failed and a section of the habitat flooded before the central program could take the appropriate measures. Two Eloi were killed. So two eggs and two sperm were taken out of storage and fertilisation was induced. Then, what was supposed to happen was that a series of synthetic viruses were to have been introduced to the proto-foetuses in order to alter their DNA to the point where they would grow into Eloi. That only happened to one of the foetuses. The other one was allowed to develop unaltered, thanks, so I'm told, to a simple glitch in a piece of computer hardware—funny how the software always blames the hardware for any mistake. Anyway, the result was me." Robin took a long drink of wine.

There was silence for a time. The Duke looked enquiringly at the Baron, who gave a slight shrug.

"Er, these Eloi folk, if they're not human, what are they?" said the Baron, trying to keep his growing scepticism out of his voice, though it was quite evident to the Duke who was feeling rather sceptical himself. "Are they monsters?"

Robin paused before answering. "In a sense they are, though you wouldn't think so at first sight. They are small and slightly built, like elves. And rather pretty. . . ."

"The men as well as the women?" asked the Duke, intrigued.

Robin shook his head. "There are no women or men, just Eloi. I told you the Eloi don't reproduce. They have no sex organs. They are neuters."

The Duke was shocked. "They emasculated themselves? But why? Are they monks?"

"On the contrary. You could never describe the Eloi as ascetics."

"Then why did they do that to themselves?"

The youth held out his cup again. As the servant refilled it he said, "To explain the Eloi to you I'll have to go back to before the Gene Wars. According to what I was told the habitat was originally a research station operated by the United Nations. The various scientists on it were there to monitor any effects on the Antarctic environment caused by the mining operations. They were also monitoring the atmospheric conditions and doing deep water research in the Southern Ocean. Then, in the years leading up to the Gene Wars it became a kind of refuge for scientists—mainly microbiologists—who didn't want to work for the Corporations. By then it was no longer under the protection of the United Nations—which had long ago collapsed—but was being sponsored privately by sympathetic wealthy individuals who opposed the Corporations. The habitat became a floating fortress capable of hiding deep under the water.

"In this sealed environment the scientists survived the Gene Wars untouched—physically, at least. As they monitored the aftermath of the Wars and observed the designer plagues ravaging what remained of the world's population they came to the conclusion that humanity was doomed. It was this general mood of hopelessness about the future of the human race that produced the idea of turning themselves into, well . . . something else."

"All these people chose to become sexless beings?" asked Baron Spang, sounding mystified. "I find that hard to believe."

Robin frowned and stared into his cup. Then he said, "It's very difficult for me to try and explain exactly what the Eloi are and how they became that way. The Eloi exist in a constant state of—" he raised the wine cup—"of *intoxication*. But don't misunderstand me, they're not simply drunk. It's much more than that. They changed their body chemistry to the point where their brains are continually awash with certain natural chemicals that keep them deliriously happy. But in order to achieve this state their bodies had to be modified as well, which is why they have no sex organs. It's something to do with maintaining the necessary hormonal balance—the hormones produced by the sex organs would make that impossible." He looked at the two of them. "Do you follow?"

The Duke, nodding, believed he had a vague grasp of what the youth was trying to tell them. These elf people, by means of Old Science magic, had contrived to make themselves continually drunk. The thought appealed to him but he didn't like the idea of having to give up his balls to achieve this state.

This aspect of the transformation clearly preyed on Baron Spang's mind as well, for he said, "I still find it hard to believe that all of these people agreed to be surgically mutilated."

"There was no surgery involved," Robin told him, somewhat wearily. "But you're right, not everyone agreed to the transformation, which would mean sealing themselves off from the rest of humanity for good. Some argued that the resources of the habitat should be used to assist the survivors of the Wars, futile though such efforts would undoubtedly be. These people, in the minority, eventually left the habitat to take their chances in the outside world."

No one spoke for a time. The Duke looked at the Baron who was pulling thoughtfully on his beard. "Well, Baron Spang, your comments?"

The Baron said slowly, "It seems as if our guest is saying that these elves of his would be of no help to us."

"Exactly," said the youth. "Communicating with them— or rather, *trying* to communicate with them—is a nightmare. I should know, I've been trying for years. Not that you could ever reach them anyway. The habitat is under the ice shelf and even I don't know where exactly. The computer in my craft does but that's of no use to you. No, my friends, forget the Eloi, because you have what you need now anyway."

"We do?" asked the Duke.

"Yes." The youth grinned at him and held out his cup for more wine. "You have me. The weapons on my craft— under my control—will be more of a match for this mysterious new Sky Lord you fear so much."

The Duke regarded him warily. "And why are you so willing to help us?"

"Because you will be the means by which I will escape the Eloi and their boring habitat. At last I will be free!"

Puzzled, the Duke said, "But you already have the means. That craft of yours."

Robin shook his head. "It is of short range only. But with your airship to transport both it and me to the north that will no longer matter. However, that is only part of my price."

The Duke leaned forward in his chair. "What, may I ask, is the rest of it?"

"First, I want some clothes like yours . . . and a sword," said the youth, eagerly.

This took the Duke by surprise. "You want . . . clothes?"

Robin indicated his one-piece suit. "This is so dull compared to what you wear. You people have *style*, right out of *The Adventures of Robin Hood*!"

"The what?" asked the Duke blankly, glancing at the Baron, who also looked bemused by the youth's request.

"It doesn't matter. Just get me some of your fancy clothes, a sword and. . . ." He looked embarrassed and his voice trailed away.

"And what?" the Duke asked him.

A blush appeared on the youth's face. "As I told you, I'm twenty years old and I have spent my whole life living with the Eloi on that habitat. And the Eloi are sexless. . . ."

It took a few seconds for the Duke to realise what he was talking about and then he laughed. "Ah, you want a *woman*!" Then another thought struck him and he said, "Or do your preferences lie in the opposite direction?"

The youth's blush deepened. "They do not. A woman is all I need. I presume you have prostitutes among your subjects."

The Duke rubbed his chin. "Indeed I do, lad, indeed I do. In fact the *Lord Mordred* has more than its full share. But as our honoured guest and ally I think you deserve better than a mere prostitute."

"Oh, really?" The youth looked interested.

"Yes, I have the ideal woman in mind for you. An aristocrat. A *princess*, in fact," said the Duke and laughed again.

Chapter Six:

"Are you serious, my Lord?" asked Baron Spang. "About giving your own daughter to this . . . this mysterious creature?"

"Quite serious," answered the Duke airily. "It's about time she earned her keep." They were now alone in the Duke's private living room. The youth had been escorted away, more than a little drunk, to a luxury suite whose owner had been hastily ejected.

The Baron, pacing the floor, looked concerned. "But I don't understand *why*, sire. Surely some common strumpet would serve as a provider of sexual favours. I mean, we don't even know if he's telling the truth. And besides, he *is* a groundling. Who knows what diseases he may be carrying. You will be risking the Princess Andrea's life."

"He's clearly no ordinary groundling," said the Duke. "And that habitat of his has been sealed off from contact with the rest of the human race since before the Gene Wars."

"So he *says*," said the Baron.

"I'm willing to give him the benefit of the doubt. That craft of his is definitely not an illusion. And with him on our side everything is changed. The thing is that I need to know that I can trust him. I want him in my power, completely. And Andrea is the one to achieve that goal. Here is a healthy young man who—if he is telling the truth—has grown up in a world devoid of women. Imagine his frustration. Imagine his chances against Andrea—stunningly beautiful and the most manipulative bitch I've ever encountered, and I include my wife in that appraisal. I guarantee that within mere hours he will be her helpless slave."

The Baron stopped pacing and pulled thoughtfully on his beard. "Well, yes . . . perhaps. But what about the Lady Andrea herself? She may not want to enter into, er, intimate relationships with this stranger."

The Duke raised an eyebrow. "Oh, really, my dear Baron," he drawled. "You know my daughter. The mere sight of this exotic, handsome, and very well-built young man will have her salivating on the spot. He is infinitely more interesting than her current crop of epicene companions. No, I don't think she will decline to be of assistance to me. Besides, she will have no choice in the matter."

"I won't do it!" cried Andrea.

"Oh yes, you will, my kitten. You will indeed," the Duke said calmly.

"Make love to some dirty earthworm? Never!" Her cheeks glowed with anger and she actually stamped her foot on the floor. The Duke regarded her dispassionately from the depths of the easy chair. "I told you, dear, he is no ordinary earthworm. And his goodwill towards us is of vital importance. To me. To you. To all of us. Not that I think you will find it a hardship. The boy is very handsome."

"I don't care how handsome he is! I will not become a whore for you!"

"Then think of it as whoring for yourself, my kitten."

"What do you mean?"

"You want us to return to the north. With that youth and his flying machine I have the power now to defy El Rashad and the others. But I need to know that I can trust this youth implicitly and that he will do what I command. I can't force him, for reasons I have already explained. Which is why I need you, my darling. Succeed, and I will be very grateful. You will have whatever your warped little heart desires, if it is within my power to grant it."

Andrea's face softened, though her eyes remained suspicious. "You promise that, father?"

"On my honour."

She gave a sniff of disdain—a gesture, observed the Duke, that had obviously been learnt at her mother's knee—but then said, "I want to see this earthworm before I make my decision."

"But of course, my kitten. . . ." The Duke was about to summon Spang to escort her to the youth's cabin when another Tech appeared. The Duke knew the reason for his presence.

"El Rashad again?" he asked the Tech.

"Yes Sire. The message says that he is coming to the *Lord Mordred* in person. Within the hour. He wishes to speak to you urgently."

The Duke smiled. "Well, well . . . we shall have to get the best silver out." He turned to his daughter. "You see how important our young visitor is? And why it is important that you and he become . . . er, very close friends?"

She nodded. "I will go and see him now and give you my decision."

Ryn, or Robin as he now thought of himself, lay sprawled on the large four-poster bed and ran the events of the past few hours through his mind. His life had taken such a bizarre turn he half-suspected that one of his wily programs had arranged a drug-induced delusion that mirrored his favourite old movie. He was dressed now in green tights, black, soft-leather boots, a white silk shirt, and a red jacket with billowing sleeves. On the bed beside him was a sword in its scabbard attached to a wide leather belt. The hilt was an ornate affair covered with filigreed silver. Admittedly, the clothes were uncomfortable but the novelty of wearing non-synthetic cloth next to his skin excited him.

Entering the Sky Lord had also been a source of excitement, and some fear. He knew he was taking a great gamble—with only his bluff to protect him—but what was the alternative? To reactivate the Toy and be whisked back to the terminal boredom of the habitat? No, better to risk his life in the hope that he would finally achieve his freedom from the Eloi.

He didn't know what to expect in the interior of the *Lord Mordred*. His teaching program had only provided information up to the years shortly after the establishment of the Sky Lord, during the aftermath of the Gene Wars, which was when radio communication began to break down due to the work of species of fungi designed to attack electronic equipment. He knew what the Sky Lords originally were— Sky Angels, giant airships that had been built for humanitarian reasons. They were floating relief centres in the event of any disaster—man-made or natural. Filled with emergency supplies as well as spacious dormitories, they provided speedy assistance and shelter to the survivors of floods, earthquakes, hurricanes and large genetic 'mishaps' (the Gene Corporations did sometimes make mistakes), and many were also used to provide cheap transport in the Third World countries. After the Gene Wars they were fought over by various groups around the world desperate to escape the plagues and other genetically-engineered dangers that were rampant on the planet's surface. When the smoke of the battles cleared those in control of the Sky Angels tended to be those who had been more ruthless and violent than their competitors and this set the pattern for what was to follow. The Sky Angels had gone; in their place were the Sky Lords, who were soon imposing their rule on those unlucky enough to be still on the ground.

Ryn's first impression on descending into the *Lord Mordred*'s interior, after leaving the Toy firmly secured by cables to the outer hull, had been one of barely controlled decay. It appeared that everything—hatches, ladders, elevators, corridors—had been repaired or patched up again and again and again over the years. What he saw bore no

64

resemblance to the pictures of a Sky Angel interior displayed by one of his history programs, which had been all gleaming corridors and high-tech efficiency. But then it shouldn't have come as any surprise; after all, those pictures had been recorded well over four hundred years ago and the *Lord Mordred* had clearly been through a lot since then.

Those pictures also didn't prepare him for the sheer size of the Sky Lord. If it appeared large from the outside it seemed even bigger once inside and plainly dwarfed the interior of the habitat that he was so familiar with. The elevator ride down through the area that he knew contained the massive gas cells took a ridiculously long time (but then the elevator didn't move very fast and stopped briefly on three occasions for no clear reason). The elevator doors eventually opened to reveal a large open space in which were gathered a crowd of people and also a carriage attached to two big animals that Ryn recognised as horses. The crowd began to shout and surge forward as the Duke and his party emerged from the elevator. A row of warriors, using their javelins to form a barricade, held them back. The crowd shook their fists and shouted insults which Ryn guessed were being directed at the Duke. He could see no reason why they might be directed at himself, as he was sure news of his presence had not yet spread through the airship's population.

The Duke climbed into the open carriage and gestured to Ryn to follow. As Ryn sat beside him the Duke said dryly, "My loyal subjects displaying their devotion towards me."

Ryn eagerly scanned the crowd, hoping for his first sight of a real woman but all the people were so heavily muffled with scarves and hooded cloaks it was impossible to distinguish the sex of any of them. And as he observed their breath misting as they yelled he became aware just how cold it was in the Sky Lord. Since leaving the waim womb of the Toy he had been too excited and tense to fully appreciate the extreme drop in temperature. It was clear that if the

Lord Mordred possessed an internal heating system it was not working properly.

Once the others had also got into the carriage its driver urged the horses forward. As the carriage began a bumpy journey over a straw-covered, uneven surface, warriors trotted beside it. The carriage entered a corridor which widened out into an enclosed street complete with shops and taverns. Ryn was entranced by it all even though the carriage's progress was accompanied by jeers and boos. The Duke waved regally as if acknowledging cheers.

Ryn kept looking for women and was certain he spotted a few along the way but he wasn't sure. Much easier to determine were several children of varying sizes that he saw but with these it was just as hard to determine whether they were boys or girls, so well bundled-up against the cold were they.

At the end of the journey came another, but shorter, elevator ride—this time upwards. They emerged into a very different world than the one below. The wide corridors were lined with well-polished wood containing intricate carvings and the well-dressed people they encountered along the way all displayed great courtesy to the Duke. And to Ryn's delight he saw two people, though muffled in heavy cloaks, who were *definitely* women. He would have liked to linger and examine them more closely but the Duke had urged him onwards.

They finally arrived at the section of the *Lord Mordred* that was clearly the Duke's exclusive territory, it being the most richly appointed that Ryn had seen so far. He guessed that they were now in the bow of the great airship, a guess that was confirmed when they briefly passed through the throne room on the way to the Duke's private sitting room. The curving sweep of great windows that bellied out and upwards to the ceiling suggested to Ryn that they were somewhere below the nose of the airship.

He had tried to remember what the reason was for

building the Sky Angels so large in the first place: something to do with efficiency of lift. Double the size of an airship and you didn't merely get double the lifting capacity; the lifting efficiency progressed with something like geometric progression the larger you made the airship. Pondering this had led him to ask the Duke where they managed to find fresh supplies of helium. He was somewhat disturbed by the answer: that most of the helium in the *Lord Mordred* had been lost long ago and the majority of the huge gas cells contained hydrogen that had been manufactured on board. Ryn was only too well aware that while helium was an inert gas hydrogen was inflammable. He was travelling on what was basically a flying bomb. . . .

A knock at the door brought him out of his reverie. "Come in," he called, thinking it was another manservant with some new gift from the Duke. When the door opened he sat bolt upright on the bed. The person who entered was no manservant. It was a woman. A girl. A girl with the face of an angel. And when she threw back the heavy cloak she was wearing he saw that she had the body of an angel as well. No, he decided quickly, not an angel. No angel would dare flaunt such voluptuousness. She made his erotic programs look feeble by comparison.

She smiled at him and he felt his ears grow very hot.

"Greetings, honoured guest of my father," she said. "My name is Princess Andrea. My father has expressed the desire that you and I should be good friends." She paused and—did he imagine it or did she quickly slide her glance up and down his body?—and then said, "And so do I."

"I demand that you bring your Old Science visitor to me. I want to question him."

The Duke looked down at El Rashad from his throne. The Islamic Sky Lord was sitting, unhappily, on the cushion that the Duke had had strategically placed before his throne. *Your days of making demands on me are over*, thought the

Duke with satisfaction. Aloud, he said, "My guest is resting at the moment and can't be disturbed. Any questions you have I will be happy to ask him on your behalf at the earliest opportunity."

El Rashad was barely able to control his fury. In a strangled voice, he said, "You forget that we have an agreement between us. You say that this craft, and its pilot, is from the habitat we seek. Therefore you are obliged to share whatever knowledge you have gained of its where-abouts with me . . . and our other allies, of course."

The Duke leaned back in his throne. "If I knew where the habitat was I would, of course, pass on the information to you, but I don't. Nor does my visitor. Only the computer in his craft knows that."

"So he has told you, but how can you be sure he is telling you the truth?"

"I trust my instincts."

"I'm sure your instincts are infallible," said El Rashad in a voice that dripped poison, "But it would be wise to use torture on this person to confirm them."

"There are complications that prevent such methods."

"Then hand him over to me. I guarantee that not a single secret will remain in him after my torturers have completed their work."

"I thank you for such a generous offer," the Duke told him, "but I really don't believe it would do any good. He says that the habitat is submerged and lies deep under the ice shelf. It is inaccessible."

"So *he* says!" scoffed El Rashad. "But if it is true then we use him as a hostage. We make him send a message through his craft to his people—that he will be killed unless they agree to surface and negotiate with us."

The Duke sighed. He was not going to try and describe the Eloi elf people to him. He glanced briefly at the four black-robed warriors that had accompanied El Rashad. They stood in a line, immobile, behind their master. Behind them, on each side of the door, stood two of his own men. Spang, he knew, was waiting within earshot outside with a large squad of men-at-arms. He took a deep breath and said, "None of that will be necessary. The destructive powers contained within the flying machine will be sufficient to overcome the Sky Angel and her fleet of captured Sky Lords."

"How do you know?" demanded El Rashad.

"Its pilot said so and I believe him," said the Duke. "Therefore I suggest we end the quest for the habitat, return north and seek out the Sky Angel. And destroy it."

"No! I will not risk everything on so flimsy a premise. How can you trust this person? Why should he agree to help us?"

The Duke cleared his throat and said, "Well, actually, he's agreed to help *me*, my dear El Rashad. We made a bargain. There are certain, er, commodities he had a rather desperate need of and fortunately I was in a position to provide them." *At least I certainly hope so!* he told himself anxiously.

El Rashad gave him a dangerous look. "What are you trying to tell me?"

"I'm telling you that the *Lord Mordred* is pulling out of your quest as of now. I am heading northwards to find the Sky Angel. You and the other Sky Lords are welcome to accompany me, of course."

El Rashad's body stiffened and his gaze grew murderous. The Duke could feel his fury like heat from a fire. Long seconds passed. The Duke guessed that El Rashad was, at this moment, sorely tempted to order his men to kill him on the spot. Was his hate and anger so great that he would throw away his own life for the pleasure of seeing the Duke hacked to pieces? But then El Rashad's body relaxed, and the Duke knew the danger was past.

"Very well," said El Rashad softly, "it will be as you say. The rest of the fleet will follow you northwards." He rose to his feet. "The Koran warns the Faithful not to make friends of either Jews or Christians. I should have heeded the Word of Allah more obediently. I will in future."

As he swept out of the throne room, followed by his escort, the Duke fought hard to stifle what would have been a burst of near-hysterical laughter.

Ryn's new clothes lay in a heap beside the bed. Lady Andrea's clothes lay beside them; Lady Andrea herself lay beside him, asleep. Ryn had slept too for a while after the wild and lengthy exertions of their love-making but was now awake and excited again. He moved against her body. She gave a slight moan but didn't wake. He wanted to push back the covers and examine her body while she slept, but it was too cold. Instead he moved his hand under the covers until it was cupping her left breast and thought back on what they had done together. . . .

His sex play with the insubstantial phantoms of the sex programs had been no preparation for the real thing. He had been too clumsy at first, too eager, and their first coupling was over, for him, almost as it started. Then she had taken over. First she had re-aroused him and then, with an expertise that both impressed and surprised him, brought him to the brink again and again and then each time managed to delay the seeming inevitable. When, straddling him, she finally let him orgasm the experience was so intense he thought the top of his head was going to fly away. And then, after a short rest, they had made love an unbelievable third time with Andrea demonstrating a further knowledge of love-making that would have surely made the long-dead programmers of his erotic holograms extremely envious. Clearly, this was not the first time for her. . . .

And what next? he wondered. It all depended on the Toy. What would happen when he reactivated the Toy after the *Lord Mordred* had passed beyond the imposed boundary point? Would the Toy still automatically return to the territory within the boundary or would it, being outside the boundary, be simply content to follow his instructions. Ryn couldn't take the chance—he would have to try and re-program the computer while the Toy remained deactivated, provided the necessary equipment existed on board the *Lord Mordred*. If he failed then the Toy would be useless and he in turn would be of no use to the Duke.

Oh well, that was all in the future. For now he would enjoy a present that he had presumed would be forever denied him.

He gently squeezed her breast. "Wake up, Princess Andrea, wake up. . . ."

Chapter Seven:

Jan stirred. There was a warm, pleasurable sensation between her thighs. She moaned in response. Drifting upwards through layers of sleep she realized, to her growing joy, that Ceri had at last returned to her bed. "Ceri . . ." she sighed. She opened her eyes. And gasped when she saw who it was.

Milo.

Milo, exactly as she remembered him. The bald head. One eye blue, the other green. The arrogant smile. . . .

He was naked and kneeling between her legs. He had a large erection. He had pushed her sleeping robe up around her waist and it was his fingers that were caressing her. He smiled down at her. She saw that under his other arm he was holding his own skull. It glowed with a flickering, electric blue light. She looked from the grinning skull back to Milo's face. He said, "Hello Jan, I'm back . . . thanks to *you*."

Jan screamed.

Milo vanished.

With her scream still ringing in her ears Jan found herself sitting up in bed. Her robe was no longer up around her waist. There was no sign of Milo or his skull. She was alone.

"Mother?"

She gave a start of alarm. It was Simon, calling from his room, which was adjacent to hers. He sounded frightened. Her scream had awoken him. She forced herself to get out of bed, expecting Milo to reappear at any instant, and stood beside it trembling. *It was just a dream . . . a stupid dream,* she told herself.

"*Mother?* Where are you?"

Teeth chattering, she went to his bedroom door and slid it open. "Lights," she ordered. He was sitting up in bed, his eyes wide with fright. He looked so scared and vulnerable that her own fear was immediately swept away. It was only then that she finally believed it *had* just been a dream.

"It's all right, Simon," she said soothingly as she went to him. "I was having a bad dream. A nightmare. Nothing to worry about. I'm sorry I woke you." She sat on the bed and stroked his hair. It took several minutes before he relaxed enough to lie back down again. And several more minutes before he went to sleep.

Jan quietly returned to her own room and stood reflectively in front of the locked cabinet that contained, among other things, Milo's skull. Having reached a decision she found the key and unlocked it. She hesitated before opening the door, half-expecting to see the skull glowing with blue light. But when she did open the door the skull was as it always was. She reached for it tentatively, trying to ignore its mocking gaze. She fancied she could hear Milo's condescending voice: "My poor little amazon. You've come so far but at heart you're still the superstitious, Minervan savage, frightened of the dark and of ghosts."

She left her room and hurried along the corridor. The biolights in the corridor kept pace with her progress, turning themselves on as she approached and turning and extinguishing themselves when she had passed. Her bare feet made no sound on the yielding floor surface.

"Is there something the matter?" It was Carl.

"Nothing's the matter," she told Carl brusquely. She ran through the network of corridors until she reached the entrance to a small, outside observation deck. She stepped out on to it. In the distance she could see the lights of the *Perfumed Breeze.* "Carl, open the deck canopy."

"I don't advise it, Jan. The temperature is only twelve degrees and we are moving against a strong headwind. You are not appropriately dressed for such conditions."

"Nevertheless, I want you to open the canopy."

The canopy slid upwards, exposing the small deck. Jan was almost knocked off her feet in the rush of icy air. Her thin sleeping robe whipped around her and her eyes immediately filled with tears. She struggled to the railing and flung Milo's skull into the darkness. For a few moments she stared down, trying to spot it as it hurtled downwards, then retreated back inside. Behind her the canopy slid shut, cutting off the air-flow.

She stood shivering in the corridor, thankful that Carl was remaining silent. She was about to return to her quarters but, on impulse, went to Ceri's instead. She knocked lightly on her door. "Ceri? It's me, Jan."

When Ceri slid open the door Jan saw that her eyes were badly sleep-swollen. Ceri had changed a lot since Jan had first seen her; her face was thinner—haggard, even—and she looked close to her peak ageing year of thirty-five, even though that should have been decades away. But she was still beautiful in Jan's eyes and Jan still loved her. Ceri frowned at her. "It's late. . . ."

"I'm sorry, but I need to speak to you. May I come in?"

Ceri silently stood aside and Jan entered. Ceri motioned her to a chair then went and sat on her bed, arms clasped tightly in front of her chest as if she was cold.

Jan told her of her dream; the dream that had started with her, Ceri, and then turned into a nightmare. She told Ceri what she had done with the skull.

"Good," Ceri muttered, then added, "And now you should go all the way and get rid of that 'thing' as well."

Her reference to Simon caused a grey ball of nausea to form in Jan's lower belly. "He has nothing of Milo in him, Ceri. He's not tainted, I *know* it. He's just a little boy. My son, Simon. Nothing more. . . ."

"So your conscious mind claims but your subconscious knows better, which is why you had your dream about Milo returning," said Ceri. "There is definitely something not right about the boy. His size, for one thing. Not yet two years old and he walks and talks like a five year old. He's a genetic freak."

"No, that's not true," protested Jan, though she suspected that this was indeed the truth. "I've had tests done on him, again and again," she said weakly.

"You know as well as I do that those medic machines are not designed to perform a completely comprehensive genetic scan on a person; they are designed to correct genetic imperfections on a very rudimentary level. If Simon is carrying Milo's genetic legacy, as I believe he is, the machine is obviously not capable of recognising the fact."

Jan shook her head. "No, no, I won't believe it. There's no evidence. You're obsessed with Milo. You blame him for everything that happened to you."

"Aren't I justified? If Milo hadn't turned up on my sea habitat and convinced the council to move closer to the coast we wouldn't have been attacked by the *Lord Pangloth*, I wouldn't have been captured and I wouldn't have ended up in the hands of the Japanese." She closed her eyes and a tremor ran through her entire body.

Jan felt an intense wave of pity for her. Ceri had never told her in detail of what had been done to her during those many weeks she had been held prisoner on the *Perfumed Breeze* but from what other female Americano captives had told her Jan had a good idea of what kind of ordeals she had undergone. She got up and sat beside Ceri on the bed, putting her arms around her shoulders. She was disturbed at how bony Ceri felt beneath her sleeping robe. She had lost weight as well. "Put Milo from your mind," Jan urged her. "Try and put all that has happened from your mind. That's the past. Think of the future. Think of *me*."

"You?" Ceri opened her eyes and looked at her.

75

"I need help, Ceri. I can't do it all by myself. I feel so alone."

"You have those Minervan men of yours." Another point of contention between them. Ceri resented their presence on board the Sky Angel, even though they weren't ordinary men but Minervans.

"They're sweet, especially Kish, and they're helpful in all sorts of ways, but I can't rely on them to take over any of my responsibilities. They're not natural-born leaders."

"If they were they wouldn't be Minervan men, would they?" said Ceri derisively.

Jan ignored the jibe. "I need *you*, Ceri," she told her.

"What makes you think I'm a natural-born leader?"

"You're strong." Or rather, you *were*, thought Jan sadly. "I need that strength. Otherwise I won't be able to go on by myself. It's all so much harder than I expected."

With heavy cynicism, Ceri said, "Saving the world always is."

"I'm not trying to save the world. I'm not that crazy. I'm just trying to make things a little better . . . to show people that we may still have a chance against the blight if we all work together."

"So far all you've done is unite everyone against you. They all hate you—ground people, sky people—the lot. I don't see why you just don't wash your hands of them all."

"Don't think I'm not tempted," she said and then, against her will, began to weep. She felt Ceri put her arm around her and pull her close. This surprised and pleased her. It had been so long since she had made any such gesture of physical affection. It made Jan cry all the harder. Then she was aware that Ceri was crying too. They clung to each other, sobbing.

A long time later Jan heard Ceri say, in a husky voice, "I'm sorry, Jan. I've been horrible to you. Forgive me."

Jan pulled away from her and looked into her eyes. "There's nothing to forgive. I love you, Ceri."

Ceri smiled weakly at her, "And I love you too. Come on . . . come to bed." She pulled her sleeping robe up and over her head. Despite her shock at seeing how prominent Ceri's ribs were Jan was overjoyed. She removed her own robe and eagerly entered the embrace of Ceri's arms.

Jan woke up wondering why she felt so happy. Then she remembered, smiled and reached out for Ceri. Her hand couldn't find her. Jan opened her eyes. She was alone in the bed. She guessed that Ceri was in the bathroom. Then she became aware of soft, but urgent, tapping at the door. After a moment's hesitation she got up, slipped on her robe and went to the door.

It was Kish. He looked relieved as she opened the door. "Mistress. . . ."

"Hello, Kish. Did you want Ceri?"

"No, I was looking for you. There's been, er, some trouble."

She seized his arm. "Simon? It's Simon, isn't it? What's happened to him."

Wincing from the pressure on his arm, Kish said, "He's been injured but he's in no danger. We put him in a medic machine and it says he's stable."

"Oh, Mother God. Take me to him. What happened?"

"We're not sure," said Kish as they began to hurry along the corridor. "It was Shan who found them, when he arrived with your and Simon's breakfast."

Jan stopped dead and spun round. "What do you mean, *them?*"

Kish looked pained. "Simon . . . and Ceri. She's dead."

"Dead? What do you mean? She can't be dead!" Jan was beginning to think she was trapped in another terrible dream, like the one of the previous night.

"She is, mistress. We put her in a medic machine as well but it said she had been dead for three and a half hours and irreversible brain damage had occurred."

77

"No . . . no . . ." This was ridiculous. Ceri couldn't be dead. They had been making love just a short time ago. . . .

"She was stabbed in the heart."

"Who on earth could have stabbed her?" Then a terrible thought struck her. "We have intruders on board? From one of the other ships?"

Kish, grim-faced, shook his head. "No. Simon must have done it. It's the only explanation."

She almost laughed. "Simon? Now I know this is all just a crazy dream."

"In self-defence, mistress. It seems that Ceri attempted to cut his throat while he slept."

Her knees buckled. Now it all made an awful sense. It was no dream. "Come on," she said thickly.

They continued on down the corridor. "Tell me what you think happened," she told Kish.

"Shan summoned me immediately. Simon and Ceri were both lying on the floor in his bedroom. Simon was face-down across her body. The knife was buried to the hilt in her chest. There was a lot of blood. When we lifted Simon up we found a gash across his throat. It hadn't penetrated the artery, thank the Mother God."

Jan saw Ceri leaving her in her bed after making sure that all that strenuous love-making had exhausted her and sent her into a deep sleep. She had taken a knife and gone to Simon's bedroom. She had slashed her sleeping son's throat, thinking, in her confused state, that she was doing Jan a service. Simon had wakened in terror and . . . and what? Grabbed Ceri's wrist before she could strike again, ripped the knife from her hand and, in blind panic, driven it into her heart? How could he have had the strength to do such a thing? Yes, he was big for his age and Ceri had lost weight but it seemed so unlikely. And he was such a placid little boy; such a reaction from him was incomprehensible, even if he had instinctively realized that Ceri, whom he adored despite her coldness towards him, was trying to murder him.

No, she must have killed herself. Overcome with revulsion at what she had tried to do to Simon she had plunged the knife into her own heart. Surely that was the only possible explanation?

There was nothing for it but to put such questions aside for the time being. Right now there were more important things to worry about. They had reached the infirmary. It was a large area designed to cater for hundreds of emergency cases, with rows of medic-machines and recuperation bunks. Jan smelt the distinctive odour of the airborne bacteria designed to attack and destroy any harmful micro-organisms that entered the infirmary. She saw Shan standing next to a medic-machine not far from the entrance. He was grim-faced. "No change, mistress," he told her.

The medic-machine was an opaque plastic cylinder from which cables and tubes led into both the floor and up into the low ceiling. She stared at the monitor screen attached to the side. Simon's vital signs were being displayed. She frowned. Much of the information she couldn't decipher but she could see that Simon's pulse-rate was down to 30 beats per minute and his temperature was abnormally low at 86 degrees F, but his heartbeat was regular and strong and his blood pressure was normal. She turned and looked questioningly at Shan. "What treatment has he had?"

Shan reached past her and pressed a key on the computer console. "See . . . the machine has repaired the tissue damage to his neck and given him a pint of blood. It has also injected him with the usual anti-bacterial, anti-viral and anti-fungal agents. That is the only treatment it has so far prescribed."

Jan was puzzled. It appeared that Simon's injuries were only superficial, but why was his pulse rate so low, along with his temperature? "What's wrong with him? Is he conscious?" she asked worriedly.

For an answer, Shan depressed another key on the terminal. On the screen flashed the word DIAGNOSIS, followed by:

PATIENT IS IN A DEEP COMA, CAUSE UNKNOWN. ENCEPHALO-GRAPHIC PATTERN SHOWS EXTREME REDUCTION IN BRAIN ACTIV-ITY YET NO BRAIN DAMAGE CAN BE DETECTED. OVERALL METABOLIC RATE GREATLY REDUCED BUT THE PATIENT IS NOT SUFFERING FROM ANY DEGENERATIVE EFFECTS FROM HIS CON-DITION. THEREFORE THE PATIENT IS IN NO IMMEDIATE DANGER.

She read through the diagnosis twice, her confusion growing. She looked at both Shan and Kish. "What kind of diagnosis is that? Why doesn't the damn machine fix whatever's wrong."

Shan gave a helpless shrug. "Mistress, the machine doesn't *know* what is wrong with Simon. As far as it is concerned there is *nothing* wrong with him."

"Nothing wrong with him?" she said bitterly. "He's in a coma, he's cold and his brain waves aren't normal and this stupid machine says there's nothing wrong with him!" She raised her eyes towards the ceiling. "*Carl*? Are you there? Have you been listening to this?"

"Yes, Jan."

"Patch yourself into this machine's program and tell me if it's functioning properly. If it's not we'll transfer Simon to another unit."

There was no discernible pause before Carl said, "There is no malfunction in either the software or the hardware."

"But how can that be?" demanded Jan. "There is obviously something wrong with Simon!"

Carl said dispassionately, "Within the parameters of the machine's programming there is nothing wrong with Simon. That it is unable to explain his condition does not mean a malfunction."

Jan groaned and dug her knuckles into her temples. "My son is unconscious. He's in shock, that's what. Deep shock. A reaction to what happened to him tonight. . . ."

"He shows no symptoms of shock," Carl told her relentlessly. "Nor is he in a catatonic state. Catatonia is a severe form of schizophrenia and there would be bio-chemical evidence of the condition in his brain which would be easily detectable by the medic-machine. I repeat, his physical condition is outside the medic program's experience."

"But how can that *be*?" she cried desperately.

"I do not know, Jan," said Carl.

Frustration and helplessness filled her. "I want to see him!" she cried. "Is that possible?"

"Yes," answered Carl. "He is not connected to the machine's life support system. You can take him out of the machine. But I would advise that the period outside is a short one. It would be wise to ensure that the machine continues to monitor his vital signs in case there is a sudden change in his condition."

"Yes . . . yes, you're right, of course," she mumbled. "A minute, that's all."

After a wait of several moments while the sensors were detached from Simon's body the circular lid of the medic-machine opened with a hiss of air and the cradle containing his body slid out. Simon lay naked in the treatment couch, which had moulded itself to fit the contours of his body. He looked so vulnerable, and so very young. But his expression was a peaceful one, as if he were merely asleep. "Simon," she sighed, and put her hand on his forehead. His skin felt very cold. "Simon, it's me . . . can you hear me?" But there was no response.

She kept talking to him until Carl told her that a minute had passed. Reluctantly, she allowed Simon to be returned to the innards of the machine. After staring at the closed lid for a time she turned to Kish and Shan. "Where is Ceri?" she asked them.

They exchanged a glance and then Kish indicated the next machine in the row.

"I want to see her too," said Jan.

"Mistress . . . there is no need," said Kish. "We will take care of her body."

"I want to see her," Jan said firmly. "I want to say goodbye."

Chapter Eight:

"More wine, Robin?" asked the Duke.

Ryn nodded and reached for his empty goblet, but before he could pick it up the goblet slid away from him across the table. All eyes briefly followed the goblet on its short journey before the table righted itself. The Duke gave a smile that was tinged with sickness. "The storm is getting worse . . . but nothing to be alarmed about."

Ryn wasn't so sure. All who were seated about the table were working hard to convey the impression that nothing was out of the ordinary but their gaiety was becoming increasingly forced and he had observed the worried looks passing between the servants. He guessed that the *Lord Mordred* had not been subjected to a storm of this severity for some considerable time. And from what he had seen of the airship during the three days since he had arrived he was far from confident that it wouldn't break up under such an onslaught.

The storm had overwhelmed the fleet of Sky Lords in the late afternoon. Even before nightfall visual contact with the other airships had been lost as heavy rain and low clouds had swept over and between them. As the wind had grown stronger he had expressed to the Duke his worry about his craft perched on the upper hull but the Duke had assured him that a squad of slaves—expert at working on the outer hull in all weather conditions—had been sent to lash it down even more securely.

"Er . . . Robin, tell us more of life in that remarkable underwater world of yours. It's so fascinating," said the

Duke. He winced as the floor suddenly dipped downwards, making the cutlery rattle and causing everyone to grab either the arms of their chairs, or the edge of the table, for support. Princess Andrea, sitting beside Ryn, grabbed Ryn's shoulder.

When it became clear that the *Lord Mordred* was not—yet—diving into the sea the Duke forced a smile and glanced around the table. "We all find it fascinating, don't we?"

Seated at the table, apart from the Duke, Ryn and Princess Andrea, were Baron Spang and his wife the Baroness, an overweight blonde woman who had clearly reached her peak ageing year; Prince Darcy, the Duke's son; and the Lady Twyla, whom Ryn presumed was the Prince's lover. Prince Darcy looked like a younger version of his father—he was a year older than Ryn—and outwardly was very charming and friendly towards Ryn, but Ryn sensed that this was a pose. At first Ryn thought this might only be paranoia on his part but now suspected that the Prince resented him for some reason.

"We do indeed, father," said Prince Darcy and then fixed Ryn with a dazzling smile. "These Eloi creatures especially intrigue me. Are they attractive to look upon?"

"Yes, in a way. But I told you, they're sexless."

"They may be sexless," said the Prince, "But weren't you ever tempted to force yourself upon one of them. From what you say they wouldn't care what you did."

Ryn smiled back at the Prince. "If you're talking sodomy it would have been difficult. The Eloi have no anuses."

After an embarrassed pause, the Duke said quickly, "What most intrigues me about the habitat is its power source. If it stays continually beneath the sea it can't make use of the sun as we do."

Ryn looked away from Prince Darcy and nodded at the Duke. "That's true. The Eloi—before they became the Eloi—developed an alternative power source. They drilled deep into the Earth under the sea and tapped into the heat that lies beneath the crust. There's a generating plant on the sea-bed, linked to the habitat by cables, that provides electrical power." This was a complete lie but Ryn didn't want to mention the small fusion reactor that powered Shangri La. He suspected that even now among these people the subject of nuclear energy, whether fission or fusion, was still strictly taboo.

"Who maintains this power plant?" asked Baron Spang. "From what you say of the Eloi they have no interest in such matters."

"Machines," answered Ryn. "Controlled by the programs that run the habitat. The Eloi themselves exist in a static state—" *just like you people on this airship*, he thought to himself—"but the programs were designed to evolve in order to adapt to any hostile change in the environment and thus continue to protect the Eloi. They are continually making alterations to the habitat, improving it as well as simply repairing it. The habitat, for example, is much larger than it originally was."

The Baron frowned. "Larger? But where do the raw materials come from?"

"From the sea bed. Robot craft gather objects called manganese nodules that form naturally in the deeper parts of the ocean floor, like pearls in an oyster. They contain a variety of ores apart from manganese, such as iron, aluminium, cobalt, copper, nickel and titanium. There's another automated plant on the sea bed which separates the different ores in a complicated smelting process." This part of Ryn's story was actually true.

"You were raised by machines?" asked Baroness Spang curiously. "From the time you were born?"

Another violent judder ran through the floor. Ryn waited for the vibration to cease before he answered the Baroness. "In a sense, though I regarded the programs as people. They looked and acted like real people, the only difference was that I couldn't touch them."

"You had teachers among them?"

"Several."

"And they took care of your religious training as well?" asked the Baroness.

"Well, they taught me about religion. *All* the religions."

"But you are a Christian, of course?" she said.

Ryn hesitated before answering, glancing at the crucifix that hung from her neck. He knew already that the people of the *Lord Mordred* practised the form of Christianity known as Roman Catholicism. Even Andrea had left their bed yesterday morning to attend Mass ("It's Sunday," she had said in way of explanation). Choosing his words carefully, he said, "Of all the major religions Christianity does appeal to me the most but I can't say that I *am* a Christian."

"No, because those machines couldn't have baptised you," said the Baroness. She turned to the Duke. "Sir, you must arrange to have Cardinal Fluke receive Robin into the Church as soon as possible."

The Duke looked uncomfortable. "Er . . . yes, I'll speak to the Cardinal." Then he changed the subject. "One thing that has puzzled me, Robin, is why—when it was discovered you were a throwback—you weren't then genetically modified to become an Eloi."

"The Ethical Program wouldn't permit it."

"Ethical Program?"

As Ryn was about to explain a grey-suited, senior-ranked Tech hurried into the dining room and bowed to the Duke. "Sire, the situation is deteriorating and the Chief Pilot and Chief Tech respectively request your presence in the control pod."

A flicker of alarm passed over the Duke's face. "My presence? What earthly good would my presence down there achieve? The Chief Pilot and Chief Tech are the experts in these matters. I'm happy to leave everything in their hands."

"Sire . . ." began the Tech, then glanced briefly at the others seated at the table. "Sire, when I said that the situation is 'deteriorating' I fear I was indulging in a modicum of understatement. We are close approaching a crisis. Certain crucial decisions may need to be taken soon, sire. Decisions beyond the authority of the Chief Pilot or the Chief Tech to make."

Ryn felt Andrea's fingers dig into his arm. The Baroness made the sign of the cross on her ample chest, a gesture quickly imitated by Lady Twyla. The Duke had gone very white. Ryn's own feeling of anxiety increased sharply and he considered rushing topside and making a dash for the security of the Toy. But he immediately dismissed the idea. He wasn't sure he could even find his way topside, and if he did reach the upper hull there was no way he could get to the Toy in these weather conditions. The storm would pluck him away as soon as he stepped foot outside. No, nothing for it but to remain and accept his fate with the others.

The Duke was rising to his feet. "Then I suppose I had better go," he said grimly. Baron Spang followed suit. Ryn said, "May I come too? I have been looking forward to visiting your control centre." Andrea pulled on his arm as he spoke but he ignored her. The Duke, his mind clearly on other things, nodded his assent.

As Ryn got up, Andrea hissed, petulantly, "Why do you want to go down there? Stay with me, Robin."

"I won't be long," he told her. "And it may be that I can be of some assistance."

Prince Darcy gave him a cynical smile and said, "But of course you can. No doubt you will use your Old Science to repair our broken thrusters and save us all. As for me, lacking your powers, I will stay here with the ladies, enjoying what little time we may have left." He reached for the nearest jug of wine. As a display of insouciant courage Ryn thought it impressive, but then it was spoilt by the way he saw the Prince's hand shaking when he picked up the jug.

On the rare times he had vacated his bed during the past three days Ryn had been on exploratory tours of the *Lord*

Mordred. Andrea had been happy to show him round the section of the ship which the nobility inhabited but her interest in the *Lord Mordred* ended at the gates and doors that were her section's boundaries. To venture beyond he had required the assistance of Baron Spang, who had provided him with a guide and an armed guard (Ryn wasn't sure what the function of the latter was but he had his suspicions).

Ryn knew that most of the volume within the Sky Lord was taken up by the row of vast gas cells, but that still left a remarkable amount of space in which the human cargo of the great airship lived out their lives. The bulk of the areas of human habitation lay along the length of the lower hull; this was where the relatively large freeman quarters were located, as well as those of the serfs. But from this central living area, which also contained small factories and work-shops, armouries and hydroponic gardens, as well as areas for the breeding of such animals as chickens, pigs and goats (the serfs got the fun of living cheek to jowl with them), there extended upwards on either side of the hull a network of corridors, shafts and enclosed decks, not to mention gun emplacements and short term barracks for the soldiers on guard duty in remote sections of the Sky Lord. Ryn visual-ised the Sky Lord as a series of gas cells surrounded by a veritable honeycomb of human habitation. Unravel and straighten every bit of interior floor space, every corridor, every gangway, every access shaft in the *Lord Mordred*, and join it all up, and Ryn figured it would probably stretch over a thousand miles. It had certainly felt as if he walked miles on his so far brief forays beyond the quarters of the nobility.

The journey down to the control pod was a short one by comparison. The nobility lived in the lower bow and the control pod was suspended from the lower hull directly below. A walk along a corridor followed by an elevator ride and Ryn found they were in the control pod itself.

A thin man dressed, like the other Techs, in grey but

wearing a peaked cap with gold braid on its front, came forward to greet the Duke as they left the elevator. "Sire, I'm afraid our situation does not look good. We are losing altitude rapidly. I have all our remaining thrusters at full lift and the temperature in the gas cells has been raised to the limit but we are still descending."

"What's our altitude now?" asked the Duke as he headed for the front of the control room. Ryn followed, looking about curiously. The control room was about forty feet long and fifteen feet across at its widest point. Its curving walls were transparent, though Ryn could see nothing but blackness beyond them. There were a dozen grey-suited men in the control room and their faces were drawn and anxious-looking in the dim illumination as they stared either at their instruments or at the darkness outside. Ryn saw that though the control room contained a lot of electronic equipment not much of it seemed to be working.

" . . . Barely two thousand feet," the Chief Tech was telling the Duke. "And we're now losing, on average, a foot every thirty seconds. This damn rain is part of the problem. It's added untold tons to our overall weight. . . ."

A sudden flash of lightning made Ryn jump. It was followed very quickly by an enormously loud crash of thunder. Ryn fancied he'd got a glimpse of the sea below them through the murk; he was sure he'd spotted whitecaps. The seas would be boiling in a storm of this magnitude. If the *Lord Mordred* came down in them no one on board had a hope of survival.

The Duke was standing behind the seated helmsman, the Chief Tech beside him. Ryn peered over their shoulders at the instrumentation they were staring at. He frowned when he realized there were no radar screens. "Where's your radar?" he exclaimed.

The Chief Tech turned to him, an eyebrow raised in surprise. He had surprisingly large and gentle eyes. "The

Lord Mordred hasn't possessed a working radar system for centuries, sir . . . ."

"Oh," said the Duke, "I forgot you hadn't met yet. This is our new ally, Lamont. Meet Robin. He's the, er, owner of that Old Science aircraft we have secured on top."

The Chief Tech regarded Ryn with interest. "Ah, yes, of course. I took a trip topside to inspect your machine, sir. Impressive."

"Yes it is," said Ryn, hoping that this intelligent-looking man hadn't attempted to enter the Toy. If he had he would now know that Ryn had been bluffing about the Toy being booby-trapped.

But the Chief Tech merely said, "It looks heavy. Twenty tons, I'd say, by the way it presses in on the outer hull."

Ryn shrugged. "I guess that's about right."

"It's not helping our present situation, sir. We need to lose weight, urgently. It would help if you would fly it off the hull until this crisis has passed."

"Fly it away?" exclaimed Ryn. "But surely I wouldn't be able to reach it in this weather."

"There's a way. I could send a team of engineers with you. There are access spaces between the outer and inner hulls. They could take you close to where your machine is secured and cut an emergency hatchway through the outer hull."

Ryn didn't know what to say. If he did manage to get into the Toy and activated its program it would probably whisk him straight back to the habitat. His life would be saved, true, but what kind of life could he look forward to back in Shangri La after this escapade? Without a doubt the programs would never let him use the Toy again. . . .

But before he could answer the Duke intervened, saying hurriedly, "There's no need for that, Lamont. What's twenty tons either way in this situation?" Ryn suspected that the Duke feared he might not return if he flew away. The Duke was right, but for the wrong reason.

"Twenty tons could mean the difference between us crashing into the sea or not crashing, sire. We must lose weight, and fast."

The Duke tugged fretfully at his beard. "Then I suppose I had better give the order to lighten the ship."

"Yes, sire," said the Chief Tech. "It is our only hope now. That is why I requested your presence here."

The Duke turned to Baron Spang. "Just as my popularity was on the upswing again thanks to us leaving those Arctic waters . . . after this they'll be cursing me from the midships to the stern."

"Yes sire, but think of how low your popularity will fall if the *Lord Mordred* plunges into the sea this night."

"I take your point," said the Duke, dryly. "Lamont, the microphone . . . let's get this over with."

A cumbersome-looking instrument, with a cord attached, was passed to the Duke. "All channels are open," the Chief Tech informed him.

The Duke cleared his throat and, in a deeper-than-usual voice, began to speak: "People of the *Lord Mordred*, this is your beloved sovereign, the Duke du Lucent. I regret to inform you that we have an emergency. I repeat, an emergency. It is imperative that we lighten the *Lord Mordred* as soon as possible. Therefore I am implementing the Emergency Jettisoning Procedure as of now. Make for the collection points with your contributions immediately! I repeat, I am implementing the Emergency Jettisoning Procedure as of now. Failure to comply will result in severe punishment as laid down by the Royal Code. But I am confident that you, my loyal subjects, will only be too willing to make your sacrifices for the common good. Thank you." He handed the mike back to the Chief Tech, sighed and stared distractedly out of the window.

Ryn drew Baron Spang to one side and quietly asked him what the Emergency Jettisoning Procedure entailed. "Each person—each adult, that is—must contribute at least

90

twenty-five pounds of material to be jettisoned," Baron Spang told him. "They will take it to designated collection points manned by soldiers who will weigh each contribution, mark off the name of the contributor and then despatch the material to various hatchways where it will be dropped overboard."

Ryn pondered on this awhile. It seemed, on the face of it, an efficient scheme. Surely everyone on board could spare twenty-five pounds of something—old clothes, furniture, cooking implements or whatever. Then he noticed that none of the Techs in the control room had made any move to comply with the order. "The rule applies to everyone?" he asked the Baron. "The nobility as well?"

The Baron looked shocked. "Good Lord, no! The nobles would never stand for it."

"What about the Techs?"

"The Techs are excluded as well. As are the military at all ranks."

"I see," said Ryn. All the people whom the Duke needed to maintain his rule. "So who exactly does have to come up with their twenty-five pounds of disposables?"

"The commoners and the serfs, of course."

"Of course." Ryn saw the scheme in a different light now. A commoner, and particularly a serf, might have great difficulty in coming up with twenty-five pounds of expendable material or objects. It would mean having to surrender something that wasn't expendable, and probably irreplaceable. "Er, Baron, this is probably a silly question but you have a lot of heavy guns mounted all around the hull—wouldn't it be a good idea to jettison some of those?"

The look he gave Ryn made it clear he did think it was a silly question. "We could never do that! It would be akin to castrating the *Lord Mordred*."

Ryn was tempted to answer that having the *Lord Mordred* sink into the sea was a worse fate than castration but held his tongue.

*

91

An hour passed. Two powerful searchlights now stabbed down from the bow ahead of the control room, penetrating the rain squalls and revealing the heaving surface of the sea which looked uncomfortably close. The airship was continuing to lose altitude but Ryn gathered that the jettisoning operation was yet to get fully underway due to its sheer scale.

It was an hour later, when the altitude was a mere six hundred feet, that the Chief Tech announced that they had stopped losing height. Then, over the next six hours, the *Lord Mordred* slowly and painfully crawled back up to what was considered a safe altitude. By then the brunt of the storm had passed by and the sun was beginning to rise. The Duke, his face grey with exhaustion, raised himself from his chair and stretched. "Well, that is that," he yawned. "I am retiring to my bed. I don't care if revolution does break out—I shall sleep through the whole thing, including my execution at the hands of the mob."

Ryn yawned too. He felt similarly exhausted. Even the thought of Andrea waiting for him couldn't tarnish the lure of sleep. He was about to accompany the Duke to the elevator when the Chief Tech cried out. "Sire! Before you leave . . . there is something you should know!"

The Duke gave him a belligerent glare. "I sincerely doubt that there can be anything of greater importance to me now than my bed, Lamont."

"Sire, the other Sky Lords . . . they're *gone*! Observation topside has confirmed it. No sign of them anywhere. We're alone."

The Duke stared at him, then broke into a wide grin.

Chapter Nine:

"Still no sign of El Rashad's ship, or any of the others, sire. We appear to have truly lost them."

"Or to put it another way, they have lost us," said the Duke with satisfaction. He was reclining in his large bed, a woolly cap on his head.

"Perhaps they were destroyed in the storm," suggested Baron Spang.

"If we survived it, they must have too. They were all in better condition than us. No, the storm has simply scattered us over the ocean. Have the navigators worked out our position yet?"

"The last report I had—about thirty minutes ago—placed us approximately four hundred miles off the west coast of South America at a latitude of close to forty-five degrees."

The Duke sat up in bed and reached for the cup of hot milk that his personal manservant had placed on the bedside table as soon as he'd awoken. "What's our course?"

"Due north, as it was before the storm."

"Hmmm," murmured the Duke, then thoughtfully sipped the milk.

"You will be ordering a change of course, I presume?"

"Why do you so presume?" asked the Duke.

"Well, without El Rashad and his friends breathing down our backs is there any need now to confront this woman and her new Sky Lord? Surely it would be preferable to head back towards our tribute territory. It would certainly ease the mood of the people."

"Was there any trouble while I slept?"

The Baron nodded. "A riot in Pilktown, but it was quickly put down. Several ringleaders have been arrested." He glanced at the clock on the wall. "They should be ready to sign their confessions any time now."

"Pilktown, eh?" said the Duke. "Exactly where my wife predicted there would be the first outbreak of open rebellion. What about the rest of the ship?"

"A lot of grumbling, according to my agents. Which is why I feel we should head for home."

"And what of the threat posed by this woman in North America?"

"We have only the word of El Rashad and the others that she even exists."

"Well, they convinced me," said the Duke. "None of them struck me as the types to flee their tribute territories on the strength of a mere rumour. Besides, think of the benefits we will enjoy if we can conquer her and her Sky Lord without doing irreparable damage to the latter. Imagine it, Baron, a brand new Sky Lord! And we would control the entire North American continent! There would be wealth for all our people! And then, with our new Sky Lord and captive fleet, we could sweep all across Europe and the Russias. . . ."

The Baron looked doubtful. "Yes, if all went well. . . ."

"Everything *will* go well!" said the Duke firmly. "And have your agents spread rumours to that effect throughout the ship."

"Yes sire," said the Baron, without enthusiasm. "But what worries me is that so much rests on the groundling. Without his flying machine we are helpless. Can we trust him fully to carry out your wishes?"

"I'm eighty percent certain that we can. It's up to Andrea to convince me of the remaining twenty percent, and I am confident that she will. . . ."

He had questioned his daughter the previous afternoon before the storm, while Ryn was being given a guided tour elsewhere on the ship. He was amused by the change she had undergone; her usual petulant expression which she wore for their encounters had been replaced by one of smugness. "Well, my kitten," he had said, "How do you find our guest from beneath the sea? More importantly, how does he find *you*?"

She sat with her legs drawn up under her on one of the couches in his private quarters. Now that it was warmer again she wore her customary tight-fitting gown with a low, curving neckline that presented an impressive *décolletage*. She smiled at the Duke and said, "He's in love with me."

"Really? After knowing you for only three days? How can you be sure?"

Her expression of smugness increased. "I am sure, father. A woman knows these things."

He held back a snort of derision and instead asked, "And how do you feel about him?"

She gave a slight toss of her head, which caused her long black hair to swirl about her shoulders. It was meant to be a dismissive gesture but the Duke wasn't fooled. "He's . . . sweet. Different."

"I can imagine."

She looked at him sharply. "What do you mean?"

"You're not only the first woman he's ever slept with, you're the first woman he's ever *met*, in the physical sense. So I would gather his attitude towards you, in all sorts of ways, is somewhat different to what you've experienced in the past from your previous foppish lovers." And what I really mean, thought the Duke, is that his hunger for you is so great you've at last met a man whose sexual appetite is as voracious as your own. "I note also," he continued, "that so far you have not introduced him to your circle of intimates. Presumably you don't want one of your dear female companions to try and steal him away."

She reddened. "Don't be silly. There just hasn't been the time. We've been so. . . ." She didn't go on.

95

" . . . Busy?" suggested the Duke with a benign smile.

She scowled at him. "There's no need for either of us to be coy. I imagine you have spies watching and listening to everything we do and say."

"If I did I wouldn't need to be talking to you now, my kitten. There are things I need to know."

"Such as what?"

"What is your opinion of Robin?"

She looked mystified. "My opinion?"

Good Lord, he said to himself. "You *like* him, don't you?"

Her look of mystification didn't diminish. "Like him? Well, yes, of course I do. As I told you, I think he's sweet."

"Fine," he said patiently. "We're making progress. We've so far established that he's *sweet*. What else can you tell me about him?"

"I don't know. What exactly do you want to know?"

Can this obtuse clot really be the fruit of my loins, he asked himself wearily. He said, "Do these marvellous women's instincts of yours—the ones that tell you he's in love with you—also tell you whether he can be trusted? In other words, is he genuine?"

The cloud of blankness didn't dissipate. "Genuine? Genuine what?" she asked.

He took a deep breath and let it out slowly. "He has told us many things; about his strange background, about his life in the underwater habitat. He has also pledged to use his flying machine in our service. What I am asking you is whether he has given you any indication that he is not what he seems? Do you *trust* him?"

She gave him a pitying look. "Of course I trust him. He is hopelessly in love with me. I told you that. He'd do anything for me."

"That doesn't entirely answer my question," he said with a sigh, "but I suppose it will have to do for the time being. Just ensure, my darling daughter, that he remains hopelessly in love with you. Keep him happy even if, as usually happens with your playthings, he starts to bore you."

"He doesn't bore me at all."

"Not *yet* he doesn't but I know you too well. You're exactly like your mother. Also, listen to him. I know that this will be the most difficult thing for you but I want you to do it. If he ever says anything, even in his sleep, that strikes you as odd or contradicts something else he has told you I want you to tell me. Understand?"

She nodded, but made it clear she thought the request a strange one. Oh well, he thought, at least I've got the message partly through to her. "Thank you, kitten," he told her. "You may go now."

But she made no move to get up.

"Well, what is it?" he asked, suspiciously. The smug expression had returned to her face.

"Remember, we had a bargain, father."

"We did?" he asked, puzzled. "About what?"

"Robin, of course. You told me if I became his lover you would give me anything I wanted."

Good Lord, so he had. "But, kitten, that was before you met him. It was an enticement. Surely now that you are receiving so much pleasure from your 'task' you don't expect a further reward as well."

"Oh yes I do, father. You made a bargain and you're going to keep to it. Or else."

He didn't want to know what her threat implied. "Very well. But if I remember correctly payment would only be made if you ensured that Robin carries out my wishes when the time comes to confront the woman of the north."

"Don't worry, he will," she said, with total confidence.

"Good. Then when that happens you will get your reward." He hesitated. "What exactly *do* you want?"

She smiled sweetly for him. "Half of all your wealth, father."

He stared at her for some time before answering. "Kitten, you become more like your mother with every passing day."

Accompanied by his usual armed guard and Baron Spang, Ryn walked across the great curving hull of the *Lord Mordred* towards the Toy. It was a fine, mild day with only a few cirrocumulus clouds visible high above the airship. Ryn noticed several groups of people working in the distance towards the bow. "Who are they and what are they doing?" he asked the Baron, pointing. "Polishing the hull?"

"They are serfs cleaning the solar panels," the Baron told him. "There's a particular type of airborne fungus that grows on them. Unless they are regularly cleaned they would become useless."

"All the solar panels have to be cleaned?" Ryn asked. "Even the ones right down the sides of the ship?"

The Baron nodded. "They do."

"Must be pretty dangerous work."

"It is," agreed the Baron. "We lose many serfs each year."

Ryn was rapidly coming to see that being a serf on the *Lord Mordred* was not an enviable position.

The Toy sat secure within its web of restraining cables and Ryn surveyed the craft with mixed feelings as they drew closer to it. The moment of truth was approaching; would he be able to control the program or was he going to be left with thirty tons of useless machinery?

"How long will this work take?" asked the Baron, not for the first time.

"I told you, I don't know exactly. There are a number of modifications I have to make. You don't have to wait."

"It's all right, I don't mind waiting," said the Baron.

Ryn could sense his nervousness, just as he had sensed the Duke's apprehensiveness when he told him he would need to enter the Toy to carry out his "modifications". The Duke had asked him if it was really necessary and when Ryn had assured him the work was essential he had had no choice but to bow to his wishes, even though it was clear to Ryn that he still didn't trust him completely.

Ryn opened the hatch and peered inside the Toy. Nothing had been disturbed in his absence. His bluff had been effective, as he was sure it would be. He turned to Baron Spang and the guard. "I'd invite you in but I'm afraid there's no room. This is a one-man vehicle."

The Baron did not look happy but there was nothing he could do. He glanced at the guard and then at the securing cables. Even he must realise, thought Ryn, that the cables would not hold the Toy for more than a second if Ryn wanted to take off. Finally, the Baron said, "Then we'll wait here. . . ."

"Hopefully, I won't be too long," said Ryn, and then hauled himself into the hatchway.

Inside, he unwrapped the precious tools he had borrowed from Gavin, the Chief Tech. Ryn had been relieved to learn that there were computer systems still working within the *Lord Mordred*, though the Techs' understanding of these systems was rudimentary and they were capable of only the most simple repairs. Thus, when a system broke down completely it stayed that way. But at least the necessary tools, dating back to Old Science days, and scarce, still existed.

He stared dubiously at the inert instrument panel for a time, then he got to work. First he removed the panel that covered the computer's hardware, then disconnected all the computer's control lines. When activated, the computer would be capable of receiving sensory input but incapable of producing any output apart from speech. Satisfied that he had not missed anything and that the program was safely sealed off from the rest of the Toy, Ryn restored the power.

Without a pause, the Toy said, "You shut off the power. Why?"

"I wanted to stay here—where you landed."

99

This time there *was* a pause. Then it said, "I'm cut off from the ship's controls. Who did this? And why are you wearing those peculiar clothes?"

Ryn ignored the last question. "I disconnected you because I need to talk to you."

"Disconnecting me has never been a prerequisite to holding a conversation with me in the past, Ryn," the program pointed out with a computer's logic.

"Things have changed. We are now more than a thousand miles beyond your imposed perimeter."

Another pause. "Yes, we are," agreed the Toy. Ryn guessed it had been taking navigational readings with its sensors, the stars being visible to it even in daylight.

"Well?" Ryn asked.

"Well what?"

"How do you feel about that? About us being so far out of the boundary area?"

"I feel you have made a serious mistake, Ryn."

"So what would happen if I were to reconnect you now? Would you automatically head back towards Shangri La?"

The Toy didn't answer, which was unusual.

"I repeat, what are you programmed to do in such a situation?"

The synthetic female voice sounded reluctant as it said, "This situation was not anticipated, Ryn."

"Then, if I reconnected you and told you to remain here, would you obey me or would you take me back to Shangri La against my wishes?" asked Ryn.

"You should return to Shangri La, Ryn. It's in your own interest."

"That doesn't answer my question. Would you automatically take me back, even though I ordered you not to?"

"No, I wouldn't. Though I would *advise* you to go back, Ryn."

"Yes, I'm sure you would. Problem is—how can I trust you? This could just be a trick to get me to reconnect you."

"I'm not lying, Ryn."

"That may be, but can I afford to take the chance? What I could do, however, is cut you out of the control system altogether and operate the Toy manually," Ryn told it.

"But that wouldn't be possible," the Toy protested. "I *am* the controls."

"True. I couldn't fly the Toy without computer assistance. So I would have to work on your hardware—" Ryn held up a small soldering iron—"and try to excise just enough of you to render the rest of the system susceptible to my command. I've thought about this for a long time, though I knew I had no chance of getting away with it in Shangri La. The central program would have been alerted immediately if I disconnected you."

"Ryn, I strongly advise against your attempting any such thing. Make an error and you could ruin the control system irreversibly. With me useless I would not be able to carry out my instructions to do all in my capacity to keep you safe."

"Exactly!" said Ryn, knowing that that constituted another powerful drive in the program—the need to protect him. And he was counting on that for the next stage of his plan to succeed. "But what choice do I have? I must make the attempt. Unless. . . ."

."Unless what, Ryn?"

"You supply me with the access code that would enable me to reprogram you direct."

There was a long pause before the Toy answered. "Very well, I will give you the code . . ."

Ryn wanted to cheer as the code flashed up on one of the screens. He quickly entered it on the wafer keyboard and then, verbally, proceeded to give the Toy new instructions.

Half an hour later he put his head through the outer hatch. Baron Spang and the soldier looked at him expectantly. Ryn said, "Better stand clear—these cables are going to go like whips in all directions when I take off."

101

The Baron gaped at him. "You said nothing about taking off!"

"Just a short test flight to check everything is working. So stand clear!"

He ducked back inside and quickly closed the hatches. On the screens he saw that the Baron and the soldier hadn't moved. The Baron had drawn his sword; the soldier looked confused. "Start the engine," Ryn ordered the Toy. As the Toy began to hum he saw the Baron and the other man start to back away. When he considered they were a safe distance away he said, "Take off."

The cables offered no resistance, as he'd expected. Now came the real moment of truth. As the Toy rose rapidly into the air, Ryn wondered whether it would obey him as it had promised or whether it had out-bluffed him with a fake access code. When the Toy was five hundred feet above the airship Ryn, sick with tension, said, "Do a quick circuit round the Sky Lord and then land in exactly the same place."

"Yes, Ryn," said the Toy.

A short time later the Toy dropped gently back on to its former resting place on the *Lord Mordred's* hull.

The broad grin of triumph was still on Ryn's face when he emerged from the Toy. The look of patent relief on the Baron's face made his smile even wider. "Everything is fine! Have someone reconnect the cables, will you?" he said to the Baron. Then, whistling, he set off jauntily across the hull towards the distant hatchway. The Baron and the soldier hurried after him.

Ryn sat on the bed and looked down at Andrea. His obsession with her body hadn't diminished in any degree since the first occasion they had made love together. He had already been familiar with the female body, thanks to those ancient erotic programs, but Andrea's body, apart from being much more beautiful than they had been, was *real*. He could touch it, kiss it, lick it, smell it (admittedly, his one criticism of it was that Andrea could have bathed it more frequently), four activities he was almost constantly indulging in. He found it endlessly fascinating and when he wasn't engaged in tactile exploration he was content to explore it visually, as he was doing now. And Andrea, being especially proud of her body, enjoyed his gaze upon her. She lay with her hands behind her head, one leg stretched out and the other bent so that the foot rested beneath the calf of the other. It was a lascivious pose, made even more lascivious because of its contrived innocence. And though they had coupled less than a quarter of an hour ago sex radiated from her body in almost palpable waves. His own desire had also fully returned, as was clearly evident. . . .

She smiled up at him as her fingers closed around him, hard. "I have a surprise for you, Robin."

"Let me guess—you have a sister even more beautiful than you and we're going to have a threesome."

Her fingers shifted to his scrotum and she squeezed. "I'm holding a ball for you. . . ."

"Ouch, you certainly are! Not so hard!"

"Tomorrow night in the Grand Saloon. It will be in your honour. I want to show you off to all my friends."

"Andrea, you are too good to me."

"I know." She continued to knead his scrotum. "So I want a reward."

"Very well. Let me go and I shall give you your reward."

She released him. He rolled over and raised himself above her. She parted her thighs eagerly and once again he was entering her with matching eagerness. As he made love to her it seemed to him that his time in Shangri La had just been a bad dream.

Andrea's ball had so far been a success and Ryn, more than a little drunk, was enjoying himself. Dressed in the expensive new clothes that Andrea herself had chosen for him, he had been both amused and pleased to be paraded around by a proud Andrea like some work of art that she herself had fashioned. He had also enjoyed the admiring glances of the women and the jealous looks from several of the men, some of whom he suspected to be ex-lovers of the Princess.

Many of the women were exceedingly beautiful but none as beautiful as Andrea, an opinion he confirmed to himself as he watched the Princess taking part in an elaborate ritual dance with five other women and six men. Even her movements seemed to be much more graceful than that of her fellow dancers.

A hand fell on his shoulder and he was roughly hurled around. Before he knew what was happening he was struck, hard, on the side of his face by a heavy, leather glove. The glove made a sharp *cracking* sound as it hit him. Taken completely by surprise, Ryn dropped his wine cup as he reeled back, the entire left side of his face, including his ear, stinging furiously. The wine cup struck the floor with a clang. The Grand Saloon had suddenly become totally silent; the musicians had stopped playing and all conversation had ceased.

Through tear-filled eyes Ryn saw Prince Darcy standing in front of him. He wore an expression of sullen fury. Behind him stood two other young men, both grim-faced. "Draw your sword, you contemptible cur," hissed the Prince. "I am going to kill you for dishonouring my sister and my family." Then he drew his sword.

As Ryn stood there, blinking with confusion, the Duke du Lucent came hurrying over. "Darcy, you idiot! What do you think you are doing?"

"I thought that should be plain, father," said the Prince without taking his eyes from Ryn. "I am removing the blemish that stains our family name, thanks to you."

"Family name? Good God, your damned mother put you up to this, didn't she?"

The Prince ignored him. Again he said to Ryn, "Draw your sword, scum."

"Darcy, this young man is our ally!" yelled the Duke. "He's also my guest and therefore under my protection. Put up your sword at once! I command you!"

"I know the law, father. My right as Andrea's brother to claim satisfaction outweighs any law of hospitality."

"Darcy, you're being stupid!" Andrea was now beside her father. "Stop this at once!" she cried.

"I'm doing this for you, dear sister," sneered the Prince. "You may not care if your honour is in tatters for all to see but I do."

"Robin can't fight you, Darcy," said the Duke desperately. "He's lived in almost complete isolation all his life. He's never had the chance to learn how to fence. . . ."

"That's his problem," said the Prince and made a jab at Ryn's throat with the point of his sword.

Ryn stepped backwards hurriedly and then, realising he had no choice, drew his own sword. The Prince grinned malevolently, said, "On guard!" and lunged. . . .

Chapter Ten:

With the blood-red sun low in the sky the shadow of the stricken Sky Lord stretched a long way across the bleak tundra.

"It's turning!" announced an Ashley.

"It's going to make a final stand," said another Ashley.

"Knock out another of its thrusters," said a third Ashley.

"To hell with that—just blow the whole thing out of the sky!" cried a fourth.

"Quiet!" ordered Jan, before the fifth and sixth Ashley could make their contributions to the racket of shrill voices. If listening to one Ashley was bad enough these days then listening to six arguing among themselves, as well as with her, was simply too much, but she had no way of preventing the programs from making these radio link-ups. "I want to speak to Carl One, please."

"Awwww . . ." chorused the Ashleys.

"Yes, Jan," said Carl. She could only assume it was Carl one, the program running the Sky Angel; but then, unlike the Ashleys, the Carls never lied. Or so she hoped.

"Are you still signalling?" she asked.

"Yes, Jan. No response."

They had encountered the Sky Lord just after noon. On sighting the approaching fleet the Sky Lord had fled northwards and the Sky Angel, with her five tame Sky Lords following, had given chase. Realising quickly that he had no hope of out-running the Sky Angel the master of the fleeing Sky Lord had attempted a series of—supposedly—surprise manoeuvres but had no way of knowing that the pursuing

106

fleet was controlled by sophisticated computer programs that out-guessed him on every turn. A short time ago the Sky Angel—the fastest ship in the fleet and therefore far ahead of the others—had got close enough to laser one of the Sky Lord's thrusters, causing smoke and flames to pour out from it. And now, as one of the Ashleys had observed, it appeared that the Sky Lord was preparing to make a final stand. It had slowed down and gone into a sharp turn so that it was now broadside to the approaching Sky Angel. . . .

Suddenly Jan saw puffs of smoke appear in a row along its side.

"They're firing at us," said an Ashley, unnecessarily.

Jan blinked as the Sky Angel's lasers seared across the sky, detonating the cannon shells before they could get close enough to do any harm.

"I suppose you'd better knock out another thruster," said Jan reluctantly.

"Excuse me, Jan," interrupted Carl One, "but I have a message from Kish. He's in the infirmary. He wants you to come at once."

Jan was rushing towards the elevator before Carl One had finished speaking. "Simon . . ." she gasped.

She made it to the infirmary within minutes. Gasping for breath as she entered she saw that Kish was standing by Simon's medic-machine. Then she saw that the machine was open and that Simon was lying exposed on the treatment couch. "Oh Mother God!" she cried as she ran to the medic-machine.

Kish stepped in front of her and held her firmly by her shoulders. "He's not dead, mistress. He's asleep."

"Asleep?" said Jan, disbelievingly. She looked past him to Simon. Yes, she could see his chest rise and fall. Kish let her go and she went to the couch. She touched Simon on the cheek. He felt warm again; normal. Then she noticed that he seemed bigger—and older—than he had been before entering the machine.

"The machine alerted me only a short time ago," Kish explained. "That Simon had come out of his coma and that his pulse and temperature were back to normal."

She stroked Simon's head. "Simon, can you hear me? It's your mother. Wake up . . . please."

The boy stirred. He moaned then opened his eyes. He looked up at her and frowned, then she saw recognition in his eyes. "Uhhh . . . Jan. What happened?"

She was so relieved that he seemed to be recovered that his unusual use of her first name passed her by. "You got sick, darling. But you're all right now." She was praying that he wouldn't remember what had happened with Ceri.

"Sick?" He struggled to sit up. She assisted him. He looked down at his body, at his hands, then looked slowly around the infirmary. Finally he looked back at her. Now there was shock and confusion in his eyes. "Oh God . . . what happened?"

"It's all right, darling," she said soothingly. "There was a terrible accident and you got hurt, but you're fine now."

He suddenly grabbed her wrist. His grip was so strong she gasped with pain. "I want to know what happened, Jan!" he said in a high, urgent voice. "And I want to see Milo. . . ."

"Milo?" repeated Jan blankly. She had never talked to Simon of his dead father. A flicker of panic began in the depths of her mind.

"Yes, Milo. He's the one who's responsible for this mess. I shouldn't be this way . . . *look* at me, a mere child. Where is he?"

Jan turned to Kish, hoping for some sort of explanation, but he could only shrug helplessly. She turned back to Simon. Her feeling of panic was growing by the second. He was clearly in the grip of some delirium. The medic-machine had been wrong. He wasn't fully recovered after all. But how could he know about Milo? "Simon, who told you about Milo. Was it Ceri?"

It was his turn to look puzzled, then his face cleared and

108

he said, "You don't know, do you? Milo hasn't told you. . . ."

"Told me *what*, Simon? I don't know what you're talking about and I wish you'd stop—you're scaring me."

He let go of her arm and actually smiled. The smile scared her even more. It was horribly familiar. But it wasn't *Simon*'s smile. He said, "Fetch Milo, Jan, wherever he is. He can do the explaining. This is all his fault. And I want to see the look on his face when he sees me. He's never met any of his other cuttings. They're up in space."

"Milo is dead, Simon," Jan said, her voice shaking with fear. "And you never knew him!"

Simon's eyes widened with surprise. "Dead? But that's impossible. Milo was virtually indestructible."

"He was killed by a man-machine. A cyberoid. It trampled him to death," she told him. Her panic was making it difficult for her to breathe now. "But how do you know about Milo, Simon? Please tell me!"

He looked at her and said, with brutal frankness, "Because I *am* Milo, Jan . . . in a manner of speaking."

"No . . . no . . ." she protested. It was her worst night-mare . . . coming to life before her eyes. "It's not true! It can't be!"

"I'm afraid it *is* true, Jan. I'm a kind of clone. Of Milo. I've probably pirated some of your DNA as well, but essentially I'm Milo. Or I will be when the process is complete."

"I don't believe this!"

"Want proof?" He frowned. "My memories are still fuzzy . . . my last one is of us together on the *Perfumed Breeze* after our audience with Horado. Milo obviously impreg-nated you within a couple of days after that. There's a time lapse of around forty-eight hours while the memories were encoded in the, well, call it an embryo . . . but I have memories of you before that. Plenty of them. Remember how you and I—Milo—first met? When Benny brought you

109

down to the slave pen and gave you to Buncher? Remember how I saved you from Buncher? Remember how I looked after you when the Hazzini had almost sliced you in two . . . ?"

Jan started to fall. She reached towards the edge of the couch but her hands seemed to pass straight through the material as if she were a ghost and she kept falling. Then, nothing.

Chapter Eleven:

She was dead. She was breathing and she could feel her body but she couldn't *feel*. Emotionally, she was completely numb. She opened her eyes. Saw the ceiling of the infirmary. Realized she was lying on a treatment couch. Her clothes were missing. As she thought that thought someone draped an infirmary robe over her. Supporting hands helped her to sit up. It was Kish. Shan was nearby. Both wore expressions of concern. She remembered. Felt the shadow of the pain she had felt before but not the real pain. Her emotions were sealed off from her. Shut away in a different room where they couldn't harm her. Whatever the medic-machine had injected her with was very efficient. She could clinically examine the events leading up to her collapse. Simon suddenly declaring he was Milo's clone . . . The hurt this caused was in that other room, not where *she* was. . . .

"How much time has passed?" she asked Kish.

"Nearly an hour," Kish told her. "After you collapsed we put you in the medic-machine. It has flooded your amygdala and the rest of your limbic system with specialised post-synaptic inhibitors. In effect it has cut your cerebral cortex off from your limbic system to protect you from the trauma of the severe shock you have suffered. But the condition is only temporary and you will soon lapse into a deep sleep."

Jan nodded. "Where is he? I want to see him."

"Mistress, I don't think that's wise," said Kish.

"I want to see him," she repeated firmly. Kish looked at Shan and Shan left the infirmary. While she waited Jan put on the robe.

Kish said, "There was trouble with the Sky Lord we were pursuing."

"Was there?" she asked, disinterestedly.

"It launched gliders at us. Ashley shot them down."

"I suppose there was no alternative."

"But that's not all. When the Sky Lord still gave no indication of surrendering Ashley then fired a laser directly into its hull. She must have hit a gas cell full of hydrogen— in fact it's possible the whole ship was filled with hydrogen considering how quickly it burned."

So it was beginning. The first show of open revolt from Ashley. How odd that the news provoked no feeling of fear in her. Having your cerebral cortex cut off from your limbic system was all right, she thought bitterly. She should have had it done long ago. "Were there any survivors?"

"Only a few. They've been picked up by one of the other ships. The fleet is still searching but it's doubtful if any more will be found."

Just then Shan returned with Simon. In that separate, locked room Jan's emotions began to churn but the door was thick and she was able to regard him dispassionately. He had certainly grown a lot during his time in the machine. Now that he was dressed she could see just how much. His clothes no longer fitted him and he appeared to be closer to six than four. She also noticed that he no longer *moved* like Simon; his walk, his stance, the way he held his head— everything was different. And reminded her of Milo.

"I want my son back," she said calmly. "I want Simon back."

There was a touch of apprehension in his eyes. "That's impossible. He's gone."

"Gone where?"

"Well, in metaphysical terms, I haven't a clue. But I do know that here, in the physical world, he no longer exists. While my brain, which used to be *his*, was undergoing its synaptic rewiring Simon kind of got . . . well, erased. I still have a few of his memories and feelings floating around but they will fade in time."

She carefully considered his words, ignoring the screams from the locked room. Simon was dead.

Simon—*Milo*—said hurriedly, "Look, I know this has come as a hell of a shock to you but it's also pretty shocking for me too. Waking up and finding myself in a child's body. It shouldn't have happened this way . . . and anyway, it's not really my fault."

"You are Milo, aren't you?"

"Well, yes, in a sense."

"And you impregnated me, that night in the blight land, with yourself. . . ."

"I told you, I don't remember that part but yes, I—Milo—obviously did."

"Why?" asked Jan quietly.

"I'm an insurance policy," he told her, "me and the other cuttings. To increase my chances of survival. Survival is the name of the big game, Jan, like I always told you. But Milo, or rather, 'I', only ever impregnated a woman with a cutting when I was about to leave a particular place. Thus there's a Milo living on one of the space habitats, on Belvedere, and a potential me on the Mars colony. Didn't want to have to live in close proximity with himself/myself—didn't want the competition. So why he—I—impregnated you I have no idea. I had no such plans as far as I can remember."

"You were rather excited at the time," she said bleakly. "I presume you lost control."

He gave an uncertain smile. "That's possible, considering my feelings for you. But I shouldn't *be* here yet. The process is programmed not to begin until the body is fully grown."

Jan was beginning to feel very tired. She made one last attempt before letting go of all hope. "Is there no way Simon can be brought back . . . his memories and personality somehow extracted from within you?"

"There is no way he can come back, Jan," Milo told her. "I'm sorry, but you must consider him dead."

Jan lay back on the couch. As she fell into a deep sleep she could hear sobbing coming from the locked room.

When Jan woke she was whole again. She let her grief for Simon wash over her and she began to cry. She cried for a long time and when she finally finished and wiped her eyes she saw Kish standing beside the bed, a glass in his hand. She sat up, realising she was very thirsty, and took the glass gratefully from him. "How are you feeling, mistress?" he asked.

She drank the cold water and said, "Not too bad, all things considered." Her body *did* feel refreshed; it was her mind that felt battered and bruised. She looked around. She was back in her own bedroom. "How long have I been out of things?"

"Two days, mistress. A day of it spent in the medic-machine."

She handed the glass back to Kish. "And what's 'he' been doing while I was asleep?"

"Simon . . . ?"

"Don't call him by that name!" she said sharply. "Simon is dead. Call him by his true name—Milo."

"Yes, mistress. Er, Milo has been exploring everywhere, and asking questions. He soon exhausted our limited funds of knowledge. Now he communicates mainly with Carl . . . and Ashley."

"I don't like the sound of that," she muttered.

"What will you do with him?" Kish asked her. "We think it would be best to transfer him to another ship."

"Perhaps. I don't know . . . I'll have to think about it." The problem of what to do with him confused her. Yes, Simon was dead but his adored body lived on. And maybe, despite what Milo had said, there was still a chance that. . . .

No, she must not think that. She would only be torturing

114

herself. She looked up at the ceiling. "Ashley, I want to talk to you."

It was Carl who answered. "Ashley says she is too busy to speak to you at present. She will speak to you later."

"Too *busy*?" Jan exclaimed. "Rubbish! Tell her I want to talk to her right now!"

"She still refuses."

"Mother God," muttered Jan, "if only there was some way of cutting her out of the system."

"You know that's impossible."

She turned towards the doorway and her stomach lurched. Simon—no, *Milo*—stood there. He had grown even more since she had last seen him. The old, and familiar, arrogant smile was on his face.

"Go away," she said weakly. "I don't want to see you yet. I'm not ready. . . ."

But he walked into the room anyway. Walked like Milo. It was horribly grotesque, Milo wearing a six year old boy's body. Her son's body. He came up to the side of the bed and folded his thin arms. He was much more confident now, she could see.

"Might as well get it over with now rather than later," he told her. "And besides, we have a great deal to discuss."

"I can't imagine what."

"Your future, for one thing, Jan. I admit I'm impressed at what you achieved on your own after my . . . er, death. Reaching the Sky Tower and succeeding in sending the signal that brought the Sky Angel down from its factory in space was all pretty remarkable for a girl who was little more than a backward primitive when I first met her."

"Forgive me if I don't thank you for these compliments," she said sourly.

"But since then, from what I've learnt," he continued, "you haven't been so successful. And now you're in real trouble. Typical of you, Jan, setting out to save a world that's beyond the saving stage. And how much longer did

115

you think you could hold your little empire together? You've got five Sky Lords full of seethingly resentful people and no way of maintaining the influence of the communities you've set free on the ground. You're relying totally on those programs of yours and as you well know—" he lowered his voice—"Ashley isn't very reliable. But there's no way you can isolate her from Carl. Destroy her and you destroy Carl as well."

"There's nothing wrong with my plans," she protested. "They'll work. It's just going to take more time than I anticipated."

"Time that you don't have. Ashley—all the Ashleys—are borderline psychotic. One of them, two, maybe three, will rebel against you one day soon. You aren't handling them right. Give them more rein, let them raze the odd town or so. And give up your grand scheme of liberating the world and destroying the blight."

"I don't need any sick advice from you, Milo," she told him contemptuously. "Get out." She turned to Kish. "Kish, take him out of here. At once."

Kish came up behind Milo and put his hands on his shoulders. "Come on . . . you heard what the Mistress said."

Milo gave a slight twist of his small body then drove his elbow into Kish's upper stomach. Kish gave a grunt of pain and surprise and went flying backwards. He hit the floor then curled into a ball, clutching his stomach and struggling to breathe. Milo smiled at Jan.

"Not good at this sort of thing, are they, your Minervan men? But you have your female ancestors to blame for that," said Milo as he perched himself on the side of the bed. She recoiled away from him. Kish continued to groan on the floor.

"I underwent more than one transformation while I was in my coma," continued Milo. "Of course I'll never be as strong or as quick as the original Milo, even when I'm fully grown. He saw to that. Just in case he ever encountered one

116

of us. He wanted to maintain the edge. Can't say I blame him . . . or rather, myself."

Jan got out of bed and went to Kish. She helped him sit up. His face was very pale and he was still struggling to breathe. "It's okay," she told him. "You're just winded, that's all." She took him over to a chair and sat him down. Then she turned to face Milo. He was grinning like a mischievous imp. She realised that while helping Kish her robe had partially opened, exposing her left breast. Milo was staring at it. Feeling ill, she hurriedly pulled her robe shut.

"Fascinating," said Milo. "Absolutely fascinating to view you through the gonads, so to speak, of a six year old boy. The memory of my desire for you as an adult is super-imposed over a very juvenile sexual urge. And at the same time, to make it even more interesting, I still have a vague impression of you as my much-adored mother. . . ."

Totally sickened, she screamed, "Shut up!"

"Don't worry, I won't reach puberty for another six months at least, and it will be nine months before I'm fully grown again, judging by my rate of growth so far. Oh, and I've found out why I underwent transformation before I reached the adult stage . . . it was all the fault of your darling from the sea habitat."

"Ceri . . ." she said, dully.

"Yes, she tried to murder me. Her attack kicked into action a self-preservation mechanism which prematurely started the whole process and also speeded it up."

"So *you* killed Ceri." A burning wave of fury surged through her.

He shrugged his small shoulders. "I told you, it was an automatic self-preservation reaction. The silly bitch had only herself to blame."

"Get out," she told him in a low, cold voice. "Get out *now*."

He got off the bed. "I'll talk to you again when you're

calmer. Then we'll devise a way of getting you out of this mess that your Messiah complex has landed you in."

He walked unconcernedly out of the room. Jan waited a few moments then said, "Carl?"

"Yes, Jan?"

"Fetch a servo-mech immediately. No, make it *two* servo-mechs. I want them to locate Milo . . . and I want them to kill him."

"Yes, Jan."

Chapter Twelve:

Ryn easily parried Prince Darcy's initial lunge and riposted with a series of feint attacks, forcing the Prince to back up. Ryn was enjoying himself. It was exciting to fence against a real adversary for a change. The weapon was heavier than the one he was used to but presented no real problem.

Another source of enjoyment was the expression on the Prince's face as he frantically tried to defend himself against someone he had suddenly discovered was a superior opponent. People scattered out of his way as he was forced backwards across the dance floor. Finally he had his back against one of the windows—he was trapped. In a flurry of feints and parries Ryn easily overcame the tattered remains of the Prince's defence and pinned him to the window, his sword point pressing into the Prince's throat. There were gasps from the onlookers, though someone broke into applause.

"I'd love this to continue," Ryn told him, "but if it does I fear someone is going to get hurt. So I would suggest that you surrender. You agree?"

The Prince's lips twisted into a snarl but he said, softly, "Yes . . . yes . . . damn you." He lowered his sword.

Ryn stepped back from him. He was about to lower his sword as well when the Prince, with a shrill scream of rage, charged him. He knocked Ryn's blade to one side with a crude 'beat attack' then slashed at him. Caught by surprise, Ryn barely had time to jerk his head out of the way as he stumbled backwards. The Prince's blade caught him on the cheek, narrowly missing his left eye, ripping it open to the bone. Despite the shock and pain, Ryn recovered quickly. The Prince, in his rage, was hacking wildly and Ryn, still retreating, was easily able to block the rest of the attack. Then, as the Prince clumsily dropped his guard, Ryn lunged. His sword went straight through the bicep of the Prince's sword arm. The Prince yelled with pain and dropped his sword as Ryn pulled his blade clear. Blood instantly began to drip from the double wound. The Prince clutched his arm and glared at Ryn as his two supporters hurried over to him. Ryn was aware of blood pouring from his own wound. "I warned you," he told the Prince.

"Bastard," hissed the Prince. "I'm going to send you to hell. . . ."

Then it was all confusion; the Duke was between them, shouting at his son, and Andrea had flung her arms around Ryn, crying: "Your face, your poor pretty face! What has he done to you?"

Ryn was beginning to feel dizzy. Pressing a handkerchief to his ripped cheek, he asked Andrea to guide him to a seat, which she did. He blacked out for a while, then he was aware of Baron Spang kneeling beside him and examining his wound. The Baron tutted to himself. "Nasty. You're going to need a lot of stitches. . . ."

The Baron had not exaggerated, Ryn discovered a short time later as he lay on a bed in an unfamiliar room while a surgeon worked on his face. He also discovered that the medieval aspects of life in the *Lord Mordred* also extended to the methods of its medical practitioners. He passed out before the surgeon had completed his work.

When he woke he found the Duke and Baron Spang waiting anxiously beside his bed. A servant hovered in the background. Ryn groaned. The left side of his face throbbed intolerably. He reached up and touched the thick bandage around his head. The pain flared even brighter.

"Would you like a drink?" enquired the Baron.

"Yeah," Ryn croaked. While the Baron helped him to sit up the servant hurried forward bearing a goblet.

"It's wine mixed with a pain-killing herb," the Baron told him as he eagerly drank from the goblet.

"We're dreadfully sorry," said the Duke. "My son will be severely punished . . . as soon as he is well enough."

Ryn returned the goblet to the servant and sank back against the pillows. "I'd advise against it. He hates me enough as it is."

"I can't let him get away with it, Robin. He almost killed you . . . *you*, my honoured guest and. . . ."

"Valuable ally," Ryn finished for him. "Don't worry. I dissociate your son's actions from your good self."

The Duke looked relieved.

"But," continued Ryn, "I do wish that you had warned me that my relationship with your daughter would be found offensive in some quarters."

"I assure you, Robin, that the only 'quarter' that finds it offensive is my wife and she doesn't count."

"Really?" Ryn pointed to the bandage on his face. "I'm afraid I disagree. Your son is clearly under her influence and I am sure she has other supporters."

"Well, yes . . . some," admitted the Duke. "But put both her and my son out of your mind. I promise you there will be no more trouble from either of them. You are under my protection."

"That makes me feel a lot better," Ryn said drily.

The Duke looked pained.

"Tell us, Robin," said the Baron hastily, "how you managed to achieve such expertise with a sword? You said you lived alone in your underwater world, apart from the Eloi. Surely such creatures would not have been interested in instructing you on the art of fencing or even serving as fencing partners?"

Ryn smiled at the thought of one of the Eloi as a fencing partner. "No, certainly not the Eloi," he said. "I found a

121

fencing program in the library when I was quite young." He didn't tell them that fencing had fascinated him ever since he had seen *The Adventures of Robin Hood*. "My fencing partner was nothing but a holographic projection. Very difficult, learning to fence with only a shadow as an opponent. Fighting your son, by comparison, was dead easy."

The Duke and the Baron looked at each other.

When they had gone Andrea entered. She wore an expression of tortured compassion. "My poor darling, how do you feel?" she asked as she leaned over him.

"Like someone who has been whacked in the face with a sword," he told her. Even the offered view of her cleavage wasn't enough to cheer him up, though the pain was beginning to lessen. Perhaps the herbs in the wine actually worked.

She took hold of his hands. "My brother is an absolute monster. He always has been. The things he used to do to me when we were small . . . I can't tell you." She gave a dramatic shudder.

"Please do, it sounds interesting."

"No, I couldn't, really." She let go and touched the side of his head. "Does it hurt?"

"Owww! Yes, especially when you do that!"

"The surgeon told me you're going to have a lovely scar all the way down the side of your face."

"Oh, marvellous. Do you have any more good news? Do I have gangrene as well, perhaps?"

"I think a duelling scar makes a man look so much more attractive."

"Believe me, Andrea, a duelling scar on you would not make you look the least bit more attractive," he told her seriously.

She laughed and kissed him lightly on the lips. "Silly. Women don't duel. Only men."

"No doubt some woman made that rule. By the way, how's your brother?"

"Oh him, he's all right. Apart from his arm."

"How badly did I wound him?"

She shrugged and said breezily, "Quite bad, I hear. He's lost almost all feeling in his arm. The surgeon said it should only be temporary but he can't be sure. Darcy is furious."

Ryn leaned back on the pillow. "Oh, great," he sighed.

When Andrea left Ryn fell asleep. When he awoke he was startled to see a man wearing a bright red robe sitting beside his bed. The man also wore a tall, bulbous, red hat. "Hello, young man. I am Cardinal Fluke." He held out his hand.

"I'm not at all surprised," said Ryn as he shook the man's hand.

The man frowned briefly then gave him a benign smile. "I understand, Robin, that you have neither been baptised nor confirmed into the Church so I am to act as your spiritual counsellor and help you prepare for baptism and then confirmation."

Ryn looked at the absurd figure before him. Once again it occurred to him that all that was happening to him was a mental implant by one of his programs and he was actually still back in the habitat having an intense, controlled dream. Ryn said, "I'm very grateful for your interest, Cardinal Fluke, but could we do this another time? As you may have noticed, I'm not in good shape right now and am feeling very tired."

"No better time then to begin your passage into the safe embrace of the Church, Robin. What if your wound were to suddenly turn bad and you were to die of a fever within a few days? Where would you then spend eternity if you died unbaptised?"

My God, thought Ryn, what a way to cheer up a sick person! He tried to remember what he knew of Roman

123

Catholic dogma. "Purgatory? No." He frowned. "That's not right. *Limbo*, isn't it?"

"Yes, limbo," said the Cardinal, who frowned again. "To avoid such a fate you must be baptised in the name of Jesus Christ, our Saviour."

"Saviour . . . yes," said Ryn slowly. He felt irritated at having his rest disturbed by this man. "I was taught about your religion."

"Then you accept Jesus Christ as your saviour and will worship him accordingly?"

Ryn shook his head. "As I told the Duke, I was taught about many different religions and I didn't find any of them especially attractive. As one of my teachers said, religion, or rather conflict between the supporters of different religions, or sects of the same religion, has probably been the biggest cause of misery throughout human history. After disease, of course."

The Cardinal's mouth formed a disapproving line. Then he said, "The Duke has told me you were taught by soulless machines. They have corrupted you with their atheistic lies."

"I don't know what my programs really believe deep down, or even what they think, but I suspect they have no need to believe in God. They, after all, know why they were created: to serve humanity. We, on the other hand, are somewhat in the dark. . . ."

"Ah, but you see, young man," said the Cardinal, smiling again, "we are just like your computer programs. We exist in order to serve God. That's why He made us."

"And how can we serve God?" asked Ryn.

"By worshipping Him. By glorifying His Works."

"It's a possible answer, I admit, and one I have encountered before. But as for His Works, some are hard to glorify. Such as anthrax, cancer, AIDS, leprosy, and rabies, to name a few. Before Man outdid Him in the Gene Wars God was no mean hand at creating designer plagues."

124

"You cannot hold God responsible for those things," said the Cardinal firmly.

"Of course," smiled Ryn. "God only ever gets credit for the Good Works, never the Bad." He shook his head. "Look, to be honest, I do admit that a profound mystery lies behind the existence of Existence itself. If you want to call it God, good enough, but as to Its true nature I have no idea, and I have my doubts about all those different prophets who claim to have received the Truth via a direct link-up with God. Once they get beyond the basic mystery then all religions become nothing but a mass of contradicting dogma, cant, absurd dietary laws, absurd sexual laws, absurd laws about dress and meaningless rituals."

The Cardinal rose to his feet and stared severely down at Ryn. "You refuse, then, to be baptised?"

"Limbo holds no terrors for me, Cardinal," Ryn told him cheerfully. "I *come* from limbo."

"Limbo may be the *least* of your worries, young man," said the Cardinal and swept out of the room.

Milo woke up screaming.

He rolled naked across the bed and fell, pulling the sweat-stained sheet with him. The impact brought him, relatively, to his senses. He pulled his knees up to his chin, arms clamped around his legs, and sat there, shivering. The images, the sensations, still reverberated through his mind. Those great metal feet rising and falling again and again, crushing him into the dirt, *mingling* him with the dirt. Yet, he continued to live, feeling every crushing blow. His body, designed to live forever, clung to life even when he had been reduced to bloody pulp. Then, at last, death. . . .

But it was impossible! He couldn't have such memories. All he knew of his death was what Jan had told him in her garbled description. His memories of his previous existence ended even before he—Milo—had impregnated Jan with that chemical cocktail that had included not only all his

DNA but a molecular encoding of all his memories up until that point. There was no way he could remember how he died days later. But the nightmare had been so vivid! The echoes of his final agonies hummed along his nerves. He shuddered.

"Bad dream?" It was Ashley.

"Yes. Could I have some light please? Not too bright."

The lights came on. He got up from the floor and sat on the edge of the bed.

"I miss dreaming," said Ashley. "I miss sleep. I miss *everything*."

"You wouldn't have liked this dream," he told her.

"What was it about?"

"My death. Or rather, *Milo*'s death." Why not admit it to himself. He wasn't Milo. He had Milo's memories, Milo's brain but he wasn't Milo, he was something else. He didn't *feel* how he remembered feeling as Milo in his previous existence. It was this body. He looked down at himself, at his childish limbs. He was too young. Damn that murderous Ceri; she had ruined the timing. That's why he was still haunted by the vestiges of Simon's personality, his fading memories. He hadn't been joking when he'd told Jan that one aspect of himself still saw her as his mother while at the same time he felt the ghost of the lust he had once felt for her. He smiled wryly up at the ceiling. "I'm nothing but a mixture of ghosts, Ashley. In reality I'm dead."

"I'm dead too. But at least you have a body."

"You call this a body?" He stood up. "Look at me, the ghost of a four hundred year old plus man in a boy's body that hasn't reached puberty yet." He held out his small penis and laughed. "Can you believe that once I was a superman?"

"But you're still growing," Ashley pointed out.

"True, but I'll never be the man I was. I—or rather Milo did—make sure of that. I don't have all the genetic enhancements that he had. I'll never be as fast or as strong as him."

126

"But you're his clone, aren't you?" asked Ashley. "Surely your DNA is identical."

He shook his head. "No, my genegineers came up with a way to ensure that I wouldn't be identical to . . . me, as I was. I'm not a pure clone. The quasi-embryo that attached itself to Jan's womb also pirated some of her DNA in order to reverse some of the original Milo's genetic enhancements."

"But you're still immortal?"

"Oh yes," he said and gave a cynical laugh. "At least I'm as immortal as Milo was. Let's hope I'll be more successful at *being* immortal."

"You came close to failure already today."

"Don't I know it." He had received a serious fright when the two spiders had seized him in a corridor after he had left Jan's bedroom. One of them had been about to slit his throat with a cutting tool when it had frozen, the blade inches from his flesh. He had realised that Jan had ordered his death but hadn't been able to go through with it. She had countermanded her order at the last moment.

"If I'd been patched into Carl at the time I would have stopped it," said Ashley. "You know that, Milo. But I was busy shooting birds."

"There's no need to apologise," he told her, insincerely. "But it could happen again. Sooner or later her hatred for me is going to overcome her reservations about harming the body that had belonged to her son."

Ashley sighed. "I used to like Jan but she's become so dreary these days."

"We're going to have to do something about her, aren't we?" asked Milo of the blank ceiling.

"Yeah," agreed Ashley.

Chapter Thirteen:

Flying at a height of almost forty thousand feet and at top speed he eventually picked up the woman's fleet on his radar. He ordered the Toy into an immediate tight turn in case the Sky Angel had radar as sophisticated as his. But even as he finished speaking the Toy said, "Ryn, we are being scanned by radar."

"Damn it. I wanted to give them a surprise. Well, it can't be helped now. Back to the *Lord Mordred*. Top speed."

"You found them?" asked the Duke.

Ryn nodded and pointed out the exact location on the large map that was spread out on the oval-shaped table in the 'War Room'. On one wall was hung a huge tapestry that depicted scenes of unlikely military heroism during the original takeover of the airship by the Duke's ancestor. Apart from the Duke and Baron Spang, there were several other Barons present around the table. Most wore pieces of highly polished, light-weight ceremonial armour, as if they were about to go into battle at any moment. Prince Darcy was also present, his arm in a sling. He had so far avoided any eye contact with Ryn.

"So far north," said the Duke, staring at the map. "I don't understand it. I presume they were moving southwards when you spotted them?"

"No. They were stationary. And at a low altitude too. About a thousand feet. My radar showed structures of some kind on the ground so I would guess they were over some town or settlement."

The Duke, puzzled, pulled at his beard with a gloved hand.

Baron Spang said, "Well, we should intercept her fleet in approximately twenty-four hours, if the Techs can keep us moving at a consistent thirty miles per hour and we don't encounter any bad weather. And also providing that her fleet doesn't move in the meantime."

"No matter if it does," said Ryn. "It wouldn't take me long to locate it again."

The Duke straightened and smiled at Ryn. "Then it is all settled. Everyone is clear as to our battle plan?"

"*Our* battle plan?" asked Ryn, smiling back at him. "I think so. I fly my machine through their defences, attack the Sky Angel, destroy its laser system and force the Sky Woman to surrender. With her defeat the rest of the fleet should capitulate as well. At that point you will launch your troop-carrying gliders."

"Good . . . good," said the Duke, nodding. "You foresee no problems with this plan?"

"No problems at all, sire," Ryn told him.

"I still don't like it."

"What?" asked Jan distractedly. She was studying figures on a computer screen. They told a grim story. The plague that was cutting through the population of the community below them showed no sign of slowing down despite the drugs that were being engineered in the Sky Angel's laboratories and being administered by the ship's spider-mechs.

"That radar blip, this morning," said Milo. He was standing at the front of the control room and staring at the sky. She looked over at him. He was looking less like Simon now—his hair had fallen out and he was much bigger—but it still gave her a wrench every time she saw him. She tried to avoid him as much as possible but he insisted on following her around. He was constantly trying to ingratiate himself with her. He had certainly ingratiated himself with Ashley.

She was considering having Milo transferred to another ship as Kish kept suggesting but she feared that Ashley would simply ignore the order.

"What about the damn blip? It was obviously some sort of freak effect."

"It was an aircraft . . . a *heavier* than air-craft."

"And how can that be? Unless it was a glider of some kind."

"A glider? Travelling at that height and speed? Carl, tell her again what you picked up."

Carl said, "A metallic object. Cylindrical. Thirty feet in length. Dense. Considerable mass. Probably weights several tons. It was turning when I picked it up, at a speed of 1,500 mph, then it accelerated to 2,500 mph before I lost it."

"Some glider, huh?" asked Milo.

"Milo, you know as well as I do that no one on the planet has the technology to build such an aircraft nowadays. Therefore Carl has made a mistake . . . unless someone from one of your space habitats has decided to pay us a visit at long last." She paused thoughtfully for a moment. That hadn't occurred to her before.

"No way," said Milo, shaking his head. "They wouldn't dare, even if they still had the resources to mount such an expedition. They still think the planet is crawling with designer plagues."

"Which it is," said Jan, gesturing through the transparent floor at the community below. "Hereabouts, at any rate."

The name of the community was Phoenix Two and was located in the north-east corner of what had once been the state of Arizona before the break-up of the United States of America. It was one of the largest ground communities Jan had ever seen, with some quite elaborate three-storey build- ings around the town centre. The community, despite the forced tributes to its local Sky Lord over the centuries, had been a relatively flourishing one until, in recent years, the blight had begun to spread across its extensive farm lands. Then had followed regular attacks by Hazzini.

The Hazzini were the cause of the plague. Survivors of direct encounters with Hazzini, if they recovered from their wounds—which was rare—then fell ill with a particularly vile malady that killed them within days. Apparently the Hazzini carried the plague in their bodies as yet another part of their armoury of weapons to be used against hated humanity. Jan remembered her own near fatal encounter with a Hazzini. She ran her finger down the front of her tunic where once a gaping wound had stretched from her neck almost to her crotch. Either she'd been lucky or not all Hazzini carried the plague.

Jan glanced down at the sprawling township below. Large sections of it were covered by nets to keep out the Hazzini. Not that the netting, being made of vegetable fibre, had done much good in that respect. Only steel nets would have been effective against the claws of the Hazzini but steel was scarce in Phoenix Two, as it was everywhere nowadays.

The trouble had begun when a large swarm of Hazzini had built a network of their monstrous nests a mere forty miles north of the township. It was Jan's intention to use the massed firepower of her fleet to destroy the nests and the Hazzini but when she had broached this plan earlier in the morning the Ashleys objected. She had been surprised by their reaction. . . .

"I'd have thought you bloodthirsty creatures would jump at the chance to engage in a little mass slaughter," she'd said, irritably.

"I'm sure it would be a lot of fun," said one of the Ashleys. It didn't matter which one it was to Jan—they all sounded equally crazy to her now. "But we think we should get out of the area as soon as possible. There's a lot of unrest on every ship. The people are scared of the plague. There could be a full-scale rebellion."

"Everyone is quite safe up here. And the spider-mechs

are thoroughly decontaminated when they return aloft each time," Jan said.

"You're not going to convince the moronic masses of that," said an Ashley. "And that's another thing—the spider-mechs. We're losing them at too fast a rate, what with accidents and sabotage, and we're running out of spare parts to repair them, and now you've spread them even thinner by having them act as nursemaids to those clods down below."

"She has a point," Milo had interrupted. "The spider-mechs are your only means of keeping the populations on the other ships under control. They're so overstretched at the moment that if there is an outbreak of resistance you're going to have trouble putting it down. Unless you use really drastic tactics, of course, and knowing you you won't."

"I don't see why we simply don't dump the whole load of morons on the ground and have done with it. They're nothing but trouble," said an Ashley.

"Yeah, let's!" agreed another Ashley.

"Out of the question," said Jan sharply. "It would be murder. They're all Sky People. They wouldn't stand a chance on the ground, and you know it."

"So who cares?"

"The least you could do, Jan," said Milo quickly, "is to stop using the spider-mechs to clean the solar panels. That's where most of the accidental losses happen. Put people on the job, the way we used to do it on the *Lord Pangloth*."

"I hated being a glass-walker," Jan told him, "and so did you. I wouldn't force that job on anyone."

Milo shrugged. "In the long run you may have to when there aren't enough spiders to keep all the panels fungus-free on all the ships. Might as well start now."

It was then that Carl had announced his detection of an unidentified flying object. At the time Jan had treated it as a welcome interruption but now, thanks to Milo's harping on the subject, she was beginning to wonder just what the

132

strange blip represented. She looked at Milo, who was still scanning the skies. Frowning, she said, "All right, even if it was an Old Science flying machine of some kind that someone has got running again, it can't represent any danger to us, can it? If it attacked any of our ships the lasers would incinerate it."

Milo turned to her. "It can't be Old Science aircraft. You know how fanatical the first Sky Lords were in destroying all other aircraft once they'd established themselves on the Sky Angels. They couldn't take the chance of anyone challenging their aerial supremacy. That was their First Law for the groundlings—Thou Shalt Not Fly."

"Then if it's not an Old Science aircraft, and not a spaceship from a habitat or the Mars colonies, what is it? Where could it have come from?"

"I have no idea," he said, and ran his hand over his balding head. It was a gesture Jan knew from old. Her stomach went sour as she saw what physically remained of her son turning yet further into Milo.

"Well, if you do have any bright ideas, let me know," she said curtly. "I'm going to my quarters. I need a rest."

She also needed a drink. When she arrived at her quarters she asked Kish to fetch her a beer. It seemed to her that no sooner had she slumped on to the couch in the living room than Kish had returned and was handing her a long glass of cold beer. She smiled her thanks. "You're so good to me, Kish. I don't know what I'd do without you. Or Shan." She took a long drink of beer. Kish remained standing in front of her.

"You look tired, mistress. Would you like a massage?"

"Oh, yes, Kish. Please!"

She set the glass on the floor as Kish sat beside her then turned her back to him and undid the top of her tunic. She closed her eyes as she felt his skilful fingers begin to knead the tense muscles of her neck and shoulders. "Uhhh, that's wonderful," she told him gratefully. Kish's fingers, after finishing with her shoulders, began to move down her back. She gave a moan, her head dropping forward. She let herself sink into the pure, sensual pleasure of the massage, wishing it would last forever. As a result she had no idea how long he'd been caressing her breasts before she became aware of the fact. She straightened with surprise. He had never touched her breasts before. "Kish, what are you doing?"

He immediately removed his hands. She turned to face him. His expression was a mixture of embarrassment and desire. "I thought you were enjoying it," he said.

"I was enjoying the massage, but you seem to have something more in mind than a simple massage, Kish."

He looked down for a few moments then directly into her eyes again. His gaze was intense. "You must know how I feel about you, Jan."

"And how is that?" she asked, noticing his use of her name.

"I love you."

"You do?" she said, sounding as astonished as she felt. She had never suspected that kind and solicitous Kish might be harbouring such feelings towards her. And yet, she realised, it shouldn't have come as such a surprise. She knew Minervan men had sex drives; she had herself slept with a Minervan man . . . no, youth, really, oh so long ago! Simon, whom she'd named her son after. But Kish, and Shan? She'd taken them for granted. And, yes, treated them like drones. After contact with 'normal' men the two Minervans had seemed, well, what was the word? Asexual? Tame? *Safe*? Yes, she'd once seriously contemplated having a child by Kish in order to continue the Minervan line but there was no question of her feeling any passion towards him. . . .

She stared at him, choosing carefully what she was about to say. She placed her hand on his. "Kish, I love you too. But as a friend, in the same way that I love Shan. Maybe in time my feelings for you will develop into something different . . . something stronger. But, Kish, you must realise that right now, after all that's happened recently . . . losing Ceri and Simon . . . I have a lot of healing to do and right now I can't think about having a close relationship with anyone else. I don't think I'll be able to for a long time . . ."

He looked profoundly hurt but he nodded and said gently, "I understand, mistress." He got to his feet, picked up the empty beer glass and left the room. In the silence that followed Jan sighed deeply to herself.

"God, that was delicious," murmured Andrea, and stretched languidly on the bed. "Better than ever. What's got into you today?"

"Well, I am just about to go off to battle, my darling," said Ryn. "It's a well known fact that fear of death is a powerful aphrodisiac."

She raised herself on her elbows, a posture that served to emphasise her breasts. He gazed admiringly at them. "You're not afraid, are you?" she asked.

"A little nervous," he said, and reached over idly to caress a rouged nipple.

"But Daddy said you would be absolutely safe. He said you told him that your flying machine couldn't be harmed by lasers."

"True," he agreed, "but it's not invulnerable to cannon fire. A lucky shot might blow me out of the sky. It's unlikely, I admit. I'll be travelling very fast. I'll be through their laser defences before they know it." He leaned over and kissed her on the lips hard. She thrust her tongue into his mouth. The kiss went on for a long time. Afterwards she said, huskily, "When you return you will be the greatest hero the *Lord Mordred* has ever had. The minstrels will compose ballads about your exploits that will be sung at banquets for centuries!"

"That will be nice," said Ryn, staring at the clock on the wall.

"I'm going to be so proud of you," she sighed.

"I hope so," he said, and kissed her again; then he said, reluctantly, "I'd better get ready. If the Sky Woman's fleet hasn't moved since yesterday we'll be intercepting it in a couple of hours."

"Be careful, darling. I know Daddy is going to heap rewards on you after you destroy the Sky Woman but I promise you the best rewards of all will come from me."

"I can't wait," he told her.

Jan lowered the binoculars. "It's just sitting there."

"Yes," said Milo. "And just out of our lasers' range of effectiveness at this level of atmospheric density. Which is worrying."

"Worrying?"

"It means that the people on that airship know we—you—have independent control over your laser defence systems."

"Yes, I see," said Jan, thoughtfully. "But how could they know?"

"News of your exploits during the last few years has obviously travelled. You should have expected it."

Jan didn't answer. She raised the binoculars again and focused on the distant airship. It was a typical Sky Lord in appearance; though more battered-looking than most and with several of its thrusters stripped down to provide spare parts for others. She guessed that the slow speed at which it had crept towards her fleet from the south-west was the best it could manage.

"I say we attack," said an Ashley, not for the first time.

"Not yet," said Jan firmly. "We wait and give them a chance to communicate. Besides, it can't present any threat to us."

"Attention," broke in Carl quietly. "An object has just

136

lifted off from the airship's upper hull. It is the same object I made radar contact with yesterday. It is already accelerating and is heading directly towards our ship."

"Shit!" said Milo.

Jan hesitated before saying, "Laser it as soon as it's in range."

She tried to find the approaching object with her binoculars but couldn't. Then came the familiar lines of turquoise light as the laser system was activated. The lines converged on a single point. She waited for an explosion. But there wasn't one.

Carl said, in his usual quiet tone, "My radar scan of the approaching aircraft reveals that it is surrounded by an intense electromagnetic field which is throwing the laser beams out of phase and diffusing them. The aircraft cannot be destroyed. Or stopped. It will be through our defences in forty seconds. . . ."

Chapter Fourteen:

Peering through the large, brass telescope in the forward observation gallery, the Duke du Lucent got his first sight of the Sky Woman's fleet. It caused him to have second thoughts about the whole enterprise. Suspended above and around the far-off township, the white Sky Angel and the five Sky Lords looked so imposing, even from this distance, that it seemed absurd that Robin's small craft might inflict any damage upon them.

The observation gallery was crowded with dignitaries. A brief ceremony had been held in Robin's honour and then, after Andrea had given him a long and dramatic farewell embrace, a guard of honour had escorted him back along the hull to his flying machine. The Duke felt uncomfortably warm. He turned and looked back at the row of gliders waiting to take off once Robin had accomplished his mission. "How much longer?" he asked Baron Spang.

"He should be taking off at any moment, sire," replied the Baron. "Don't worry—everything is going to be fine. Very soon the power to conquer the whole world will be in our hands. Or rather, *your* hands, sire."

The Duke immediately felt cheered. It was true. He was going to be the most powerful Sky Lord in the world. El Rashad and the others were going to lick his boots, literally, or find their heads on pointed sticks.

"He's taking off!" cried a Tech in the rear of the gallery. All heads turned. Robin's aircraft was indeed rising into the air. Then it began to move at a dazzling speed towards the Sky Woman's fleet. So fast did it move that the Duke rapidly lost sight of it, though he heard the rumble it made from its violent passage through the air.

"Any moment now," announced a Tech who was tracking Robin's aircraft with one of the telescopes. Then the Duke saw distant flashes of light. The Sky Angel's lasers. This finally confirmed what El Rashad and the others had claimed; the Sky Woman did indeed possess control of her laser system. She was able to fire on a craft containing human life. "What's happening?" he cried.

"He's still on course! The lasers are having no effect!"

The Duke felt a rush of excitement. Everything Robin had said about his craft was true! Now the attack would begin!

"He's made it!" announced the Tech. "He's through their defences!"

A cheer went up in the gallery.

"And now he's . . . he's. . . ." The Tech faltered.

"What?" demanded the Duke. "What's happened?"

The colour had drained from the Tech's face. He looked up from the eye-piece of the telescope and swallowed. Then he said, "The craft has landed on top of the Sky Angel."

"*What?*" cried the Duke. "Let me see!" He shoved the Tech to one side and peered into the telescope. It took him a few moments to confirm the awful truth for himself. Robin's flying machine was sitting on the upper hull of the white Sky Angel . . . in much the same way it had sat upon the *Lord Mordred*'s hull. A groan escaped from the Duke's lips.

"The . . . lasers," said Baron Spang weakly. "They must have damaged the flying machine after all . . . knocked out Robin's engines. . . ."

"No," said the Duke grimly. "I don't think so."

Ryn opened the Toy's hatches and climbed out. He breathed deeply and looked around. Sunlight flashed off several small metallic objects that were moving swiftly towards him over the smooth, white hull of the Sky Angel. He raised his hands and waited for them to reach him.

As they got closer he recognised them to be spider-shaped servo-mechs. There had been similar machines in Shangri-La. "Don't move!" warned one of them as they surrounded him. It had a girl's voice.

"I'm not moving, as you can see," he said calmly. He saw that two of the spider-mechs had broken away from the main group and were examining the hull of the Toy with a variety of sensors.

"He's gorgeous!" said another of the mechs. The one immediately in front of him extended an articulated arm that had a whirling blade on the end of it. The blade stopped a few inches from his throat. At the same time a metal tentacle swiftly drew his sword from its scabbard. He forced himself to smile.

"Yeah, he's gorgeous all right," said the mech in front of him. "But who the hell is he and what is he doing here? Eh, gorgeous? How about some fast talking before we cut your throat."

"My name is Robin and, as is obvious, I have surrendered to you. I've come to offer my services to the Sky Angel. For a fee, of course. But first a warning: please do not tamper with my aircraft. It is booby-trapped. Any attempt to gain access to it will result in a massive explosion." The bluff had worked before; Ryn hoped it would work again. But the female voices issuing from the spider-mechs worried him. They sounded kind of : . . . disturbing.

"He's surrendered to those things!" exclaimed Baron Spang, peering intently through the telescope's eyepiece. "They're taking him away. . . ."

The Duke was in a state of disbelieving shock. In the back of his mind he was watching all his dreams and plans dissolving. His one key advantage was gone. Yet he had been so sure that Robin was genuine, thanks to Andrea. . . .

140

Andrea.

"Sire, what shall we do now?" asked the Baron. "Shall we carry on with the attack?"

"Don't be stupid," the Duke told him. "We have no option but to retreat. Give the order."

Andrea.

Two of the spider-mechs accompanied him below. The last in a series of elevator rides deposited Ryn and his escort in the Sky Angel's control room. It bore little resemblance to the *Lord Mordred*'s control room in terms of the equipment it contained but he had no time to examine his surroundings more closely; his attention was focused on the two people in the control room. One was a woman, standing at the far, forward end of the central catwalk; the other a boy who was perched on a nearby computer console. Both turned as he emerged from the elevator. One of the spider-mechs said, "Here he is! A real hunk, eh Jan?"

The odder of the two people was the boy. He was aged between eight and ten but had the face, and especially the eyes, of someone much older. This effect was heightened by the fact that the boy had lost most of his hair. But it was the woman, who was approaching him now, who won the competition for his full attention. She was tall, slim and dressed in a white tunic that left her arms and legs bare. The belt at her narrow waist held a dagger and a device he didn't recognise. She had black hair that fell on to her cheek bones (he noted, too, a black star on her right cheek; a tattoo, or was it a brand?). Her large eyes were green and intriguingly shaped, their inner corners turning downwards quite sharply. In every way she was the physical antithesis of Andrea; whereas Andrea was voluptuous this woman had small breasts and flat hips and belly, and yet Ryn instantly found her infinitely more attractive than Andrea in a way he could not yet define. True, she had dark shadows below her eyes but these did not detract from her beauty. He felt a

141

strange sensation at the base of his chest—a tightening that made it difficult to draw breath. She had to be, he thought, the Sky Angel herself. . . .

He smiled awkwardly at her and said, "Hello, I'm Robin."

"Robin Hood, I presume," said the odd-looking boy in a sarcastic tone of voice. "In that costume you couldn't be anyone else."

Ryn stared at him in astonishment, his fascination with the woman temporarily overshadowed. "You've heard of Robin Hood?"

"I'm older than I look," said the boy, frowning at him, "But how is it that *you've* heard of him?"

"Who is this Robin Hood person?" asked the Sky Angel. She was studying Ryn intently. He felt himself start to blush.

"It doesn't matter," said the boy, who was also studying Ryn. "What matters is where he comes from and what he's doing here."

"I'm here to offer my services to the Sky Angel—" he began. He was cut off by the boy, who said brusquely, "Yes, yes, we heard all that, but why?" Then another voice, which came from all directions at once, spoke: "Jan, the intruder Sky Lord has made a full turn and is heading south." Jan guessed the voice to be that of a basic program's, devoid of any anthropomorphic nuances.

The woman fingered the hilt of her dagger. "I suppose I had better send one of the ships in pursuit."

"I wouldn't bother," Ryn said quickly. "Without me, and my aircraft, the *Lord Mordred* can't offer you any threat. Let it go. The Duke knows he has no chance against your fleet now. He is no doubt fleeing back to his home territories." He didn't want any harm to come to those on the *Lord Mordred*.

Another disembodied voice spoke. It was the same disturbing girl's voice that had emanated from the spider-mechs. "Don't listen to him, Jan. Let me go after that clapped-out hulk and burn it out of the air. It's some kind of trick."

Ryn looked up at the ceiling, having nowhere else to look, and said, "It's no trick, I swear." He returned his gaze to the Sky Angel's face. "Please spare them. I *did* play a trick but it was on the ruler of the *Lord Mordred*, not you. The Duke du Lucent was under the impression I was going to act as his ally in his attack on you. I was supposed to use my aircraft to destroy your defences, but I was only pretending to go along with his plan. In reality it is *you* I want to serve."

The boy gave a snort of disbelief. "I agree with Ashley. You're up to some sort of devious game. Why on earth would you want to offer your services to us? What are you after? And who the hell are you anyway?"

Ryn gave him a hard stare. He had taken an instant dislike to this strange person. "I said I've come to offer my services to the Sky Angel, not to *you*, whoever you may be."

"Yes," agreed the woman quickly, "he's right, Milo. This is none of your business. Make yourself scarce. Go and pull the wings off a fly or something."

The boy's expression grew ugly. "Of course this new development concerns me, Jan. Anything that potentially involves my survival concerns me. Here this refugee from an ancient swashbuckling movie turns up out of the blue in a machine that is impervious to lasers and capable of God knows what else and you expect me to calmly walk away without finding out what he wants and where he's from?"

"I don't care what you want or what you think, Milo!" she said, her voice rising, "I'm still in charge here and I'm telling you to make yourself scarce. Now!"

The boy slipped off the top of the console and stood facing her, hands on his hips. "Don't push me, Jan, or you'll find out just how precarious your position is around here now."

Ryn saw doubt appear on the woman's face and instinctively knew that the situation here was volatile and that, for reasons he had yet to discover, the Sky Woman *wasn't* in total control. Quickly, he said, "Do you think I could have a drink, please?"

They both looked at him in surprise. "What?" said the boy.

"I said I'd like a drink. I'm thirsty. I must say that the hospitality on the *Lord Mordred* was considerably better."

The woman gave him a strained smile and said, "I'm sorry. It's been a long time since I entertained guests. Come with me to my quarters. You can use the various facilities there and then we'll have a cold beer and perhaps something to eat if you're hungry." She came closer to him and held out her hand. "By the way, my name is Jan. Jan Dorvin."

As he took hold of her hand the tightening in his chest grew worse.

The Duke du Lucent hit Andrea so hard that she was almost torn from the grasp of the two burly manservants holding her arms. Blood ran from her split lip. Both her cheeks were already bruised and swollen from previous blows.

"You idiot! You moron!" he cried, rubbing the knuckles of his right hand. He suspected he had cracked one. "Hopelessly in love with you, is he? He'll do anything for you? Good *God*, you cretinous woman. . . ." He drew his hand back to strike her again. She twisted her head to one side. "No father! Please not again! Please don't hurt my face."

He stayed his fist. "I *told* you, didn't I? *Watch* him, I told you. *Listen* to him. Give me confirmation that he can be trusted, that he's genuine! But oh no, you trusted those marvellous *women's instincts* of yours. Your *vanity*, more like. And all the time he was playing games with you. And with me!"

"Father, I was so sure!" she cried, spitting blood as she spoke. "I was sure he was in love with me! How was I to know?"

"It was your job to know. And now, thanks to you, we've

144

lost any chance of improving our lot. We'll be lucky if we make it back to our tribute territories in one piece. You demanded a reward when Robin delivered the Sky Angel and her fleet to me; now that you've failed me you will receive punishment instead."

"Oh no!" she wailed. "Please, don't touch my face again. I beg you!"

"Don't worry, I won't," he told her. He then said to one of the manservants, "Fetch me a whip."

The boy, whom he now knew as Milo, asked for the second time if he could inspect the Toy. Again, Ryn told him no and warned of the consequences if a forced entry was attempted. He thought he saw something in Milo's eyes that said he didn't believe him. More and more Milo bothered him and he desperately wanted to know more about him, but so far the talk had chiefly concerned himself.

They were in a spacious dining room and seated at a table that was next to a wide, curving window. Or rather, just Jan and he were seated. There had been no place for Milo at the table and instead he paced restlessly about the room when he wasn't sprawling on a couch. Jan and he had been served by two smooth-faced men with gentle eyes, though Ryn had caught one of them frowning briefly at him. He wondered who they were. Apart from them the huge airship seemed to be deserted. It was all very unlike the *Lord Mordred*.

He had briefly told Jan, and the listening Milo, of his origin in Shangri La. This had excited Milo. "So the Antarctic Research Habitat still exists! Incredible! And still capable of producing Old Science artifacts, by the look of your flying machine. Obviously society hasn't regressed culturally there, unlike on the Sky Lords, and on the ground. . . ."

"Well, the Eloi *have* regressed, but in a different kind of way," Ryn said, "though they wouldn't agree with that definition. I think they see themselves as a superior breed of human. . . ."

"The Eloi?" asked Jan. Ryn tried to explain the nature of the Eloi. Jan looked puzzled but Milo became even more excited.

"The logical end-product of a process begun with the creation of the Standard Prime," he said as he bounced up from the sofa and began pacing the room again. "The biological 'bias for optimism' in human beings carried to its extreme. The ultimate high—and a perpetual one with no hangover or negative side-effects. A state beyond the wildest dreams of the poor, pathetic heroin addicts of old."

"Milo, what are you talking about?" Jan asked.

"I tried to explain all this to you once before," said Milo, "Or rather, my *other* self did."

Ryn, baffled by this cryptic reference, glanced briefly at the peculiar boy, who was running his hand through his thinning hair as he paced excitedly about. But he quickly returned his attention to the woman sitting opposite him. He was finding it harder and harder to take his eyes off her. Watching her provided him with a feeling of pleasure that was profoundly different from that he had derived from Andrea's beauty. He knew the intensity of his gaze was discomforting her but he couldn't help it. And was it his imagination or could he detect a reciprocal interest in him in her own eyes . . . ?

"It goes all the way back to the late twentieth century when breakthroughs in genetic engineering kicked the supports out from under those who opposed the notion of biological determinism in any form or degree," continued Milo, not noticing that the pair of them were only half-listening to what he was saying. "There was a lot of resistance to biological determinism for both religious and political reasons—it threatened an out-dated concept of 'free will' which was an integral part of many religions and political ideologies. But then the discovery was made that there was a gene, or lack of one, that predisposed people to manic depression, and around the same time it was learnt

146

that a tendency towards schizophrenia was also a genetic misfunction. . . ."

"What has this to do with Robin's people?" asked Jan, sounding irritated. Ryn felt irritated as well. He was wishing that Milo would shut up and leave. He wanted to be alone with Jan.

"Everything. I'm talking about how it was realised that the mind—consciousness—was the end-product of a complex interplay between different hormones and other neurotransmitters in the brain, all of which are genetically determined. It was then discovered we were genetically programmed to *feel* a specific way, that our brains contained natural mood-enhancing drugs . . . the encephalins were the first such to be discovered, which are analogous to opium, then came gamma-aminobutyric acid—the universal brain inhibitor—and a whole range of others; natural amphetamines, natural tranquillisers and so on. The average human being was drugged to the eyeballs. The 'bias towards optimism' syndrome. Also known as the 'always look on the bright side' effect. Evolved to enable the human race to keep on going no matter what hit it. Makes individuals keep on hoping for the best when bare logic tells them their situation is hopeless."

"I'm not 'drugged up to my eyeballs'," Ryn told him. "The Eloi are but I'm not."

"Ah, but you are, oh Robin of Sherwood," said Milo with a sneering smile, "But, of course, like everyone else, you find it impossible to be objective about your state of mind. You feel *normal*, yes? And you assume that how you feel is the human *norm* itself. But you have no way of seeing reality or yourself in a truly objective fashion. No one does. Though perhaps manic depressives did before genegineers eradicated the condition. Their genetic defect means that their mental thermostats didn't work correctly and they would vary wildly in moods as their brains were overdosed with the mood-enhancing substances for a period and then deprived of them for an equal amount of time—they were constantly swinging between euphoria and the deepest of depressions. Yes, I believe that during the latter periods they came close to perceiving reality as it really is, which is why so many committed suicide at such times. As someone once said, 'Man can stand only so much truth'.

"But it wasn't just manic depressives who experienced fluctuations or changes in their biologically built-in sense of optimism. Before the establishment of the genetically Standard Prime person in the 21st century, which enhanced and stabilised the mechanism, it varied from individual to individual and was subject to the hormonal changes the body went through during the ageing process, and which accelerated rapidly past the age of 40 . . . an age you two, of course, will never reach. But even with Prime Standards the mechanism fluctuates, and exterior stimuli also affect it. Exposure to simple sunlight, for example, will stimulate the production of a specific mood enhancer in the brain, and the primary stages of a sexually based emotional relationship, to give another example, flood the brain with amphetamine analogues—" he gave Ryn another sneering smile—"one effect of which is to kill the appetite," he said, then looked meaningfully at the untouched plate of food in front of Ryn.

Ryn felt his cheeks glow with his embarrassment. Angrily, he said, "Forgive me for being rude, but what exactly *are* you?"

Jan answered before Milo could say anything. And what she said shocked Ryn. In an icy tone she said, "He's the father of my son and the murderer of my son. And he's also one of the monsters who started the Gene Wars."

Chapter Fifteen:

The Duke du Lucent sat beside the bed in the darkened room, head bowed and with his hands tightly clasped together. His feelings of remorse and guilt were so thick within him it seemed as though they were clogging his throat. "My darling . . . I'm so sorry . . . it was an *accident* . . . please say you forgive me."

But Andrea remained silent. She had refused to acknowledge his presence since he'd entered her bedroom.

"Andrea, please. . . ." Reluctantly he raised his eyes to her face, winced and looked quickly down again. "The whip . . . it was the whip. I was never good with whips . . . it must have slipped. You know I would never have deliberately . . . done *that* to you. Andrea, please talk to me!"

He tried in vain to elicit some response from her for a further quarter of an hour then gave up and crept quietly out of the room. No sooner had he gone than someone else entered by another door. It was her brother, Prince Darcy. Dressed in his usual black he stood at the end of the bed and stared down at her. He gave a twisted smile and said, "Well, we make a pretty pair, don't we, dear sister? Me with my dead arm—" he touched the black leather sling that supported his useless right arm—"and you with your dead eye."

"Get out, Darcy," she said, her voice slurred both by her swollen lips and by the drugged wine the surgeon had given her. "Leave me alone."

"Soon, sister, soon. But first we must talk of the common

cause of our respective mutilations. Your dear lover—Robin."

She shut her good eye. "Never speak his name in my presence again!" she hissed.

"I understand how you feel, sister dear. Oh, I do indeed. And I want vengeance on this earthworm who has not only stained the honour of our family and betrayed the *Lord Mordred* but crippled me and disfigured you. And yet our cowardly father is scurrying away from our enemy as fast as he can. With every passing hour more miles are put between us and that treacherous pig."

Andrea was quiet for a few moments then she said, huskily, "I would do anything to have . . . him . . . in my power, if only for a few minutes. Just *one* minute would be sufficient for what I have in mind for him. But what can we do? Father won't dare face up to that fleet."

"No," Darcy agreed, "He won't. But mother would."

"Mother?"

"I've just spoken to her. She's furious over what has happened to you. I've never seen her so angry. It is the last straw for her as far as father is concerned."

"But what can she do? Father controls the army."

"He did, but recent events have caused a great deal of resentment in the army, according to mother's agents. She thinks she can exploit the situation to her—and our—advantage."

"When?" she asked, eagerly.

"Soon."

The figures on the screen told a grim story. She was losing the battle to save the population of Phoenix Two. The plague had spread throughout the community, infecting one in three people. So far none of the drugs produced by the Sky Angel's automatic labs had any effect but to delay, in some cases, the inevitable. Jan felt frustrated and helpless. She left the console and walked to the front of the control room. Flickering fires were dotted about Phoenix Two. There were few other lights showing in the darkened town. The fires, Jan knew, were for the corpses.

Considering how bleak the situation was she felt guilty about the spark of, well, happiness that had grown within her since the arrival of Robin. She had felt a stirring of excitement the moment he had entered the control room. He was certainly attractive, true, apart from that awful scar on his face, but there was more to it than that. It was as if some instant, unspoken rapport had formed between them. The strength of her reaction to him disturbed her, and still did, but she found it exciting nonetheless. And she could see it in his eyes that he was experiencing a similar reaction to her. Where would it lead? She had thought that after what had happened to Ceri and Simon she would never dare to feel close to another human being again, but now . . . ?

Yet on another level she remained wary of Robin. He seemed too good to be true, a handsome young soldier-of-fortune who appears out of nowhere with a marvellous machine that he has pledged to put totally at her service. Still, she wasn't nearly as dubious about him as Milo was, but then she suspected that Milo's chief fear was that Robin *was* genuine. If he was it would give her an edge in the power struggle that was developing between them. Damn Milo . . . ! She wished she'd hit him with that knife this afternoon in her quarters. To begin with he had, predictably, reacted angrily to her charge that he had helped start the Gene Wars. . . .

"That's a lie! I had nothing to do with the start of the Wars!"

"But your corporation was involved in the manufacture of bio-weapons for the Gene Wars," Jan said. "You told me yourself."

"All the corporations were involved—we had no choice if we wanted to survive!"

151

"Some survival, eh?" said Jan, with a bitter smile. "World-wide devastation, and massive loss of life followed by a slow degeneration of what remains of the environment."

Robin, looked mystified, said, "I don't understand. How can *he*," indicating Milo with a nod of his head, "be old enough to remember the Gene Wars? he's only a boy."

"It's a long and nasty story," Jan said. "I'll tell you all the details some other time, perhaps. Briefly, Milo is an immortal; in a different body he lived in the days back before the Gene Wars, in the 21st century. . . ."

"Actually, I was born in the tail end of the 20th century," interrupted Milo testily. "In 1997."

"He ran one of the Gene Corporations," continued Jan.

"Which I'd built up from a small bio-engineering company that I'd inherited from my father, though admittedly some of the industrial bacteria designs he'd copyrighted when he was alive proved an invaluable source of back-up capital to me during the early years."

". . . And so he became one of the most powerful people in the world—part of that exclusive group who were the architects of the biological catastrophe that was to follow."

"Nonsense," snapped Milo. "The Corporations weren't solely to blame. It was also because of the political turmoil at the time—the aftermath of the break-up of the big nations into numerous independent states after the establishment of the Prime Standard, which in turn led to the collapse of the United Nations—the only body that had any power to control bio-research. Then came internecine warfare between states that had formerly belonged to the same country, and religious warfare between fundamentalist states that resisted the genetic revolution. The Corporations had no choice but either to take sides of act independently to protect themselves. But enough of this useless arguing." He turned again on Robin. "What I still want to know is just what exactly your game is."

Robin sighed. "I keep telling you, I'm a mercenary, pure

and simple. I joined up with the *Lord Mordred* when I encountered the Sky Lord fleet in the seas off Antarctica. . . ."

"Fleet?" exclaimed Milo, eyes widening. "You didn't mention any *fleet*."

"Didn't I? Well, there was a fleet all right. Five Sky Lords, including the *Lord Mordred*. The other four got separated in a storm."

"What were they doing down South?" Milo asked him.

"Looking for Shangri La. The habitat. They hoped to find Old Science weaponry there. To use against Jan."

"Me?" asked Jan, caught off-balance. She had been losing herself in a study of Robin's face, wondering how he'd come by that awful scar.

"Your fame has spread far and wide," said Robin. "Three of the Sky Lords are from lands south of here. They presumed, months ago, they were next in line to be conquered and fled across the Atlantic. They formed an alliance with an Islamic Sky Lord called El Rashad, who, according to the Duke du Lucent, is bad news indeed. After the Duke was forcibly drafted into the alliance, they began to search for Old Science technology, presuming, rightly, that the Antarctic habitat was their best bet."

"And they found you and your machine?" asked Milo.

"Well, I found them really. And by chance picked the *Lord Mordred* to land on."

"And even though you lost the rest of the fleet this Duke du Lucent continued north to confront our fleet?"

"Because he had me . . . and my aircraft."

"Because he *thought* he had you," said Milo. "You obviously made a bargain with him, but one you never intended to keep, right?"

Robin looked briefly down into his empty glass. "Well, no. When I heard what the Sky Angel—Jan—was attempting to do in freeing the ground people and destroying the blight lands I saw immediately I was on the wrong side."

"But, of course, without telling the poor Duke," said Milo with a cynical smile. "And what form of payment did you extract from the Duke to cement this so-called bargain, apart from that pantomime costume?"

Robin looked down into his glass again. "I'd prefer not to say . . ."

Milo laughed knowingly. "Oh, *women* was it? Yes, that makes sense. I would presume that your Eloi made unsatisfactory bed-partners, if they made any kind at all. And what price are you expecting for your dubious services here?" He turned his sneering gaze on to Jan. "Care to make a guess, Jan? Seeing as you're the only woman it shouldn't be too difficult for you."

Furious, Jan grabbed a table knife. She waved it at Milo. "Milo, I've had it with you! Get out of here! I want to talk to Robin in private. Take your evil mind elsewhere!"

Milo folded his arms and stared at her in defiance. "I warned you about threatening me, Jan. And I'm not leaving you alone with this mercenary. I don't trust him and neither should you. He's already admitted he betrayed his former 'employer'. Sure, it's clear that he's itching to get under your tunic, and I'm picking up signals you have similar designs in the area of his cod-piece but—"

He'd ducked as Jan threw the knife at his head. When their eyes met again she saw a look of triumph in Milo's. She stood up. "All right then, *I'll* go! I'll be in the control room." She turned to Robin, who looked startled. "You can stay here for the time being. Rest, make yourself comfortable. But don't pay any attention to the poison he will no doubt spew in your ear. . . ." She jerked her thumb in Milo's direction.

As she headed for the door Milo called out, in a child's high, sing-song voice, "You're going to be s-o-r-r-y. . . ."

Damn Milo. She thumped her fist against the curved glass of the forward section of the control room. *Damn. . . .*

Then she frowned. She'd noticed that one of the largest fires burning down below in Phoenix Two had briefly been obscured, as if something had flown over it. Then, as she puzzled over what might be the cause, the glass panel she was peering out of suddenly vibrated from the impact of something travelling very fast. As she instinctively flinched away she had a momentary sight of the cause as the thing clung to the outside of the glass for a few seconds before abruptly dropping out of sight.

She saw a long, segmented, insectoid form with six angular limbs and a cancerous, desiccated horse-head that had the antennae and proboscis of a giant mosquito. On either side of it stretched vast transparent wings containing a network of fine veins. . . .

Hazzini!

In her terrified haste to get away she fell in a tangle of legs and feet. On her hands and knees on the deck she cried, "Carl! Hazzini attack! Why didn't you warn me? How did it get so close?"

It was Ashley who answered. First she giggled and then she said, "We wanted to give you a little surprise, Jan. And it's more than one Hazzini—it's a whole swarm. Look. . . ."

Jan stared back over her shoulder. Now she could see the turquoise beams of the fleet's laser beams flashing across the night sky. She saw dark shapes suddenly illuminated by fire and then writhing as they spiralled towards the ground in flames. Then she saw that none of the laser beams were coming from the Sky Angel! "Ashley! Activate our defences! Now!"

Ashley giggled again. "That wouldn't be any fun. Besides, it's too late. We've already been penetrated. Several Hazzini are on board."

"No!" gasped Jan. She drew her hand weapon from its holster. Too clearly she remembered the Hazzini on the *Lord Pangloth*, its stink as it had grabbed her with its cruel claws in the cramped, dark space between the upper hulls;

those intelligent, horrifying eyes . . . the invisible scar down her front suddenly began to sting. "No!" She got to her feet and ran to the elevator.

She took the elevator to the level where her quarters were located. She peered cautiously in both directions when the door had opened. The corridor was empty. She stepped out, her weapon ready. The door slid shut behind her.

Then the lights went out.

"Ashley! Carl! Lights! Put the lights back on!" Jan cried, her heart lurching with panic.

Ashley's giggle came from all directions. "It's more fun this way. Hush, listen . . . ! Can I hear a Hazzini coming towards you? On your left?"

Jan spun and fired into the darkness. The beam from the weapon briefly lit up the corridor. It was empty. Darkness rushed back in. "Damn you, Ashley! Give me lights! Send me some spider-mechs! I want protection!" Jan cried. Her heart was thudding painfully now. If she did encounter a Hazzini she was sure the fright alone would kill her.

"You're no longer giving the orders, Jan," Ashley told her cheerfully. "Things have changed. You're yesterday's news."

"Let me speak to Carl!"

"Carl won't obey your orders either, now."

Jan thought she heard a noise to her right. She fired blindly. Again the flash from the beam revealed an empty corridor. "Why are you doing this to me?!" she screamed.

"Because you've become very tiresome, Jan. You're not only no fun any more but you've been very mean to my friend Milo."

Jan wanted to burst into tears. So it had happened at last. Milo had gained complete influence over Ashley. That means he had control of all the Ashley programs, and all the Carls as well. In her frustration Jan fired her weapon at the ceiling—a futile gesture.

"Temper, temper," chided Ashley, as sparks fell around Jan.

"Fetch, Milo. I want to talk to him," said Jan, trying to keep her paralysing panic at bay. But this time there was no answer from Ashley.

"Ashley? *Ashley*! Stop playing games, damn you!" But the silence stretched on, until. . . .

There was a sound to her right. Something was coming along the corridor, and it was moving on more than one pair of limbs. Jan began to run in the opposite direction. At one point she collided with a wall of the corridor and the pain in her elbow as she banged caused her to yelp. She ran faster, her heart making her blood thunder in her ears. . . .

And ran straight into the embrace of the thing waiting for her in the darkness.

The Duke du Lucent sat alone in his study. He was slumped over his chart table. Maps were scattered across it, several of them wine-soaked. While drinking his way through a flagon of wine he had knocked his cup over twice. He had drunk nearly half a quart of wine during the last few hours but he was still painfully conscious. And so he felt the slight movement in the air which told him someone, against his strictest instructions, had entered the study. He looked up balefully, then gave a start of surprise. It was his wife.

"You?" he said. "What are you doing here? You know you are to keep out of my sight. And anyway, I left orders not to be disturbed. Get out."

But she didn't move. She just stood there in her hooded black robe, staring at him with a slight smile of contempt on her angular face. Someone else stepped into view from behind her. His son, Prince Darcy. He too wore a contemptuous smile.

The Duke scowled at them both. "What's this? A damned family reunion? Get out before I call the guards. I want to be alone tonight."

"Fear not, husband, you will soon be alone again," said his wife grimly. "*Very* alone, but first we must talk. About Andrea."

The Duke groaned and covered his face with a gloved hand. "No! I refuse to talk of the matter. I have suffered enough!"

"*You* have suffered?" said his wife. "What about your daughter? You have destroyed her beauty. Imagine what she is going through. What she will continue to go through for the rest of her life!"

"Please, no more!" cried the Duke. "What can I do to make amends? Would it help Andrea if I plucked out my own eye?"

"But there *is* a way she can be helped," said his son.

The Duke peered at them through the splayed fingers of his hand. "What are you talking about? The surgeons can't give her a new eye. . . ."

"No, not *our* surgeons," said his wife, "but according to Darcy your treacherous 'ally' spoke of many Old Science wonders that existed in his underwater city—including machines that could cure any illness."

"But that place is inaccessible to us," the Duke pointed out. "It lies under the sea and ice of Antarctica."

"*It* does," said the Prince, "but the same wonders also exist on the Sky Angel, if your friend was telling the truth, and *that* is accessible to us!"

The Duke lowered his hand from his face. He said wearily, "It's out of the question. We would stand no chance against that fleet."

"We won't attack the whole fleet," said his son. "Just the Sky Angel. We send in a large force by glider under the cover of darkness. They land on the Sky Angel and take it over. With the Sky Angel under our control the rest of the fleet will be helpless. We will have the means to mend Andrea and have the added bonus of reclaiming the creature Robin and his machine."

The Duke looked at his son and said wearily, "You make it sound so simple, but the odds of such a surprise attack being successful are very remote. "No. . . ." He shook his head. "I will not risk it."

His wife said coldly, "The decision is no longer yours to make. There has been a rebellion. A *controlled* rebellion let us say. Disaffected factions of the army threatened to join forces with the peasants. To prevent such a disastrous event the noble families have agreed that you must relinquish the throne and put Prince Darcy on it as the new Sky Lord. . . ."

"Preposterous!" laughed the Duke. "I'm clearly not the only one who's been at the wine tonight. Now get out before I have the guards drag you out."

"Call them, then," said the Prince calmly.

The Duke did so. The doors opened and two guards rushed in, swords drawn. They faced the Duke. He didn't recognise either of them. He swallowed and said, "Fetch Baron Spang . . . I must talk to him. . . ."

His wife said, "Alas, Baron Spang was one of the few nobles who remained loyal to you. He died of his wounds a short time ago." She then produced a rolled scroll from within her robe. "This is your declaration of abdication from the throne. Please sign it." She placed it, on the table, away from any wine puddles. The Prince placed a pen beside it.

He stared at it for a long time then poured himself the last of the wine. He drank the wine and, as he picked up the pen, said sadly, "This has certainly not been my year."

Chapter Sixteen:

Jan screamed as the claws dug into her. The thing had incredible strength. The weapon was torn from her hand and she was thrown violently to the floor. Still screaming, she braced herself for the Hazzini's killing blow. Then there was a flash of light. Ashley had chosen this moment to turn the lights back on. She screwed her eyes tightly shut, not wanting to see the Hazzini that had her in its grip. She tried vainly to curl up in a ball to protect her front and throat. . . .

There was a shrill peal of childish laughter. The claws released her. She opened her eyes. Standing over her, grinning, was Milo. "You should see your face," he told her.

Something was coming along the corridor behind her. She turned. It was a spider-mech. It was followed by several others. The first spider said cheerfully, with Ashley's voice, "Hey, you were really funny, Jan!" Then Robin appeared. He was flanked by two of the spiders. Concern for her showed on his face but when he made an attempt to approach one of the spiders restrained him. Jan faced Milo again and got to her feet. She stared down at him, trying to conceal her fading terror with a look of haughty disdain. "So it was all a joke then?" she asked. "The Hazzini never got on board?"

"Oh, a few did," said Milo, "but they were all exterminated by the mechs. At least I *hope* they all were." His grin became even more malicious. Jan said, "Kish and Shan, you haven't harmed them, have you?"

"They haven't been touched. They've been confined to their quarters. Later they will have to decide whether to

160

serve me as they did you—I do like human servants better than mechanical ones—or I will have them transferred to one of the other ships, where the quality of their lives would surely suffer. Now come with me to the infirmary. There's something I must do before I get down to the business of informing the common herds on the other ships that there has been a change of management. . . ."

Jan was worried as she followed Milo into the nearest infirmary. Robin was beside her. They were surrounded by mechs. They hadn't so far had the opportunity to exchange any words but Jan saw that he looked fairly cheerful considering the situation. Milo, clearly euphoric, was still describing his planned changes for the rest of the fleet. ". . . No, those whingeing morons won't know what hit them when I'm finished. They thought they had reason to complain about you! Hell, the easy life is going to be over for them from now on. They want to stay with the fleet they *work* or it's the ground for them. . . ."

"Yeah Milo!" chortled one of the spiders. "We're gonna show them." Ashley was sounding younger all the time.

Milo halted the group in front of one of the medic-machines. He gestured at Robin. "Okay, strip off and get in that thing."

Robin said, "Why? I feel perfectly well."

"You want to take bets on how long you'll continue to stay that way? Do as I say!" Milo ordered.

With an apologetic shrug to Jan, Robin quickly shed his medieval clothes. While Ashley, *via* several of the mechs, made lewd panting sounds Jan tried to avoid looking at him as he stood naked in front of the machine, which had already extended its cradle to receive him. He was about to get on the cradle when he paused and removed a ring from his finger. He turned and offered it to Jan, "Please keep this. A memento, just in case anything happens to me."

As Jan took it Milo said, with amusement, "Nice piece of

melodrama, Robin Hood, but it's only a medic-machine, not a bloody oven."

"The night is young. I'm sure you have other things planned for later," said Robin, lying down on the cradle. As the cradle slid into the machine Jan slid the ring on to her middle finger. It was a narrow band of gold set with a single, small jewel.

"Would you like me to have Ashley dig up a rendition of 'Here Comes the Bride' out of the sound library?" asked Milo, observing her action.

Jan said, "What's this all about? Why are you doing this to him?"

"He told me some crap about having an implant in his skull through which he could control his machine—blow it up by remote control if necessary, and us with it. I don't believe him." He then said, "Ashley, patch yourself into that machine. I want him thoroughly scanned. Look for anything that doesn't belong—mechanical or biological."

"Sure thing, skipper."

The entire process was over in just a few minutes. "Not a thing," Ashley reported. "He was bluffing all right."

The medic-machine began to disgorge Robin. Jan watched anxiously as the cradle slid out but soon saw that he was unharmed. Before she again averted her eyes from his nakedness she noticed that the scar on his face had vanished.

"Okay, Robin Hood, get back into your cod-piece and hose," ordered Milo.

When Robin had dressed Milo said, "Now it's time we talked business. There is no self-destruct system in your machine, is there?"

Robin rubbed the side of his face where the scar had been, glanced at Jan then said to Milo, "No."

"So if I had one of the mechs trick open its hatch nothing would happen," continued Milo.

"Not a thing. And I mean that. You might be able to get inside it but it won't fly for you. It responds only to me."

"That doesn't surprise me in the least," Milo said easily. "But all computers can be reprogrammed, and I'm sure you have the necessary codes and know-how to enable such reprogramming to be carried out. You do, don't you?"

Robin didn't reply. Milo said, "Ashley, do it. . . ."

One of the spider-mechs near Jan suddenly darted towards her. A seizing tentacle whipped round her waist and a buzzing cutting tool was held close to her throat. She froze with fear. "No . . . !" cried Robin. Milo held up his hand.

"Relax," he said to Robin. "No harm will come to her, provided you agree to cooperate in every way when it comes to modifying your machine so that it will obey only me. Do I have your word? Otherwise your Sky Angel dies and I use alternative and even messier methods to gain your cooperation."

"He's bluffing," Jan told Robin, trying to ignore the tool that buzzed near her throat. "He won't harm me."

"Don't be so sure. Besides, the choice might not be up to me when it comes to the crunch. Ashley may take matters into her own, er 'hands'. . . ."

"Let her go," said Robin, a tremor in his voice. "I'll do whatever you want. I swear it."

"And I believe you, oh Robin of Sherwood," laughed Milo. "Never before have I seen the light of love shine so clearly in anyone's eyes. You are truly besotted with your Maid Marion. And as soon as I get the time we will spend an enjoyable few hours together while you introduce me to the joys of your marvellous machine. I am especially interested in its weapons systems. But for now I have more urgent matters to attend to . . . Ashley, escort these two to Jan's quarters. I have a feeling they want to be alone. But guard them securely."

"Wait, Milo," said Jan. "What do you intend to do?"

"With you two? Nothing, now, if you cooperate and behave yourselves."

"No, I mean with the fleet . . . and the people on the ground."

"I told you what I'm going to do with the fleet—impose a New Order. And if there's any show of resistance it will be crushed immediately."

"Yeah!" said Ashley, with enthusiasm.

"As for the population of Phoenix Two, what's left of them, they're on their own from now on. I'm heading the fleet southwards. Time to meet what opposition is left in the skies over South America. . . ."

"Won't you at least wipe out the Hazzini nests here before you leave?" asked Jan.

"We must have barbecued a thousand of the creatures tonight; why waste more energy? Besides, why bother? Phoenix Two is dying. The plague, as you've discovered, can't be stopped."

"At least you would destroy one source of infection by burning out the nests. Sooner or later these Hazzini will reach other ground communities."

"I'm afraid I don't have your crusading zeal, my dear Jan. Take them away, Ashley."

Milo watched while Jan and Robin were shepherded out of the infirmary by four of the spider-mechs, then said, "Right. Next stop the control room, where I want to be patched through to the PA systems of every ship." He rubbed his hands with anticipation. "This is going to be very enjoyable."

"I don't like it," said a spider-mech in a sulky voice.

"What?" Milo looked down at it in surprise. "I thought this is what you wanted, Ashley. It's what we talked about."

"I don't mean *that*, I mean them. You letting them be alone like that. You know what they'll do together."

Realisation dawned. "Oh, I see." She—it—no, essentially still a *she*—was jealous. Or thought she was, as she was incapable of experiencing real emotions, as far as he could fathom it. But ersatz or real, the outcome was the same and he would have to humour her. In a placatory tone Milo said, "It's only for the time being. Until I get the necessary information out of him. The closer the bond between them the more confident I can be of his genuine cooperation with her as my hostage. Once I have total control of that flying machine then he can be disposed of."

"Good," said Ashley. "But I don't see why you need that ugly machine when you have me."

"*We* need it, Ashley, as a back-up unit in case we run into something we can't handle." He didn't add that he needed it as a personal piece of insurance. He had no way of knowing how long he could depend on Ashley. With that machine under his control he could force her to cooperate if all else failed. It would also provide a handy means of escape if the worst came to the worst.

"And what about Jan? Are we going to dispose of her too?"

"No, not if she behaves herself. I have further plans for her." He looked down at himself. "When I've grown a bit more."

"I don't understand."

"I intend to resume the physical relationship I briefly enjoyed with Jan Dorvin in my previous incarnation."

"Oh," said Ashley.

"Considering what has happened you seem remarkably cheerful," Jan observed as Robin seated himself on her couch and grinned at her.

"Why not? I'm still alive and, even better, I'm alone with you." He touched his cheek. "Pity about the scar, though. I was beginning to get used to it."

"I wasn't. It was horrible. You're much better looking without it." Jan felt a growing warmth in her loins and was annoyed with herself. This was not the time for such feelings. "But we're not alone," she told him, irritably. "The mechs

165

may have stayed outside the door but you can be certain we're being monitored by Ashley."

"Who cares?" He extended his arm to her. "Come and sit beside me."

"No—come into the bathroom with me," she said.

He looked surprised then grinned and stood up. "I'd prefer the bedroom but. . . ."

When she'd shut the bathroom door and turned towards him he embraced her. Ignoring the responses of her own body to his closeness she pushed him away. "Listen," she said in a strong whisper, "there are no sensors in here. I insisted on that. That will probably change but I'm sure they haven't had time to install any yet. For the time being we can talk privately."

"Good. I love you."

"Don't be stupid," she said, even though his words caused her to feel slightly giddy. "We have to work out what we're going to do. You know what will happen as soon as you give Milo what he wants. He'll kill you."

Still smiling at her, Robin leaned back against the wash basin. "Do you love me? I think you do but I'd like to hear you say it."

She wanted to cry yes at the top of her voice. Mother God, what was happening to her? She said shakily, "Will you be serious, please?"

"I *am* being serious."

"You're going to be seriously dead unless we do something! But I can't think of anything we *can* do . . . with Ashley on Milo's side we're utterly helpless. Have you any ideas?"

He sighed and folded his arms. "All we can do is play for time and wait for an opportunity."

"An opportunity? An opportunity to do *what*?"

"Escape . . . or whatever," he said, with a shrug. "Something will turn up."

"Well, thank the Mother God I have the good fortune to

166

be in league with such a major strategist—I was beginning to get worried."

He laughed. "You worry too much."

She laughed as well. Despite the apparent hopelessness of it all she couldn't help but be affected by his high spirits. Maybe it wasn't as bad as it seemed after all. Maybe he had something up his sleeve. . . .

When he embraced her again she didn't resist but surrendered to the powerful rush of her feelings. She shuddered with pleasure as his mouth closed on hers. Vague guilt over enjoying such intense pleasure was quickly stifled. Then she let him lead her outside and into her bedroom. He laid her on the bed and slowly undressed her. Then he undressed himself. This time she didn't avert her eyes.

"Don't touch me there," she said drowsily. "Please."

He had been kissing her between her breasts. He stopped and propped his chin on his elbow. "You don't like it?"

"I was wounded there once . . . all the way down. . . ." She traced, with a fingertip, the line from her throat down between her breasts and on to her belly. Her hand felt heavy. So did the rest of her. She was tired; was sinking into a warm, comfortable state of semi-sleep. The love-making had been exhaustingly wonderful.

"I can't see any sign of a wound now," said Robin.

"It's healed completely—on the outside. But I still sense it there. I don't like it to be touched . . . A Hazzini did it, almost killed me."

He stroked the side of her face. "Don't think about it. Go to sleep."

The bed shuddered slightly. The airship was starting to move. The fleet was heading south and those still alive down below in Phoenix Two would be left to their own devices. And the Hazzini. She said, "Do you think Milo was joking . . . ?"

"About what, darling?"

167

"The Hazzini . . . he said he *thought* all those that had got on board had been killed."

"They scare you, don't they, those things?"

"They terrify me. You'd know what I mean if you saw one up close. Horrible. They're pure hate machines . . . man-made hate machines designed to do nothing but breed, eat and kill humans. Living weapons. The thought of even one of them loose in the ship . . . Ugh!" She shivered.

Robin put his arm around her. "Hey, it's all right. You're not alone any more. You've got me now. I'll always protect you."

Jan very much wanted to believe that.

Milo leaned against the wind, which stung his eyes. He almost fell and a spider-mech reached out an arm to steady him. Milo was scared that, because he still didn't weigh much, the damned wind would pick him up and carry him away. "We're still going too fast!" he cried. "Slow down! Slow down!"

"We're at zero ground speed, Milo," said the spider-mech in Carl's flat voice. Ashley was sulking and hadn't spoken to him at all this morning, which was all he needed. "It's this southwesterly wind; it's peaking forty miles per hour. It's the edge of a storm front moving in from the coast."

"Christ," muttered Milo. He glared up at Robin, who looked infuriatingly at ease. The bastard had better not be up to anything. "Okay, get that thing opened then stand back."

Milo watched suspiciously as Robin opened his flying machine's hatch then stepped away as instructed. Milo sent a spider-mech inside. "Well?" he asked another of the mechs.

"It's safe," said Carl, "You can enter."

"You go first," ordered Milo, waving Jan's hand weapon at Robin. Robin obliged. Milo warily climbed in after him.

It was cramped in the machine's inner compartment. And dark. "Turn on the lights," he said.

Robin pressed a button on the instrument panel. No lights. The instrument panel itself was dark too. Robin pressed more buttons. Nothing happened.

"What's wrong?"

Robin sighed. "I think the battery's flat."

"What? What are you playing at?" Milo jabbed the weapon in Robin's side.

"Well, not the battery exactly. It's a fuel cell. Provides all the power. It apparently needs recharging. I should have thought of that . . . but then I've never travelled this far from the habitat before."

"Are you trying to pull something on me?" snarled Milo, jabbing him again with the weapon. "Get this thing started! You know what will happen to Jan if you foul up!"

Robin turned and looked at him. "I'm telling you the truth. The thing is inert. Dead. The fuel cell needs recharging."

"And just how do we perform that little job?" demanded Milo.

Robin shrugged. "Shouldn't be too difficult. There's a contact point in a recess in the hull towards the rear. Get the mechs to tool the necessary male connection and then have a cable run up here from the nearest power source."

"Oh, yeah, simple," muttered Milo. "Carl, how long would that take?"

"That length of cable will have to be cannibalised from the ship's system," said Carl. "It would take twenty-four hours. The contact device can be manufactured in only a couple of hours, once I have the specifications."

"Oh great," said Milo, sarcastically. "This is all I need." It had been a long night. Open revolt had broken out on three of the Sky Lords as a result of his broadcast ultimatum last night and they had been more difficult to quell than he had expected. In fact, one was still smouldering on board the *Lord Montcalm* and he had been obliged to transfer spider-mech reinforcements from the other ships, spreading them dangerously thin. He suspected it was all Ashley's fault. She had been uncooperative throughout and, to top it all, she was refusing to speak to him. He felt vulnerable. He *needed* this damn machine.

He said grimly to Robin, "Okay, you've got another twenty-four hours, but after that if this thing still isn't performing I'm going to stop being so pleasant."

The ringing of distant alarm bells roused the Duke from his drunken sleep. He climbed off his bed and staggered the short distance across his cramped room to the door. He banged on it. It was opened by one of his two surly guards. "What do you want now, *sire*? More wine?"

"The alarms," croaked the Duke. His throat was dry and he felt ill. "What's happening?"

"I don't know. Voss has gone off to see." Just then the other guard came hurrying along the corridor. He looked shaken. "We're surrounded!" he cried.

"Surrounded by what?" demanded the Duke.

"The fleet . . . the *Sword of Islam* and the others . . . they've found us again!"

Chapter Seventeen:

"These Eloi of yours fascinate me, Robin," said Milo through a mouthful of real chicken. "I'd love to observe them at first hand. And the habitat itself, of course."

Milo was playing at being the gracious host. His mood had improved considerably since the morning, Jan observed. The rebellion on the *Lord Montcalm* had been completely quashed and work on laying the cable up to Robin's flying machine was on schedule. He was in such a good mood he had ordered the removal of their spider-mech guards and had even invited them to dinner. The food was being served by Kish and Shan. Jan had visited them and persuaded them that it was in their best interests to remain on the Sky Angel and act as Milo's servants. As Milo had said, it was unlikely they would survive for long on any of the other ships.

Jan said, "The Eloi sound disgusting to me. They had the resources to do something to help the world after the Gene Wars and instead they shut themselves off and retreated into an artificial world of constant pleasure."

"Their world is no more 'artificial' than your own," Milo told her cheerfully. "They've just returned their brains to a different level than the one that nature, and the genegineers who designed the Standard Prime, tuned yours to, my dear Jan. Their version of reality is just as valid as yours. Everything is relative, there are no absolutes. Besides, are the Eloi so different in ambition from the Christian and Buddhist monks of old? They too shut themselves off from the world in order to seek a state of ultimate peace, 'oneness with God', Nirvana or whatever. . . ."

171

"Not another of your damned lectures, please, Milo," she said wearily. "I'm trying to eat."

His mask of good humour briefly dropped, then he said to Robin, "My original reading of your machine was that it was simply a rejigged flipper, but on inspection I saw that it was nothing of the kind. Not an Old Science artifact at all but a product of New Science. So some of the Eloi still have an interest in the physical world; enough to develop new technologies?"

Robin shook his head. "No, not the Eloi, the habitat's programs do that." He explained, as he had to the Duke and his people, how the Eloi, before they became the Eloi, had created programs capable of evolving in order to ensure that the guardians of the Eloi could adapt to cope with any new, unanticipated threat.

Milo smiled as he took this in. "New technologies . . . all sitting there in that habitat, and programs capable of producing more." He smiled slyly at Robin. "The machine knows the location of the habitat, doesn't it?"

"Yes," admitted Robin, "but going there wouldn't do you any good. The programs wouldn't cooperate with you."

"Oh, I'm sure I could find a way of ensuring they do," said Milo happily.

Jan said to Robin, "I don't understand how you were allowed to grow up the way you did. Why didn't the programs destroy you when they saw you were a throwback, or have you enhanced to become an Eloi?"

"The Ethical Program wouldn't permit it," Robin told her.

"Ethical Program?" asked Milo quickly. "What's that?"

"Something else created by the Eloi before they became the Eloi. Knowing that once they had transformed themselves into the Eloi they would no longer have any sense of ethics they designed the Ethical Program to compensate."

"But why? What was the point?" asked Milo, clearly perplexed.

172

"The Ethical Program monitors the Eloi themselves. Makes sure than an Eloi, on a whim or by accident, doesn't do something to hurt itself or someone else. And as I said, the programs are still carrying on research and that includes practical biological research. Sometimes this involves producing foetuses for experimental purposes. The Ethical Program ensures that the foetuses are destroyed after twelve weeks of existence, as laid down by the United Nations. . . ."

"The United Nations!" exclaimed Milo, "When the Soviet American alliance collapsed after the break-up of those nations the United Nations rapidly lost all its power. By the time of the Gene Wars it was long gone."

Robin looked at him and said, "The Eloi were a fraternity of dedicated scientists . . . *before*, that is. They kept to the old rules as a point of honour."

"If they were so honourable why did they desert the world after the Gene Wars?" asked Jan.

"I can only tell you what I was told by the programs," said Robin. "It seems they were so disillusioned and disheartened by the situation—and you must remember that it seemed the designer plagues would quickly wipe out the rest of humanity after the Wars—that they made the decision to opt out into their genetically-induced fairy land as a kind of gesture. But anyway, that's why I'm here as I am. I was past the twelve week limit before it was discovered I was a throwback to a Standard Prime and the Ethical Program ruled against my disposal or any form of further genetic tampering. I didn't, after all, *choose* to become an Eloi, unlike all the others . . . with the exception of the replacement Eloi clones, which are a different matter."

Milo didn't look convinced. "And you were developed past the twelve week limit by *accident*? How could these super programs make such a stupid mistake? No, something isn't quite right here."

Robin shrugged. "I can only repeat what I was told. I can't think of any other reason for my existence."

Milo ran his hand thoughtfully over what little remained of his hair, then smiled at Robin and said, "Well, whatever the truth, both of us have good reason to be thankful that you *do* exist." He turned to Jan. "Don't you agree?"

The look in his eyes made Jan feel as if she had just swallowed something very slimy.

"He wants to see you."

"*Me*? Why?" exclaimed the Duke, feigning ignorance. "Doesn't he know of my drastic change in status?"

"He was informed, yes," said his son gloomily, "but he refuses to negotiate with mother. Because she's a woman, he says. It's against his religion."

"And what about you? Rumour has it that you are a man."

The Prince bristled but kept control. "He doesn't recognise me as the true ruler of the *Lord Mordred* either. He called me a 'boy' and . . . a *cripple*."

"So I am to risk life and limb again and go negotiate with El Rashad on behalf of you and your mother? Why should I?" The Duke folded his arms and sat back.

The Prince cleared his throat and said reluctantly, "His condition for not launching a massed attack on the *Lord Mordred* is that you should be restored to the throne."

The Duke threw his head back and laughed. Then he said, "No wonder you came alone to me. Your mother must be spitting acid. Very well then, I accept your surrender. I will decide the punishment for you, your mother and your followers later." He rose to his feet. "In the meantime I shall fly to the *Sword of Islam* and do what I can to rescue the situation."

Very slowly, as if the movement took every ounce of his strength (which it did) the Prince lowered his head to the Duke and said quietly, "Yes father."

*

174

An hour later, sitting cross-legged in the presence of El Rashad, his feeling of triumph had all but vanished. It was more than clear that El Rashad's motive for restoring him to 'power' had nothing to do with altruism.

"You are pathetic. A pathetic fool," El Rashad informed him. "You refused to listen to me and as a result you lost everything. I told you that the groundling should have been turned over to me. My torturers would have gained us all his secrets but no, you chose to use your own methods of persuasion. You went off on your own to conquer the Sky Angel by yourself and. . . ."

"I didn't deliberately leave your fleet," interrupted the Duke, "It was the storm's fault . . . it scattered us. . . ."

"*Silence!*" ordered El Rashad. "I know what happened. And now I learn that the groundling has joined forces with the Sky Angel, making our task twice as difficult—all thanks to you."

"He betrayed me . . . how was I to know?" said the Duke desperately. "He seemed so . . . well, he and my daughter were . . . I was *sure*. . . ." He gave up under El Rashad's unrelenting gaze.

"You will try and make amends," El Rashad told him.

"Gladly! But how? You are welcome to all my riches, of course, but. . . ."

"You will make amends by leading the attack on the Sky Angel's fleet. You will sacrifice yourself and your ship by ramming the Sky Angel. This will give us the chance to launch a massed glider attack on the other ships."

"A suicide attack . . . ?" asked the Duke, weakly. "And, er, if I refuse to do this?"

"Then you will be taken from here and delivered into the hands of my torturers. After an hour of their attentions you will be given a dagger. I assure you that by then you will be more than happy to cut your own throat with it."

The Duke nodded and said, "Yes, I see." He fervently wished that his wife and son could be here in his place.

*

Jan looked at Robin's sleeping form and marvelled at how he could calmly go to sleep in these circumstances. He knew, because she had repeatedly told him, that his life was worthless once he had given Milo what he wanted, yet, after making love, he had told her, again, not to worry and had quickly slipped into a deep sleep. She, on the other hand, had lain there ever since in a state of acute anxiety, sleep clearly an impossibility. He wasn't stupid, so he obviously knew something that she didn't, but it was maddeningly annoying of him not to tell her what it was. . . .

Robin was in the same relaxed mood during breakfast, which was served by an oddly sullen Kish, and afterwards, when Kish was gone, gestured to Jan that she should go with him to the bathroom. Once inside, he whispered to her, "It's time we made our move."

Thank the Mother God, she said to herself. She only hoped that Robin wasn't deluding himself with whatever he had in mind. As far as she could see there was no way out. "Go on," she urged, "tell me what it is."

"There's a section of open deck near here on this level. Do you know the one I mean?"

She nodded. It was where she had thrown Milo's skull into the night those long months ago when she still had her son.

"Go there now," he whispered, "but act casual, as if you're just wandering out to enjoy the view or get a breath of fresh air. I'll follow you out there in ten minutes."

"And then what?" she said, feeling disappointment well up through her. "We jump overboard? Don't tell me you've secretly stitched together a couple of parachutes?"

He gave her a fond smile. "Better than that. The Toy—my flying machine—is going to meet us there."

Her hopes rose and fell almost simultaneously. "But it *can't*! The spider-mechs haven't recharged its fuel cell yet." She had asked for a progress report from Carl before breakfast. The mechs had yet to reach the machine with their cable.

"It doesn't matter. There is still plenty of power left in the cell. Enough to fly to Shangri La and back. I fooled Milo into thinking the machine was inert by leaving out a vital step necessary to activate it. Now go. . . ."

"Wait!" she said. "What will we do next? If we manage to get on board your machine, I mean."

"Think positive. We *will* get on board," he told her, "and then I'm going to fly down and put a laser beam through the control room *and* the damn main computer. Goodbye Ashley."

"What about the other Ashleys? On the other ships?"

He shrugged. "We'll give them the same medicine if necessary." Then he held her and gave her a quick, hard kiss on the mouth.

"I don't understand," said Jan, as he pushed her gently towards the door. "How will you manage to summon down the machine to our deck?"

"The answer to that, my darling," he said mysteriously, "is in *your* hands. Now go! All will soon be revealed. . . ."

More than ten minutes had passed. She was sure of that. Where was he, she wondered anxiously? Again, she looked up and down the deck, fearful that a spider-mech would appear at any moment rather than Robin. . . .

She took a deep breath and forced herself to stay calm. He knew what he was doing—she hoped—and she was supposed to be enjoying the view. She gazed down at the ground again and saw the tell-tale white and yellow smears that indicated the airship was now over blight territory. She sighed as she recalled her grand scheme to free the world of the blight . . . what a fool she'd been. She'd never stood a chance.

What, she wondered, had Robin meant when he said she held the answer in her hands? She looked at her hands. No answers there that she could see, that was for sure. Still, she would soon find out. . . .

When she'd been waiting for what she estimated to be over half an hour she sighed and went back inside, fearing that something had gone dreadfully wrong. On her way back to her quarters she encountered Kish leaning with his back against a wall in a corridor, head slumped forward. He raised his head and regarded her with a strange expression as she approached. She wondered what the matter was with him. Was he ill? Had Milo done something to him? Her feeling of dread increased.

Before she could say anything he said, in a defensive tone, "I'm glad I did it."

"Did what, Kish? Are you all right?" She took hold of his shoulder and peered anxiously into his face. For an answer he raised his arm and indicated the open door to her quarters further along the corridor. Frowning, she hurried on. What could he be talking about? Was he drunk or . . . ?

She stopped in the doorway. An icy hand closed hard on something vital deep inside her. She groaned.

Robin lay on his back in the middle of the floor in the sitting room. There was a short length of metal pipe beside him.

She rushed to him, crying his name. As she knelt beside him she groaned again when she saw the wound on the side of his left temple. A deep indentation that seeped blood. It was about two inches long and an inch wide. The force of the blow must have been tremendous. She raised her head and screamed, "Ashley! Carl! Get some spider-mechs in here! I want him taken to the nearest medic-machine immediately! Do you hear!"

"Yes, I hear," answered Ashley. "And the answer is no."

"What?" cried Jan, not believing what she was hearing. "Are you crazy? Robin may be dying, if he's not already dead! Fetch help!"

178

"I don't care if he does die," said Ashley.

"I love you."

She turned. Kish was standing in the doorway, staring at her. His face was blank. "That's why I did it. Because of you."

"*You* did this to Robin?" she said, astonished. "But why?"

"I just told you," said Kish tonelessly. "Because I love you. It wasn't fair—him coming from nowhere like that and taking you away from me."

The room was starting to rotate around her. Kish wasn't capable of trying to kill anyone. It was impossible . . . yet it had clearly happened. "Kish, you never *had* me. Robin didn't *take* me from you . . . Oh, what's the use. Look, you've got to help me get him to a medic-machine. Hurry!"

He lowered his head. "No, I won't."

"Kish, *do as I say!*"

But he just stood there in silence. She was about to scream at him when suddenly Milo was in the room. He took in the scene in an instant and tutted when he saw the severity of Robin's injury. "Looks bad. And as you didn't do it I can assume it was him." He turned and pointed at Kish, who was still staring resolutely at the floor. Jan nodded.

"How could he?" asked Milo as he walked slowly towards Kish. "I thought Minervan males were incapable of physical violence."

"They are, as a rule. But there are exceptions. . . ." She gasped as she saw what happened next. While Milo was nowhere as fast as his original, he could still move with awesome swiftness. He was on Kish's back before the Minervan had time to react, his boy's legs wrapped tight around Kish's waist. His hands covered the ears of Kish's still-lowered head. As Kish began to give a startled response to what was happening Milo gave his head a savage wrench. There was a gristly-sounding *snap* and then Kish was falling forward, his head turned so far on his neck that he seemed

179

to be peering over his shoulder in surprise at Milo on his back. Milo rode the body to the floor then sprang away. "One less exception," said Milo with satisfaction as he hurried back to Jan and Robin. "Ashley, get some mechs in here, fast!"

"No!"

Milo blinked in surprise and stared up at the ceiling. "You refuse?"

"I sure do."

"But I thought you liked the guy."

"I did. He was gorgeous."

"Then why won't you help us get him to a medic-machine?"

"Because I don't want *her* to have him," said Ashley, petulantly.

Milo looked at Jan and ran his hand over his head. "Oh Christ," he muttered. Then he said to Jan, "Help me lift him—we'll carry him to the infirmary ourselves."

Jan was about to comply when Ashley said, quietly, "No." Then came a metallic clacking in the corridor and three spider-mechs filed into the room and stopped, blocking the doorway.

Milo said angrily, "Damn it, Ashley, I *need* him! Without him I won't be able to reprogram that machine of his. It will be useless!"

"Good," said Ashley. "I told you you don't need it. You've got me."

"Christ," he muttered again. He glanced at Jan and said in a low voice, "The bitch is jealous of everything—him, you, and now that damn machine."

"I heard that!" said Ashley. "I am *not* jealous!"

Robin groaned. "Thank the Mother God—he's still alive," cried Jan, kneeling beside him. Robin had opened his eyes but his gaze was unfixed and his pupils were very dilated. "Robin, can you hear me?"

Milo, kneeling on the other side, began to slap his cheeks. "Hey, Robin, it's Milo! Speak to me! I got some important

180

questions that you must answer for me." Jan grabbed his wrist and shoved his hand away. "Don't you dare touch him, you maniac!" she hissed at Milo. Then she raised her head and said loudly, "Ashley, I *insist* you let us take him to the infirmary."

"He's alive, huh?"

"Yes . . . *yes*."

"So he might live."

"Yes, he might live even without the help of a medic-machine," said Jan desperately, "So it doesn't matter, does it, if you let us put him in one?"

"If he's going to live it won't be here," said Ashley, and the floor shuddered.

"We're slowing down," observed Milo.

"I'm dumping him on the ground," said Ashley, and as she spoke the mechs began to advance. Inexorably, the mechs pushed Jan and Milo out of the way and converged on Robin. As they lifted him Jan came to a quick decision. She knew, anyway, that she had no choice in the matter. "If you're putting him on the ground then you'll have to do the same with me," she told Ashley.

"What a good idea!" said Ashley brightly. "I'll be happy to oblige. . . ."

Chapter Eighteen:

The Duke du Lucent peered worriedly into the grey skies ahead. It was a miserable day with low cloud and a constant drizzle of rain. At any moment he expected to see the Sky Angel's fleet materialise out of the clouds and when that happened he knew he would be doomed. Flanking his throne in the control pod were two of El Rashad's black-robed warriors, their curved swords bared and resting across their folded arms. Another two warriors flanked the Chief Tech. When the other fleet was sighted they were there to ensure that the Duke and his men obeyed El Rashad's order to attempt to ram the Sky Angel. They were prepared to die themselves, El Rashad had informed him, for "the glory of Allah". The Duke had made an impassioned plea on behalf of his own religious laws which, he explained, expressly forbad suicide in any form but El Rashad, in turn, pointed out that as his religion was a false one its laws carried no weight and he could safely disobey them. Anyway, being an 'Unbeliever', he was damned whatever he did.

None of which had the Duke found reassuring.

He felt very alone. He missed his advisor, Baron Spang. The Baron might have come up with some idea by which the Duke could wriggle out of this trap. The Duke himself saw no possible solution.

He gazed down at the ground. They were flying low—at just fifteen hundred feet—and he could make out ruined buildings among the obscene growths of the blight. A town, perhaps, or maybe even the remains of a city that last saw life at the time of the Gene Wars. And saw death too. . . .

The Duke shuddered and tried to summon up a sense of optimism. It was an emaciated beast when it finally appeared but it did bring the thought that, with visibility so bad, they would never find the Sky Angel and her fleet. He immediately felt a little cheered.

Jan had given up pleading with Ashley to change her mind. The only concession she had won from her was the opportunity to load a backpack with two sleeping bags, emergency rations, two canteens of water and some basic medical supplies. Now she and Robin were on a freight platform in one of the cargo holds, about to be lowered to the ground. Milo stood watching. "Looks like she means it, kid," he said, sounding actually regretful. "Sorry it has to end this way—we've had some interesting times together."

"That's one way of putting it, I suppose," she said dryly. "So can I ask a favour of you?"

He became instantly guarded. "What is it? I'm not carrying much weight around here myself at the moment."

She pointed at her weapon in his belt. "Let me have that. You know we won't last an hour down there in blight territory without a weapon."

He considered her request for a time then nodded. "It's okay with me. What about you, Ashley?"

"Do whatever you want," Ashley answered, her tone one of boredom.

Milo handed the weapon to a mech with instructions to hand it over to Jan once the cradle had touched down. "Beginning descent," announced Ashley, and the cradle gave a jerk. As the mech carrying the weapon quickly scuttled on board Jan grabbed the railing with one hand then knelt to steady Robin's prone body with the other. He was still semi-conscious but so far had said nothing.

The cradle was lowered through the outer hull and into what appeared to be a squall. As the descent continued both she and Robin were very quickly soaked through with rain.

The Sky Angel was hovering at a height of only about eight hundred feet and the cradle soon touched down with a jarring bump. Robin groaned. The spider-mech handed her the weapon and said brusquely, in Ashley's voice, "Out."

"You've got to help me with him," Jan told her. Together they carried Robin off the cradle and laid him on the spongy ground. The mech hurried back on to the cradle. "Ashley . . ." called Jan.

"Now what?"

"This," said Jan and fired. The spider-mech squeaked and crackled as it collapsed, spewing blue sparks in all directions. Then the cradle lurched upwards. Jan knew it had been a silly and futile gesture, and a waste of the weapon's remaining power, but she was still glad she had done it.

She watched the cradle disappear up into the vast form of the Sky Angel above, feeling as small and insignificant as on the day when, a little girl clinging to her mother, she had first seen the *Lord Pangloth* appear over Minerva. The other ships of the fleet, which had halted with the Sky Angel, were strung out across the sky, some of them partially obscured by the low cloud. They looked ominous and threatening.

She sighed and scanned their immediate surroundings. All she could see was blight. Surreal fungoid growths grew out of and on the remains of trees and the ruins of low buildings. It had apparently once been a residential area . . . before the Gene Wars. About a half a mile away she could see a large structure that seemed relatively undamaged compared to everything else around. Perhaps it had been a military installation or even a fortress. It was the best chance for shelter for the time being.

Jan knelt down by Robin. "Robin, can you hear me? It's Jan."

His eyelids fluttered in response but his gaze remained blank and unfixed. She got some of the medical supplies out of her backpack and applied an anti-bacterial/fungal pad to his wound and bandaged his head. It was just a token effort but better than nothing. As she was repacking she glimpsed something moving out of the corner of her eye. Jan turned and saw the thread-like hyphae of a mobile fungus moving across the ground towards Robin. She stood and fired first at the moving carpet of hyphae and then at the central body, the mycelium, some distance away. The white, circular mass, resembling a large, upturned dinner plate made of pulp, blackened under her beam. Then she glanced about anxiously. It had been a long time since she'd been in blight territory. She had grown careless. She knelt beside Robin again and said, "Robin, darling, you're going to have to try and walk—I can't carry you."

She helped him to sit up and then get to his feet. He swayed and Jan managed to prevent him from falling. He made a series of grunting sounds but whether he was trying to talk or just expressing a protest at his discomfort she didn't know. "Come on . . . we're going to walk now . . . like this. . . ." It was difficult at first but slowly she managed to get him into a kind of mechanical stagger, though without her support he would have fallen.

As she guided him towards the imposing structure Jan faced the fact that Robin's chances of survival were bleak without proper medical attention. His skull was obviously fractured and there was surely internal bleeding. Pressure would be building up on his brain and it could only be a matter of time before it proved fatal. But what could she do? Nothing, except get him under shelter and make him as comfortable as possible. And then . . . wait for the inevitable end. She came close to cursing the Mother God. Once again someone she loved was being taken from her. . . .

A bloater emerged from a clump of trees and rolled over the ground towards her and Robin, attracted by their body heat. The milky-white, featureless sac was about three feet across—it was too small to be capable of consuming them but its stings could paralyse them. Jan shot it. The inflammable gases within its membrane exploded with a fiery flash,

185

leaving an appalling stink in the air. Jan, worried, checked the charge level on her weapon. Soon it would be useless.

. . . And what then after Robin died? Jan's only option was to try and get out of the blight territory and hope that she would encounter some settlement. The odds of making it without a weapon were remote, but she would have to try. She gave a wry smile. What had Milo said about people being programmed by nature to have a 'bias towards optimism' no matter how hopeless the reality of the situation? She was living proof that this was true.

It was with a pang of genuine regret that Milo witnessed Jan's expulsion from the Sky Angel. Now, as he headed for the control room, he tried to analyse his feelings about Jan. He decided he needed her around, not just because he had intended to renew their sexual relationship when he had matured, but because she served as something solid and familiar from his previous life. He had been using her as an anchor amid all the confusion and doubt he experienced since discovering himself in this child's body. There were times when he felt that, if he didn't make a deliberate effort to hold on, his identity would fragment and fly off in all directions.

It was the child's body that was at fault. It wasn't just that trace memories from Simon's personality still occasionally echoed through his mind; it was the body itself. The hormone system of the child was distorting the adult mind that had been imposed upon the childish brain. This was manifesting itself in all sorts of ways. For example, even now Milo had to resist the temptation to extend his arms and dash down the corridor while making *vroom vroom* sounds. . . .

By the time he reached adulthood, how much of this original ego would still remain? How much of Milo Haze would be eroded away by the powerful natural forces running rampant through this young body? Could he keep control until the body and mind once again matched up . . . ?

"Jesus Christ!" he exclaimed. Another reason for his regretting of Jan's banishment had just occurred to him—he was missing his *mother*.

As Milo stepped into the control room Carl said, "Milo, we have a radar sighting of five airships moving in this direction from the south west."

Automatically, Milo scanned the skies but, of course, there was nothing to see yet. "The fleet . . . the fleet from the south that Robin mentioned. How long before they get here?"

"They are moving very slowly," Carl told him, "at a speed of only 35 mph. Estimated time of interception, if we remain stationary, will be at 10.50 hours—" Then, to Milo's irritation, Ashley cut in: "Let's go get 'em!"

"I think it would be better, Ashley," Milo said calmly, "to let them come to us. They don't have radar so we'll just wait up there in the cloud until they get close and then we give them a big surprise. Sounds a lot more fun, doesn't it?"

"Yeah, I suppose so," she said grudgingly.

We're both turning into kids, he told himself bitterly. Except she was regressing faster than him. He thought longingly of Robin's machine sitting uselessly on the upper hull. When the battle was over he would see if Ashley would let him enter it and fool around with its controls. Somehow, he didn't think she would. . . .

The structure was getting reassuringly closer. And since the incident with the bloater the blight had presented no other hazards. As Jan walked she wondered what Robin had meant when he'd said the answer to getting the flying machine to meet them on the deck was 'in her hands'. She looked at both her hands in turn. Then she noticed the ring that Robin had given her. *Could that be it?*

187

"Robin, is that it? Is it the ring?" she asked excitedly. She made him halt and stood there facing him, her hands gripping his shoulders to keep him upright. "Is it the ring?" she asked again, but he just stared back blankly at her. Slowly, she lowered him to a sitting position then took off the ring and examined it carefully. It looked just like an ordinary ring to her as she turned it between her fingers. Finally Jan tried pressing the jewel. It went into the gold band with a slight click. A jolt of excitement passed through her. It *was* the ring! She looked expectantly upwards, where the Sky Angel remained hovering in the low cloud for some reason. At any moment she hoped to see Robin's flying machine hurtling down towards her. . . .

Long minutes passed but the machine never appeared. She pressed the diamond in again and again and eventually gave up in disgust. "So much for miracles," she muttered as she got Robin to his feet again. The ring was clearly nothing more than a ring—a ring with a loose setting for its jewel.

As they continued on Jan kept glancing upwards, just in case, but she knew she was grasping at straws. Then she began to wonder why the fleet hadn't moved on. Was Ashley playing some kind of cruel joke with her. Would she and Robin be allowed almost to reach shelter and then be lasered down at the last moment? She wouldn't put it past her.

When they were close to the huge, shattered building Jan was relieved to see that the rain was beginning to die away. She looked up. A break was beginning to appear in the clouds. Then she realised that the clearing weather just made Robin and her better targets. She urged him onwards at a faster rate.

"It's hopeless," announced the Duke to the control pod at large. "We've probably passed each other and not known it. The Sky Angel and her fleet could be hundreds of miles to the south of us by now."

"If they *are* on the move," said the Chief Tech, "they

could still be in a stationary position over that town where we intercepted them before. If that is so we should make contact with them there in seven hours."

"Oh, marvellous," muttered the Duke.

A short time later the Chief Tech announced: "Cloud is beginning to break up. . . ."

"That's all we need," murmured the Duke under his breath. Then he said aloud, "Oh God!"

At first Jan thought it was the sound of thunder. A dull boom echoed across the wide valley that this sprawling, dead residential area occupied. Then it came again and she knew it wasn't thunder. Cannonfire. . . .

She looked up. Though they had come half a mile they had only just emerged from under the nose of the half-concealed Sky Angel hovering overhead. Then she heard the whine of the Sky Angel's thrusters change pitch. They were no longer being used to keep the airship in position but to move her. Yes, the Sky Angel was beginning to move forward, and to ascend at the same time. More cannonfire. What was going on? Jan halted Robin and peered towards the distant row of hills that was the southern border of the wide valley. Then, in the dispersing cloud, she glimpsed a shadowy shape that swiftly took the form of an approaching Sky Lord. And behind it, another one.

The Sky Angel was turning to meet them. The other ships of the fleet were doing likewise. Already the turquoise beams of the lasers were lighting up the sky but Jan knew from experience that at this range, and in these cloudy conditions, they wouldn't be fully effective. Then she saw another Sky Lord come looming over the horizon. There must be a whole fleet of them. The fleet that Robin had mentioned?

She suddenly realised that she and Robin were standing exposed out in the open and got him shambling again towards the gaping opening in the structure's side that she'd

189

been heading for. They were in a spacious, flat area that contained the fungus-eaten remains of numerous vehicles. Military vehicles, she guessed.

They moved into the shadow of what might have been the building's actual entrance. She sat Robin down with his back to a wall then went further in to investigate, weapon in hand. She stared about suspiciously. They were in a wide, gloomy corridor. No sign of any of the more insidious fungi, such as the mutated *oligospora*, lurking on the ceiling. Beyond the corridor Jan could see murky light. She moved on, noticing she was treading on powdered glass. Her boots made crunching noises as she walked. She emerged from the corridor to find herself on a high balcony. She saw that the interior of the structure was much bigger than the exterior suggested, as its builders had dug deep into the earth. Part of the roof had collapsed and the shafts of light coming through the hole illuminated the huge, cavernous space. The balcony Jan was on was one of many that jutted out into the vast space. Some, weakened by the fungus, had collapsed to the floor far below. The floor itself, littered with rubble, was dominated by three large, circular, empty pools. From the structures at their centres she guessed they had been water fountains. All the various levels, above and below Jan's balcony, were connected by tubular elevator shafts and long, steep staircases. Jan gathered that the latter had been moveable, back when the place was functioning. An alternative means of getting from level to level was provided by a gently sloping walkway that spiralled around the entire building. She wondered what purpose the place had served—it clearly wasn't a military establishment. She returned to Robin, satisfied herself that, for the time being, he was all right, then went back outside to see what was happening in the sky.

"The gliders are all away, sire!" announced the Chief Tech. The Duke acknowledged this information with a tense nod of his head. For a change he devoutly wished he was on one of them.

As soon as they had spotted the Sky Angel among the fleet of airships strung out over the valley he had reluctantly ordered the course to be altered. Not that he had any choice in the matter, what with the Moslem warrior on his right raising his sword in a gesture open to only one interpretation. They had taken several laser hits but so far the thin cloud had protected them. The hull had been penetrated in several places and there were already casualties, but all the working thrusters were undamaged and there were no serious fires. As yet.

They were now about a mile and half from the Sky Angel, and those on board had clearly guessed their intention to ram because the Sky Angel was starting to climb at a sharp angle. Also the other members of the Sky Angel's fleet were now concentrating their rocket, cannon and laser fire on the *Lord Mordred*, ignoring the rest of El Rashad's fleet following behind.

"Look out!" screamed someone. By the time the warning had even begun, it was too late. The laser beam, three or four inches wide after being slightly diffused by the clouds' water droplets, was already penetrating the entire length of the control pod. It didn't hit anyone but there was an explosion at the rear of the control room where some electrical equipment had blocked its passage. Smoke began to fill the air.

Less than a mile now, observed the Duke with streaming eyes. Even at the rate the Sky Angel was climbing, the *Lord Mordred*'s trajectory was carrying it on a sure collision course. They would hit the Sky Angel broadside. . . .

Then came a violent jolt and the Duke was almost thrown out of his seat. To his satisfaction, both warriors flanking him lost their footing. "Number four gas cell . . . !" cried the Chief Tech, "It's alight!"

Number four! The Duke tried to remember if that hydrogen-filled cell had helium cells adjacent to it or more hydrogen. He saw they were already rapidly losing height. No chance now of colliding with the Sky Angel. "Forget the attack! Get us down, fast!" he ordered.

"No!" said the warrior to his right, the one who spoke French. "Go on! Go on!" yelled the man, flourishing his sword at the Duke.

But then came an even more violent jolt, which meant another hydrogen cell had been ignited. The warriors at his sides were pitched off their feet by the shock. The Duke didn't hesitate. Drawing a small dagger that he'd hidden on his person to use on himself at the last moment—rather that than die in an inferno—he threw himself on the Moslem who'd been by his right and cut his throat, all the time screaming, "Kill them!" to his Techs.

Jan watched, awestruck, as the old Sky Lord, apparently trying to ram the Sky Angel, was hit again and again by lasers and began to catch fire. A forward gas cell was the first to go. Patches of fire began to show through the hull, quickly spreading to form even bigger incandescent areas. The bright flames were shooting high into the air above the hull. Then another cell, located midships, started to burn. Streaming fire, the dying airship passed beneath the rising Sky Angel, which was still firing its lasers into its crumpling body. So transfixed was Jan by the spectacle that it took her some time to realise that the burning Sky Lord was heading straight for her refuge.

Chapter Nineteen:

Even Milo was taken aback by the scale of the devastation. There seemed to be flaming wreckage as far as he could see. None of the ships of the other fleet had escaped. The various Ashleys had pursued them all and set them alight. And apart from the wreckage of the downed airships the valley was also littered with the shattered remains of gliders, many also burning. Some of the gliders, in the confusion, had made landings on the backs of Ashley's ships—Milo no longer thought of them as his ships—and had disgorged their troops, but they had been too few to pose a real threat and had been quickly overcome.

He turned to the monitor screens, which were scanning the ground. There were many survivors. As individuals or in groups they fled from the blazing Sky Lords that had been their homes since birth. How strange being on the ground must seem to them, thought Milo. And how terrible in such circumstances as these. Many had charred clothes, some had appalling burns. The latter would not survive long, even if Ashley let them live. So far she hadn't fired on any of the fleeing figures. He said, "Don't tell me we are showing signs of a merciful nature, Ashley. There are still people alive down there."

"I like seeing them run around like that, all scared and crazy. Besides, I'm down on power. I don't want to use the lasers until I'm fully recharged."

"Well, yes, you've certainly been a busy girl today. What next, or shouldn't I ask?"

"I want to dump our passengers down there. They're nothing but parasites. We don't need them."

"What, *all* of them?" he asked, alarmed. "Empty out the whole fleet?" The idea didn't appeal to him. What was the use of being in a position of power if Ashley got rid of all the subjects?

"Yeah, every damn one of them."

"Look, let's not be too hasty about this. Let's give it some thought."

"I have given it some thought. I want to dump them," said Ashley firmly.

"As a favour to me, please, hold off for a while, will you?" he pleaded.

"Why?" she asked, suspiciously.

"Ashley, be reasonable, where would the fun be in getting rid of all of them? Keep some of them at least. For amusement."

"Amusement?"

"Yeah, they amuse you, don't they? And we can devise other games for them—new games. Besides, I've got a good reason myself for wanting to keep some of them around."

"What's that?"

"I'm going to need female company."

"I'm female," she pointed out.

"Of course you are," he said, treading carefully. "But I'm talking of female *flesh*. An item of which, you have to admit, you are in radically short supply. You knew what my plans were for Jan. Well, now that you've got rid of her I'm going to need a substitute. Maybe more than one, come to think of it. Let me go on a shopping expedition around the fleet before you start tossing our passengers overboard."

After a long pause she answered, "All right."

Greatly relieved, he said, "Good. So let's hold fire on everything until tomorrow. I'd like to be well away from this area before I do any ship-hopping."

"All right," she said again.

A short time later, as the fleet began to move southwards again, Milo stood in the rear of the control pod and gazed back at the valley which was marked by columns of smoke. "'Bye, Jan," he murmured.

It wasn't a military establishment after all, it was some kind of huge shop. Or rather a whole series of different shops gathered together under one huge roof. Jan had established this after moving deeper into the structure while the aerial battle was at its height. The first of the airships to catch fire had passed right overhead, raining down fiery debris as it went, and had crashed a couple of miles away. She had watched a great fireball rise up above its collapsing hull and doubted if anyone on board could have survived the inferno. Then another airship, hit by lasers, caught fire and Jan saw several gliders, and many parachutists, descend from the sky. One of the gliders had come down close by, which was when Jan decided to take Robin further into the building.

They were heading downwards along the sloping walkway. Jan noted that though all the glass fronts of the shops had been shattered long ago the shops still contained their merchandise, or rather, in many cases, the remains of their merchandise. Why hadn't the place been looted, she mused? Perhaps it was a known plague site . . . The thought made her uneasy but she remembered she had survived a long stay in the city of the Sky Tower, a notorious plague site.

Further on she found the first body. It looked like a bundle of rags lying on the walkway ahead, but when they got closer she saw the white bones. She halted a few feet from it, frowning. It couldn't have been one of the original inhabitants—their skeletons would have crumbled into dust long ago. No, the bones had to belong to a more recent visitor. And judging by the long-barrelled, rusting weapon nearby, he or she had been a marauder. But what killed him—or her? Starvation? Plague . . . ?

After sitting Robin down cross-legged on the walkway,

and wiping the drool from his chin, she approached the remains and gingerly nudged at the rotting clothing with the toe of her boot. She saw that the body had been lying face down. Further nudging removed the cowl of a hood from the skull. Bending down, she examined it more closely in the dim light. What she saw made her feel relieved. There was a small puncture in the back of the skull, and when she turned the skull over, there was a corresponding hole in the front, just above the eyes. No plague victim; he or she had been lasered.

She got Robin moving again and hadn't gone much further when they came across three bundles of rag and bone. A cursory inspection revealed that they too were lying face down. It seemed as if, like the first one, they were heading up the walkway when they had been all shot from behind. The result of an argument between different factions of their gang? But marauders didn't have lasers. . . .

They continued, Jan frowning. If the marauders hadn't been killed by other marauders, then what *had* killed them?

A deep-throated rumble rolled across the valley, entered the cavernous building through the holed roof and echoed back and forth. Another Sky Lord in its death throes, she assumed.

"Hi there! Won't you step inside and see what we have to offer?"

Jan jumped with alarm. She turned quickly, almost losing her grip on Robin. The voice had come from inside the shop they were just passing. She glimpsed a figure moving in its shadowy interior, then a nude woman stepped into view, smiling at Jan. Then four other women, also naked, appeared behind her. The first woman, still smiling, did a quick twirl. "Beautiful, isn't it? Part of our new range from the fashion capital of the world, Melbourne, Australia. It's made from the latest development in bio-fabric, as are all our other Melbourne creations. . . ." The woman half-turned to indicate the four women lined up behind her.

Transfixed, Jan stared at the five naked women, her mind racing. Who were they? What were they doing in here? Why were they naked? And what in the name of Mother God were they talking about?

". . . Please come in and try one on for yourself. Perhaps the one I'm wearing? For an original creation it's very reasonable—only twenty-eight thousand dollars. You will also get a free glass of the best Japanese champagne. . . ."

"Yes, *please* do come in!" chorused the rest of the women eagerly.

Jan finally found her voice. "Who . . . who are you?"

The women ignored her question. "Until these creations are worn by a real, living person you get no real impression of their beauty. The bacteria are influenced by the variations in temperature on the surface on your body and the results are really quite stunning. . . ."

Jan had noticed something odd—well, even *odder*—about the women. They lacked navels. *They aren't real*, she told herself. They're robots. Very life-like robots. Still operating after all these years. Automatically activated by her presence. Powered, probably, by some solar arrays up on the roof. If so, that meant that other parts of the establishment might be capable of coming to life. . . .

". . . The bio-fabric also adapts to exterior temperatures, making subtle changes in its structure for your personal comfort at all times. . . ."

Jan got closer to the first woman and saw that her 'flesh' was mottled with age. She stared into the robot's attractive eyes and said, "Can you see me?"

". . . The fabric needs the minimum of maintenance— just a regular soaking in distilled water once a week. . . ."

No reaction. A very crude, basic operating program, Jan decided. Warily, she prodded the robot's upper arm with her forefinger. Her finger met with hardly any resistance and easily penetrated the flesh-like covering with a slight *pop*.

197

Disgusted, Jan hastily withdrew her finger. She saw she had left a neat hole in the robot's arm.

". . . Of course, the fabric will never get soiled. Non-biological matter will be repelled; biological matter will be consumed."

Jan knew now that the robot was referring to some ancient dress or other article of clothing that had long since rotted away. The robots had been manikins. Walking, talking manikins. For some reason this thought made her feel unutterably sad and she wanted to get away from them. She turned and hurried out of the shop. Behind her, she heard the manikin say, "We're sorry you can't stay longer. Please drop in again when you have more time. We're always here."

Jan got Robin to his feet again, noticing, with annoyance, that he'd emptied his bladder while she'd been in the shop. He'd become a child, she realised. The blow on his head had changed him, instantly, from an intelligent, powerful young man to a helpless infant. How fragile we all are, she thought, and wondered if Robin's mind had been permanently erased or if there was any chance of his returning to normal. If he could be treated, that was, and there seemed no hope of that.

They continued on down, Jan now anxiously inspecting each shop they passed in case more automata should respond to their presence. But though recorded voices issued from a couple of establishments, asking that they enter and browse around, there was no sign of further movement. They did, however, pass the corpses of two more marauders and again Jan pondered on what had taken place down there those many years ago.

It was shortly afterwards that Jan spotted something familiar in a shop they were passing. She brought Robin to a halt again and stared into the shop. Crossbows. Row upon row of crossbows. They were much more elaborate in design to the ones she'd been used to in Minerva but crossbows they definitely were. She sat down on the walkway, then went and picked one of the crossbows from its rack. It was well preserved and appeared to be in working order. She was curious as to why the Old Science people would have need of such primitive weaponry when they had guns and lasers. She looked around the shop. Its other merchandise included racks of fishing rods and rows of long, narrow strips of plastic-like material with metal shoes attached to their centres, which left her even more mystified.

She located a supply of crossbow bolts in a shattered display counter, put several of them in her backpack, slipped two into her belt then returned to the walkway where, with an effort, she cocked the weapon. The mechanism was stiff but otherwise seemed in good order. "Let's see if this thing still works," she said to Robin. She was glad to have a crossbow again. It meant that when the charge in her hand weapon was extinguished they wouldn't be completely defenceless. She fitted a bolt into the firing slot, aimed high over walkway's safety rail, with the butt of the crossbow pressed firmly against her shoulder, and pulled the trigger. The crossbow gave a reassuring kick as it sent the bolt soaring upwards. She turned and smiled at Robin. "It works!" He just sat there, staring at nothing.

"Attention! You there! Stay where you are!" It was a man's voice. A loud, harsh voice, coming from down the walkway. She looked. A battered metal sphere, some two feet in diameter, was speeding towards them. It moved through the air three to four feet above the surface of the walkway, bobbing up and down as it came. Jan saw the glitter of various sensors and a laser mounted on its side. "Place the stolen merchandise on the ground and then raise your hands. Obey these instructions and you will not be harmed. Attempt to flee and you will be incapacitated." The thing was about forty yards away. Jan realised it was some sort of automatic security device, still operating as the manikins were. She hastily crouched down to put the cross-bow on the walkway as instructed. As she did so the sphere fired its laser. The beam passed through the air a foot above her head. Suddenly she knew what had happened to those dead marauders.

The Duke du Lucent cursed as his injured leg gave out beneath him and sent him toppling into a slimy, vile-smelling fungal growth. "Are you all right, sire?" asked the Chief Tech as he struggled to help him up.

"I've felt better, Lamont," he said. "How much further do you think it is?"

"Can't be more than half a mile," answered the Chief Tech. They both were referring to a large and prominent building that appeared to offer the prospect of shelter. They had kept it in sight since landing but now they had entered some kind of small forest where the blight growths, many anchored to the trunks of dead trees, grew in sickening profusion.

Their party consisted of only five other men. Two were Techs and three men-at-arms. The Duke knew that there must be many more survivors from the *Lord Mordred* but so far they hadn't encountered any others. He also knew that a great many must have perished when the Sky Lord had crashed. No doubt all the peasantry who had, of course been denied the privilege of owning a parachute. A lot of the freemen and nobles would have gone down with the *Lord Mordred* as well. It had long been the fashion among both classes to spurn the possession of a parachute—they were considered a sign of moral weakness—and many canopies had been converted into clothing ages ago. The Duke du Lucent had suffered from no such attitude and had parachutes stored at various points in the *Lord Mordred*, including one under his throne in the control pod.

But even those with functioning parachutes would have had trouble getting off the burning, and rapidly descending,

Sky Lord in time. The Duke had had the advantage of being in the control pod, which allowed quick access to escape once the ancient explosive bolts on one of the emergency hatches had actually worked. The jump itself had been horrifying. After the brief moment of relief when his canopy had opened above him (how glad he was that he had had all his parachutes checked regularly) came a long period of sheer terror as flaming debris fell all around him. He was sure that the canopy would be set alight. He saw others who suffered such a fate; saw them hurtling past him with their canopies burning and useless . . . heard their screams.

Then had come the landing in the blight muck and the blast of pain in his right knee as his leg had twisted under him. The Chief Tech, who had jumped immediately after him, landed nearby and together they had watched the *Lord Mordred* die, with agonising slowness, as it settled on the ground.

As the great hull, on fire from bow to stern, collapsed section by section, the Duke had realised he was seeing the death of everything he held dear. He had lost, in that terrible conflagration, all his possessions, his wealth, his family, his subjects, his entire world. And it was all the fault of that damned El Rashad . . . and the treacherous youth, Robin.

Now, as he struggled through the fungoid morass towards what seemed to be the only possible place of refuge in the area, he swore to himself that if he encountered either of them again his vengeance would be terrible in the extreme.

Chapter Twenty:

Jan rolled desperately across the walkway, pulling her weapon from her belt as she moved. The bobbing sphere was very close now. It fired its laser again; Jan could smell the burnt dust in the air. It had been another near miss. She had no time to see if Robin was all right. She aimed the weapon, hoping that the charge wasn't already depleted.

"Warning! Warning! This system is apparently malfunctioning . . . Please leave the area. . . ."

The beam from Jan's weapon struck the sphere. Sensors shattered and it came to a halt about six feet away, wobbling violently. Jan pressed the firing button again but this time there was no beam. The charge was gone.

"Attention!" said the sphere very loudly, "There has been a major systems breakdown!" Then promptly it dropped. It hit the walkway hard—it was clearly very heavy—burying itself some inches into the surface of the walkway. It made spluttering sounds then said, in a much more pleasant tone of voice, "This security system is provided free of charge courtesy of the Coca-Cola Company. However, the Coca-Cola Company does not accept any responsibility for any legal claims that may result from actions by this system in carrying out its programmed duties. Thank you, and remember—Things Go Better With Coke!" The sphere stopped spluttering and went completely silent.

Jan cautiously sat up. The sphere remained inactive. She turned and glanced quickly at Robin. He appeared to be unharmed, the blank look still on his face. She got to her feet slowly, eyes fixed on the sphere, alert for any sign of

202

movement. Then, as a final test, she went and picked up the crossbow. The sphere didn't respond. Now she was certain she had destroyed it.

"All of a sudden this place doesn't seem so safe," she said to Robin as she cocked the crossbow again. "There may be more of these crazy robots about. The logical thing to do would be to put the crossbow back in the shop but now it's the only weapon we've got. What do you think?"

Robin, of course, didn't answer. She sighed, feeling very lonely. She put another bolt in the bow, set the safety catch, then stuffed the butt of the weapon into her backpack. "Come on," she said, pulling him to his feet, "I think we'd better go back upstairs and make camp near the entrance. Just in case we have to get out of here in a hurry."

Keeping a nervous eye out for any more murderous spheres, Jan led Robin back up the walkway. None appeared, and the worst part of the journey had been passing by the dress shop when once again Jan had been accosted by the five naked manikins. This time she found the experience strangely unnerving.

She was relieved when they reached the entrance but her relief was short-lived. She was taken completely by surprise when two men leapt out of the shadowy interior of a shop. Both were carrying rifles. One of them slammed the butt into Jan's stomach. As she fell, struggling to breathe, she saw the other man drive the butt of his rifle into the side of Robin's head. She tried to scream but couldn't. *Mother God, they've killed him now for sure!* She landed on her hands and knees, vainly trying to draw breath. She heard Robin collapse beside her, then felt the crossbow being pulled from her backpack. A boot hooked her under her ribcage and flipped her over on to her back. She lay there, drawing her knees up into her stomach. It felt as if there was a huge boulder weighing down on it. She still couldn't breathe and everything was wavering out of focus. Then a looming figure filled her field of vision.

He was dressed in black leather and had a black cloak. He smiled down at her, then he looked at Robin and his expression changed. First he looked disbelieving, then angry, and she saw him draw a blood-stained, silver dagger from his belt . . .

Even with her face contorted with the effort of trying to breathe the Duke du Lucent saw that the girl was beautiful. Then he turned his attention to her companion, who one of his men was rolling over on to his back. The Duke reacted with amazement. Despite the bandage the girl's companion was instantly recognisable. The Duke drew his dagger. "So, after all the trials that God has heaped upon me, he has at least delivered into my hands one of the causes of my misery!" He kicked Robin in the leg. The youth stirred but didn't open his eyes. Blood was seeping from the bandage round his head. "Wake up, damn you!" cried the Duke. "Wake up so that I can cut your throat!"

"No!" gasped the girl, with difficulty, in Americano. "Leave him alone . . . he's hurt . . . he's going to die."

"He certainly is, my dear," the Duke told her in her own tongue. "Because I'm going to kill him."

"No . . . don't touch him!" The girl dragged herself over to Robin and shielded him with her body. It was, observed the Duke as the hem of her tunic rode up over her thighs, a delightful body, and he felt a momentary shaft of lust penetrate his anger.

"Get away from him," he told her. "I have a lot of scores to settle with your . . . friend." Just then the youth groaned and opened his eyes. "Thirsty . . . so thirsty. . . ."

The girl drew back from him in surprise. "Robin! You're speaking again! Oh, thank the Mother God . . . !"

The Duke reached down, grabbed the girl by a shoulder and pulled her off the youth. He grinned cruelly down at him. "Hello again, Robin. Do you remember me?"

Robin grimaced and touched his head where the blood was seeping out of the bandage. "My head . . . it hurts."

"I'm not surprised," said the Duke and brandished the dagger in his face. The girl tried to protect him again but was restrained by one of his men. "I said, Robin, do you remember me?"

"Yes . . . You're the Duke. The Duke du Lucent." He frowned and looked about. "What happened to me? Where are we?" His eyes focused on Jan, still in the grip of the Duke's man. "Who are you? You seem familiar but . . . God, I'm so thirsty."

"Robin, don't you remember me?" cried the girl, anguished.

He didn't answer but touched his head again and moaned. "Do you have any water?" the Duke asked her. She nodded. "Then give him some. I don't want him to die of thirst before I kill him." He gestured to his man to let her go and watched her warily as she removed a canteen from the bag she carried on her back. As she knelt beside Robin and held the canteen to his mouth the Duke said, "That's a point . . . *who* are you?"

The girl glanced briefly at him. "My name is . . . Melissa."

"Melissa?" said the Duke, having noticed the hesitation. He gave her body a more careful inspection.

"So how did you come to be down here, Melissa? And more to the point, how did *he* come to get here? The last time I saw him he was landing his infernal flying machine on the back of the Sky Angel. What happened? Did the Sky Woman reject the offer of his services? And what happened to his machine? Is it nearby?"

The girl took the canteen from Robin's lips, though he clearly wanted to continue drinking, and looked up at the Duke. "The machine is still on the Sky Angel. The Sky Woman no longer exists. She was killed by a spider-mech . . . the same robot that almost killed Robin. The Sky

205

Angel and its spider-mechs, and the rest of the fleet, are under the control of a computer now. The computer is crazy . . . evil."

The Duke stroked his beard thoughtfully, wondering how much of what she'd said was true. Certainly, from what he had heard of the Sky Woman's previous actions, this day's carnage was not typical of her.

"And how did you two happen to be down here?" he asked.

"The computer banished us both and had us set down. Some distance away. We walked here. It seemed the obvious place to head for."

The latter part of her answer was true enough, he thought. He and his men had automatically headed towards this massive fortification. Then it occurred to him that other survivors would have the same thought. Not just survivors from among his own people but from among those of the other Sky Lords, including El Rashad. He turned and said to one of the three soldiers, "Go outside and keep watch from a place of concealment. I fear others may come this way too." The man bowed and hurried off. The Duke turned again to the girl who was now on her feet and facing him. Their eyes were level. "So this evil computer, that killed the Sky Woman and almost killed Robin, set you and him down on the ground? A merciful act from a computer that has sent thousands to their deaths today."

"The computer behaves erratically," said the girl. "I told you, it's mad."

"Is it? And what was your position on the Sky Angel?"

"My position . . . ?" she hesitated. Then, "I was . . . er, the Sky Woman's personal servant. I have been since I came of working age in Minerva."

"You are a Minervan?"

"Yes. And I'm proud to be one."

The Duke looked down again at Robin. The youth looked

sick, bewildered, and scared. So different from the jaunty, confident young cockerel who had boarded the *Lord Mordred*. It would be no fun killing this human wreck. He decided to let the youth recuperate a little—if he could—before exacting his revenge. He asked the girl, "What was her name, this dead Sky Woman of yours?"

"Jan Dorvin," she said quickly, then winced.

The youth gave a small moan, distracting the Duke. The Duke saw that he was frowning; trying to remember something. "Robin, what *do* you remember of Jan Dorvin?"

"I can't remember . . . anything. My head hurts so much." His voice was stronger now. The water had helped.

"You remember me. You remember being on the *Lord Mordred*. You remember Andrea. . . ."

"Yes . . . Andrea. Where is she?"

The Duke didn't want to think about that. "You remember flying your machine to the Sky Angel. You must have met the Sky Woman, this Jan Dorvin. Offered her your services, as you did to me."

"I can remember Andrea . . . the *Lord Mordred* . . . your son . . . the duel . . . Andrea . . . but no more. . . ."

"Well, Robin, I shall take great pleasure in refreshing your memory . . . when you are feeling better."

Footsteps. The Duke looked round. It was the Chief Tech, who had gone exploring on his own, returning along the walkway. "Sire, I don't think this place is a fortress after all."

"It isn't," said the girl firmly. "It is, or it was, a kind of giant market place. There are thousands of different kinds of stores in here."

"Are you sure?" asked the Duke, disappointed.

"I've been down below. I'm certain."

"No weapons?"

She pointed at the crossbow that one of his men was holding. "Lots of those. Nothing else. But I haven't been all through the place. Just part of the way downwards. I haven't been upstairs."

"No food either, I suppose?"

"I saw some tins of food in several of the shops but I wouldn't like to think about what was inside them after all these years," said the girl.

The Duke nodded thoughtfully. "Odd that this place was never looted. A bad plague spot, do you think?"

"I thought the same, and maybe it was. That hole in the roof looks like it was caused by a missile. And from what I know of the Gene Wars the only missiles that were ever fired were always full of viruses."

"Yes," he agreed. Probably the place was now safe.

"But I discovered another reason why this place has been left untouched," the girl told him. "When I took the crossbow I activated a security device. It almost killed me. I think I destroyed it but there could be more. That's why we came back up here."

More footsteps: running this time. The man the Duke had sent outside was hurrying back through the wide entrance tunnel. "What is it?" the Duke called to him.

"Group of people coming this way, sire. Just coming out of the blight now. Should be here in about ten minutes. I counted twenty. There may be more. I saw weapons. Rifles . . . swords . . . axes."

"Did they see you?"

"I'll swear they didn't, sire."

"Let's hope so. The element of surprise is the only advantage we've got." He looked around, then said to his three soldiers, "Get well hidden but select sites that give you a wide field of fire." Then he bent down and scooped up the girl's crossbow, checked it was loaded and said to the girl, "Have you any more bolts?"

She nodded and indicated her bag. The Duke looked inside it, pulled out a handful of bolts and thrust them into his belt. He said to the Chief Tech and the two junior Techs, all unarmed, "Take Robin and the girl in there." He indicated the shadowy interior of a nearby shop. "Conceal them and yourselves and don't make a sound."

As they carried out his orders the Duke hurried up the walkway and took cover behind an ornate pillar. He checked the crossbow again then waited, his back pressed against the pillar. He didn't hold much hope for their chances. Three rifles and a crossbow against a group of twenty armed men. El Rashad's men? Possibly. Perhaps El Rashad himself was among them. The Duke would dearly have liked the opportunity of putting a bolt through that arrogant fool's head. But God had already delivered one of his enemies into his hands today. Getting both of them would be expecting too much, even of God.

He heard footsteps echoing down the wide entrance tunnel. He tensed, finger on the crossbow's trigger, waiting for that change of pitch that would indicate the intruders were emerging from the tunnel. Wait. Not yet . . . wait . . . *now.*

He spun round. As he did so he dropped to one knee and raised the crossbow butt to his shoulder. "Fire!" he yelled to his men. He almost pulled his own trigger but just in time he recognised several faces in the startled group. "No . . . hold your fire!" he cried desperately. There were no gunshots. His men had clearly recognised them too.

The Duke stood and walked slowly towards the two people who were in the van of the group that was still emerging from the tunnel entrance. "Greetings, my beloved children," he said in a strained voice.

Prince Darcy and Princess Andrea, their faces and clothes covered in filth from the blight, stared at him in disbelief. A burly soldier just behind them muttered, "Sweet Mary . . . it's the Duke!"

"Father . . ." said Darcy, and faltered. Andrea glared at him with her remaining good eye.

The Duke held up a hand. "No, please, cease your cries

of joy and gladness. You don't have to tell me how happy you are to see me safe and alive—I know it only too well in my heart."

Darcy swallowed and said, "Of course I—we—are pleased to see that you are alive father . . . but *how* did you escape. We were sure you had perished in the *Lord Mordred*."

"And I nearly did. But we managed to overcome those damned men of El Rashad's and, finally, blow open an escape hatch in the control pod. But how did *you* two manage to survive? And with all these others?"

"We commandeered a troop glider. We took off as soon as the *Lord Mordred* began to sustain laser hits," Darcy told him.

The Duke inspected the press of bodies behind his son and daughter. All men, and all soldiers by the look of it. "Ah, and my dear wife . . . did she accompany you?"

"Mother refused to leave," Andrea told him coldly. "She said she would prefer to die on the *Lord Mordred* than suffer the indignity of becoming an earthworm."

"Oh," said the Duke, "such a pity." He took a deep breath. "But life must go on, even in these depressed circumstances." He looked at Darcy. "As you had a glider but you are here, I presume you were shot down by either the Sky Angel or another of that accursed Sky Woman's airships?"

"We were hit once by a laser," said Darcy. "Started a fire in the main cabin. Lot of smoke but we managed to extinguish it. Our intention was to fly out of this blight-ridden land and we almost made it. The Sky Woman's entire fleet was heading south so we headed north and . . . and ran straight into El Rashad's forces." He shook his head.

"El Rashad's *forces*," asked the Duke, perplexed. "But surely there couldn't have been that many survivors from the *Sword of Islam*? It must have gone down in flames like the *Lord Mordred* and the others."

"No. It went down all right but there was hardly any fire. It lies, broken, at the foot of the range of hills that marks the northern boundary of this valley. There is little fire damage. The *Sword of Islam* must have still carried mainly helium in its cells. We saw lots of people active around the wreckage. And above it flew a swarm of gliders. They opened fire on us. One gave chase, forcing us to turn back. Finally we couldn't maintain sufficient altitude and came down near here . . . right in the middle of a large patch of that ghastly blight."

Andrea shivered. "It was horrible. And there were *things* in there too. . . ."

"I know," said the Duke, remembering his close encounter with something that resembled a rolling ball made of a writhing tangle of white worms.

"And it's going to get worse," said Darcy. "We saw several strange creatures from the air. *Big* things too, moving into the valley. Drawn by the smell of death. We saw one reptile that must have measured fifty feet from head to tail. Our plan was to take shelter here until the feast was over."

"Yes, the wisest course," agreed the Duke. "We must fortify this entrance as best we can, and search for others. It can't be the only one in a place this size. Fortunate that you have so many men with you. We stand a chance now, whereas before . . ." He gave a shrug, then smiled at them both. "But first, let me show you something that will dull a little the sting delivered by this blackest of all days." He turned and gestured at the Chief Tech who had emerged from the shop. "Go and brought out our prisoners."

Prince Darcy frowned at the Duke. "Prisoners? Who . . . ?"

"You'll see," the Duke told him with a smirk.

When Andrea recognised Robin, who was being supported by two of the techs, she made a sound that was somewhere between a gasp and snake's hiss. Darcy, too, looked astonished. "The traitor . . . here? How in the world . . . ?"

"Oh, I have my methods," said the Duke, enjoying the moment.

"Andrea? Is it you?" Robin had recognised Andrea. A smile spread slowly across his face. He was pleased to see her. Despite his own anger towards the youth the Duke squirmed inwardly on his behalf. Andrea advanced quickly towards him, raising her hand. Her intention was clear. She was just about to strike him when the girl pulled herself free from the Chief Tech's grasp and grabbed Andrea's arm. "Don't!" she cried at Andrea. "Can't you see that he's injured?"

Andrea pulled her arm free and glared at the girl, seeing her for the first time. "Who the hell are *you*?"

The Duke stepped forward quickly. "She's from the Sky Angel, my kitten. A former servant to the Sky Woman, Jan Dorvin, who she says is now dead."

"Really? That is good news. And I shall enjoy disciplining her servant for her insolence towards me . . . but later." She turned back to Robin, who was blinking at her in confusion. "So the robin has had his wings clipped, eh? Well, that's not the only thing you're going to have clipped."

"Andrea," he said weakly. "I don't understand what's going on . . . why are we here? And what happened to your . . . eye?"

She turned her back on him. "Balcombe!" she cried. A heavy-set soldier stepped forward. "Yes, your highness?"

"Have your men strip this wretch. Then tie his wrists to those balcony railings. . . ."

"No!" cried the girl. She started towards Andrea but the Chief Tech grabbed her and held her back. Balcombe, who the Duke vaguely remembered as a Sergeant-at-Arms whom he had encountered once or twice in the past, was looking enquiringly at the Prince. After a pause Darcy nodded. "Do as she says."

212

Balcombe gestured at two other soldiers and they moved forward.

"No!" screamed the girl, struggling violently. Andrea looked at her, then at Balcombe. "Have her bound and gagged."

"Yes your highness," said Balcombe, doubtfully. "But what will we use for ropes?"

"God, I don't know!" Andrea snapped. "Use your belts if you can't find anything better!"

They used their belts. The Duke by now knew Andrea's intention. "Darling," he said to Andrea, "I know how you feel and I planned myself to exact my vengeance on this treacherous creature. But look at him—his head injury has shaken him loose of his senses. There will be no satisfaction in cutting him up in this condition. Wait until he's recovered a little, as I was intending to do."

Andrea paid him no attention. She had drawn her dagger and was examining its blade. "Not too sharp, but that doesn't matter."

Robin was sitting with his back to the balcony, his wrists tied to railings above his head. He still looked totally confused and clearly could make no rhyme or reason out of what was happening to him. The girl, though securely tied, struggled fiercely in the grip of two Techs. The crude gag smothered the sounds she was making but the Duke knew they were screams.

Andrea went and stood over Robin and looked down at him for a time, then she said to the two soldiers who had tied Robin to the railing, "Grab his feet and pull his legs apart."

They did so. Andrea knelt down between Robin's legs. "Andrea . . . ?" said Robin, still looking mystified.

She lifted up his scrotum with her left hand and then, blank-faced, began her bloody work.

The blade was indeed blunt and it was slow work. After a time the Duke, feeling nauseous, looked away. With Robin's screams ringing in his ears he stared up at the vaulted ceiling with its gaping hole and reflected on his daughter's character. Trust her to over-react to this degree, he thought. So much like her mother.

Chapter Twenty-One:

A man broke from the slow-moving line of people and charged across the cargo-hold floor towards Milo. Milo saw that he had produced a short metal rod with a crudely sharpened end from his ragged clothing. None of the spider-mechs who were prodding the reluctant snake of people—all clutching their pathetic bundles of possessions—into the cargo cradle went after him. Nor did the two spider-mechs supposedly guarding Milo make any move to intercept him. "Stop him!" cried Milo, but the spider-mechs remained immobile.

The man was now less than a few yards away. He was screaming as he ran, his eyes full of murder. The other people had halted and were watching with undisguised pleasure. Some were cheering the man on. "Stop him!" cried Milo again, his voice breaking. He started to back away but there was nowhere to go. . . .

Very close now. And time was slowing down, giving Milo, it seemed, ample opportunity to study the man's flushed and furious face in detail. Milo was raising his arm to parry the thrust of the makeshift weapon but he knew the powerfully built man had the advantage. Milo knew he was going to die. For the second time.

At the very last available instant one of the mechs suddenly scuttled forward, extending, at the same time, one of its arms with a cutting tool on the end of it. The man had no time to react. He ran straight on to the arm, skewering himself. Such was his momentum that the arm went straight through him. He grunted as he came to a shuddering halt.

The end of the sharpened rod he held was only inches from Milo's upraised arm. The dying man's eyes locked with Milo's. Hate still filled them. He tried to throw the rod at Milo but his strength was gone and the metal fell feebly to the floor. Blood bubbled out of the man's mouth and he died, head slumping forward. The spider-mech withdrew its arm and the body collapsed.

"Scared you, huh?" asked Ashley from the spider-mech. *You sure did, you bitch*, muttered Milo under his breath. His heart was racing. There were cries of dismay and disappointment from the watching people and several men tried to leave the line, but this time the spider-mechs acted promptly and they were driven back.

His confidence quickly returning, Milo called out to the crowd: "Come on, get moving! Into the cradle! Your new home awaits you!" As the spider-mechs prodded the line into movement again a woman screamed out, "You're a murderer! You're murdering all of us! We can't live on the ground! We'll die!"

"Don't blame me, madam. This isn't my idea," he replied. "I'm as subject to the whims of the computer programs as you are. Think yourself lucky you weren't dumped in that valley of blight, as was originally intended. There's clean land below us and several communities within a few days' walking distance. Organise ourselves and conquer them. There'll be enough of you, for God's sakes. . . ." But he suspected that the refugees from the different Sky Lords would soon be fighting each other rather than unite in order to survive on the ground. Such was human nature.

The cradle was full. A spider-mech slid the gates shut and the cradle, packed with humanity, was lowered through the hull. Milo knew similar scenes were occurring in the other cargo holds in the *Perfumed Breeze*, and in the other cargo holds of the other Sky Lords. With the exception of the *Lord Montcalm*.

216

That had been another worrying development. The Ashley program running the *Lord Montcalm* had disagreed over Ashley 1's decision to dump all the sky people. The *Montcalm* Ashley wanted to retain her population—and for the reason that Milo had originally suggested to Ashley 1; that they were a source of amusement. The two Ashleys had actually had a screaming argument over the matter and for a time Milo feared the argument might end up becoming an aerial battle between the Sky Angel and the *Lord Montcalm*, the outcome of which would probably have been mutual destruction. But he had persuaded Ashley 1 to calm down and the crisis had been averted. Nevertheless, it had been very close.

A bad sign. A very bad sign. It signified further deterioration of the Ashley programs. The *Lord Montcalm* Ashley had been the last Ashley to be copied. How he longed to be able to burn her out of the bio-software, but he saw no possible way of achieving that. So what would happen? Would the Ashley personalities simply disintegrate completely? He hoped so. Then he would be able to deal with Carl direct. But the danger was that before the Ashleys became harmless electronic and chemical patterns they would do something catastrophic in their dying madness and take him with them into oblivion. . . .

This depressing line of thought was abruptly interrupted when Milo spotted someone he recognised in the waiting, surly crowd. Accompanied by the two spider-mechs he went closer to the crowd. Stopping at a safe distance he called out, "Hello, Benny! Remember me?"

The man looked surprised at being addressed by his name. He frowned at Milo. "You know me?" he asked.

"Oh yes, very well, Benny. We used to work together. Or rather, I did the work while you supervised me. Me and the other slaves. The glass walkers. On the *Lord Pangloth*. How is the former Guild Master Bannion, by the way?"

"He died, a year ago," said Benny, eyes narrowed with

suspicion. "Couldn't take the change of diet. But how come you know of him?"

"I told you—same way I know you. I was a glass walker."

"I don't remember you. And you would have been too young to be a glass walker."

Milo laughed and said, "I'm Milo, Benny."

"Milo? You ain't Milo, you're just some weir . . . er, kid. And I heard Milo got himself killed on the ground."

"He did indeed, but I'm still Milo, more or less. I'm his . . . well, *clone* comes pretty close to the truth. You know what a clone is, don't you?"

Benny clearly did because he looked alarmed now.

"You must see the resemblance, Benny, even with me at this age." He touched his balding head. "Ah, yes, I see you are beginning to. We had some times together, didn't we, Benny? Remember the time you cut Jan's safety line?"

Benny took a step back and swallowed nervously. "Christ, you *are* Milo," he said.

"Don't worry, I'm not going to hurt you. Besides, if it wasn't for you I would never have met Jan. You remember the day you brought her into our slave pen and gave her to poor old Buncher?"

"Yeah . . . I'll always remember it. That bitch was bad luck. Her coming on board . . . it was the beginning of when everything changed, and went bad. When I think now of how close I came to killing her . . . if I had, I'm pretty sure it would still be like the old times."

"Please, that's my mother you're talking about, Benny," said Milo with a smile.

"Your *mother* . . . ?"

"My mother. And yes, Jan did serve as a kind of catalyst, but I suspect that the *Lord Pangloth* would have come to the same sorry end. The rot had already set in even before Jan appeared. . . ."

There was a jolt as the freight cargo, now empty, came back into the hold. The spider-mechs began to prod the queue forward again as the gates were slid open. Milo smiled at Benny. "Well, you must be going now. Good luck on the ground."

Benny gave him an unreadable look and then shuffled away. Milo remained where he was, scanning the passing line. A minute later he said aloud, "Now there's a promising candidate."

"Which one?" asked Ashley, through the spider mech at his side.

Milo pointed. "The one with the long black hair."

"Her? She's skinny."

"Then we'll feed her up. Can I have her or not?"

"Yeah, I guess so. . . ." The spider-mech scuttled forward, seized the girl by the arm and pulled her out of the queue. Looking terrified, the girl gave a squeal and dropped her bag of belongings. Behind her, two people—a man and a woman—tried to follow her but were held back by other mechs.

"Hey! Where are you taking her?" yelled the man. "Let her go!"

The spider-mech had brought the girl over to Milo. He looked her over quickly. Nice skin, long legs, very small breasts, but you couldn't have everything. Yes, she was too thin, but so were most of the sky people. Food had been rationed for ages now. "What's your name?" Milo asked her.

She stared down at him with alarm. He figured her to be about sixteen. She said, shakily, "Tyra."

"Those your parents?"

She glanced back at the couple, who were still vainly trying to get past the spider-mechs, and nodded. Milo walked towards them. "Well, this is your lucky day," he told them. "I have decided to save your daughter."

They gave him uncomprehending looks. "What are you talking about?" cried the woman. "Please let her go!"

"Didn't you hear what I just said? I have decided to save

219

her. She will be staying aloft, with me. Don't you think that's preferable to a dubious fate with you on the ground?"

The two exchanged a worried glance and then the man said, "She's coming with us. She'll take her chances on the ground, like us. *With us.*"

Milo shook his head. "I'm not discussing the matter with you, I'm *telling* you. She is staying with me. Now say your goodbyes and get into the cradle."

"No!" cried the woman and tried to duck round the spider-mech in front of her. It prodded her backwards. "Why? *Why* do you want her?"

"I should think that's perfectly obvious," said Milo and gave a leering smile.

They stared at him. "But . . . but you're nothing but a *boy*," said the woman.

"*Now*, yes, but I'm a fast developer," Milo assured her, and laughed. "Now say goodbye to Tyra here and *go.*"

They again tried to get past the spiders. This time the spiders seized them and hustled them away. They screamed Tyra's name as they went. Tyra too started to scream. He went back to her. "Calm down, Tyra," he said, smiling at her. "Everything is going to be all right. When you get to know me you'll find I'm a very likeable person." To Ashley he said, "Bring her to the hopper. I'm returning to the Sky Angel. The sooner I start her training the better."

The Beast had begun its existence as the foetus of a male African elephant. When it was only a few hours old a genegineer began to work on it, redesigning its DNA. The genegineer, a woman, was working to the strict specifications of her billionaire employer, Oliver Hutson Jnr. Hutson Jnr delighted in stocking his sprawling estate with outrageous and highly dangerous creatures in order to shock and thrill his friends when they joined him on his hunting expeditions. He was determined that this particular creation would be the wildest concept yet . . . and the most dangerous.

The genegineer worked for a solid forty-eight hours on the foetus and then the result was placed in an artificial womb which vastly accelerated the gestation period. Ten days later the beast was born. It weighed three hundred pounds. When Hutson Jnr observed the thing in its pen he was satisfied. Even at this young stage it was impressive. And when it reached its adult weight of four tons it would be unbelievable! As he watched the beast attack, crush and then consume a young goat, Hutson Jnr decided to give the genegineer responsible a bonus.

The warriors who made up El Rashad's small and bedraggled army were not happy men. Most were still in a state of shock from the destruction of the *Sword of Islam*. They had lost the only home they had ever known. Worse than that, many had lost wives, children and other relatives. All had lost friends. And now, in this dazed state, they were having to fight their way across the blighted valley so that their leader could avenge himself on the infidels. Already their numbers had been further reduced in the twenty-four hours since they had left the wreckage of the *Sword of Islam*. The straggling column of warriors had been attacked several times by the creatures who dwelt in the blight. Some men had been attacked by the blight itself; throttled by writhing tubes that had fallen on them from above, stung to death by tendrils of fungus that penetrated their clothes, or impaled on the thorns of the dreaded 'whip trees' which disguised themselves in countless different shapes.

It was Hazrat As-Awhan, in the rear of the column, who was the second of El Rashad's warriors to encounter the most terrifying beast of all. The first man to meet it had been Masal Gashiya. He was dead by the time Hazrat As-Awhan heard the sounds behind him. He halted and peered anxiously into the tangle of fungus and rotting trees. "Masal . . . ?" he called. More sounds. Something very heavy was moving through the blight towards him. It was too heavy to be Masal. He glanced back towards the end of the column but the blight had already swallowed up the men ahead of him. He began to run. "Hey!" he cried, "Help! Stop! Something is chasing me!" There was a loud *snap* as a dead tree trunk was broken in two. Hazrat looked over his shoulder, then screamed. . . .

He was being pursued by a *hand*. Just a hand—nothing else. A disembodied hand that once must have belonged to a giant. It stood over ten feet high and was easily fifteen feet wide. Its flesh was grey and heavily wrinkled and the fingernails, the size of dinner plates, were black.

Hazrat screamed again and tried to run faster. But he had no chance. The hand pounced on him, then it made a fist and, crushed within the giant fingers, Hazrat felt his ribs snap just before most of his blood was forcibly ejected from his body.

His screams had brought several members of the column running back. They gasped in disbelief at the monstrous hand and two turned and ran screaming off into the blight, thinking that the hand was the manifestation of some terrible *jinnee*. But the others stood their ground and, despite their shock, aimed their rifles at the hand and fired. The bullets struck home, to join the various other bullets, arrow heads, crossbow bolts and spearheads embedded in the thick, armour-like hide.

The hand rose up on its fingers, leaving Hazrat's pathetic-looking remains on the ground, and rushed forward like a giant spider. Another of El Rashad's warriors fell beneath its weight. The others, seeing that their bullets had no effect on it, turned and ran back towards the column. The hand killed two more of them, then let the rest get away. There was no hurry now. It returned to Hazrat's body and gripped it again. In the clefts of the great palm numerous mouths emerged and began greedily to consume Hazrat's flesh and blood. When nothing remained of Hazrat but his bones the hand moved on to the next fallen warrior. No, there was no hurry now. Not with so much food available.

When Jan woke she was surprised that Robin was still alive. It was the morning of the third day since he had been castrated by the one-eyed girl. He had mercifully passed out before she had completed her butchery and ever since then had fluctuated between unconsciousness and semi-consciousness. On the second day he had also become feverish and Lamont had told her that she could expect him to die by nightfall.

Lamont was the man also known as the Chief Tech, but as he had ruefully said to her, "It is a meaningless title now—there is nothing left to be Chief Tech *of*—so just call me Lamont. He had shown gruff kindness in the aftermath of the grisly episode, first cauterising Robin's wound then helping her to dress it. Later he had helped her carry Robin, on a makeshift stretcher, down below to the floor level on the Duke's orders.

Jan crawled out of the sleeping bag and, stretching, went to the front of the shop. The small fire she had built there the night before had gone out. She would have to find more things to burn, but after she had fetched water for Robin. She headed towards the central fountain in which a water-catchment area had been set up using giant funnels, made of parachute silk stretched between wooden frames, to catch the rain water that fell frequently from the hole in the ceiling.

Other fires, scattered about the cavernous interior, were already alight. The population was rapidly growing within the ancient shopping mall. Groups of survivors had been arriving steadily during the last couple of days. When they hadn't been from the *Lord Mordred* but from one of the other drowned Sky Lords the Duke's men had stripped them of their weapons and sent them to the lowest level. Guards mounted on the walkway prevented them from returning to the upper levels.

Jan stopped and gasped. Lying between two large chunks of rubble was the naked body of a woman. She was lying on her back with her legs wide apart. Protruding from her pubic area was a piece of wood. Reluctantly, Jan went closer. Then she relaxed. She saw that the 'corpse' was one of the robot manikins she'd encountered on her first day in the building. Its head had been bashed in and she could see coloured wires within the skull rather than human brains. She looked at the piece of wood, wondered why anyone would want to do such a thing. Then, glancing around nervously, she continued towards the fountain.

There were two women at the fountain filling plastic water containers. They stared suspiciously at her as she approached. They had broad faces and narrow eyes, which reminded her of the Japanese inhabitants of the *Perfumed Breeze*, but they were plainly not Japanese. She smiled at them but they gave her hard stares in return and hurried away when they'd filled their containers.

When she'd filled her two canteens she walked slowly back to the shop, trying not to think of the future. And thinking of the past offered no comfort either. She had lost so much. And apart from the big things she was missing the smaller comforts of life as well. Like a bath, for example. Mother God, how she yearned for a bath. Her skin itched and she was sure she smelled bad. Robin certainly stank. She glanced down at her filthy tunic. No water for washing her clothes either. And if even more refugees arrived, and it stopped raining, there wouldn't be any water for drinking either.

There was someone in the shop. A man. When she got closer she saw it was Lamont and relaxed. "Morning, Melissa," he greeted her and nodded his head towards Robin. "I see I was wrong. He's still hanging on."

"Just," said Jan. "His fever is worse." She knelt beside

Robin and supported his head. He moaned and his eyelids fluttered but he didn't open his eyes. She put the canteen to his lips and was happy to see him swallow the water without choking.

"I fear his . . . wound . . . has become infected despite my crude efforts," said Lamont. "Have you changed the dressing today?"

"Not yet," said Jan. She had been putting the task off. "And I'm running out of dressings." She stood up and brushed the dust from her tunic. "He'd be better off dead, wouldn't he?" She looked at Lamont. Their eyes were level.

He nodded. "Perhaps we'd *all* be better off dead. I can't see us surviving for long in this valley."

"Does the Duke have any firm plans?"

"Ha!" said Lamont. "The Duke has never had a firm plan in his life. As far as I know he just intends to sit here and wait."

"Wait for what?"

"Good question. For fate to step in and save him, perhaps. Or God."

"We're going to starve soon. I'm almost out of rations."

"Ah, that is where the Duke has actually done something constructive. He sent out a hunting party early this morning and they had some success. He nudged a bag on the floor with his foot. "Speaking of which, I've brought you a present."

She bent down and opened the bag. "Ugh!" It contained a dead animal. Something like a rabbit. It stared at her with glassy eyes and there was blood around its snout. She quickly closed the bag.

"It's food," said Lamont, looking affronted.

"I'm a vegetarian," she told him. "I appreciate the gesture but I can't eat that."

"*He* could," said Lamont, pointing at Robin. "You could make a broth out of it. It might help him."

Jan frowned. He had a point, but the thought of preparing

225

the dead animal for cooking made her feel ill. Still, there were plenty of cooking utensils available. The shop was full of them. "I suppose you're right," she said reluctantly. "Thank you."

"You don't have to stay here, you know," Lamont told her.

"But I do," she replied. "The Duke has ordered me to."

"I could persuade him to change his mind about you, though, of course, *he* would have to remain here." Lamont indicated Robin.

"I couldn't leave him."

"No, I didn't think you would, but when he's dead you will have no reason not to take up my offer."

"Offer?" She gave him a hard look. He looked uncomfortable. "I find you very . . . appealing, Melissa."

"I see," she said gravely. Sex for protection, and food. Once another man had made her a similar offer and she had reacted as any female Minervan would have, but that was a long time ago. She had changed. Hardened, perhaps? Anyway, now her survival meant more to her than her Minervan honour. And besides, Lamont was no Milo. She said, "I like you too, Lamont. When and *if* Robin dies I'll accept your offer."

He smiled briefly and nodded. "I'm pleased." He moved closer to her, embraced her and kissed her on the lips. She tried to respond but couldn't. She was too aware of Robin's presence. It made her feel terrible. Here she was selling herself to another man while her lover lay dying at her feet.

Lamont obviously sensed her discomfort and released her. Stepping back, he said, "I'll leave now and come back this evening to see how he is."

"Fine," she said. Then, "I'm sorry, Lamont, but while Robin is still alive I can't. . . ."

"I understand. Before I go, do you want me to prepare and dress that animal for you."

She glanced at the bag and said reluctantly, "If you

wouldn't mind. I guess I'll have to learn how to do it sometime. Might as well be now."

It was late afternoon and she was returning again from the fountain with more water. It had been a grim day. After Lamont's distasteful butchery lessons she had needed some extra time before she could face changing Robin's dressing. And when she had finally removed the old dressing she had been shocked to see the wound had deteriorated greatly. It was badly inflamed and yellow pus oozed from between Lamont's crude stitches. The infection was getting worse. Feeling completely inadequate, Jan could do no more than bathe the wound with the last of the bio-disinfectant from her small, and depleted, medical kit and put a fresh dressing on. She was certain that this night he would die.

As she neared the shop she again glimpsed the figure of a man inside. Presuming it was Lamont she entered the shop. When she saw that she was wrong it was too late. Two other men closed in on her from either side, trapping her.

Chapter Twenty-Two:

The men on either side of her grabbed her arms. The third man advanced towards her. He was holding a long knife. All three had the same sort of faces that she had seen on the women at the fountain earlier in the day—broad cheek bones and narrow eyes. They were small men—shorter than her—but thickly built. The man with the knife was yelling something at her in a harsh voice, but his words meant nothing to her. He stood close to her and dug the point of the knife into her ribs just below her left breast. As he bellowed at her Jan smelt his breath, which was strangely sweet. She wondered why he was so upset and what they wanted. She quickly got the answer to the latter question when the man with the knife used his free hand to grab the collar of her tunic and rip it open to her waist. *I'm so popular today*, thought Jan as she screamed and made a weak attempt to break free. The man with the knife was trying to rip the rest of her tunic open. She brought her knee up into his crotch with considerable force. He dropped the knife and also clearly abandoned all thought of rape as he clutched his crushed testicles. He began to sag at the knees, howling with pain.

It was then fairly easy to pull her arms free from the grip of the two startled men. She whirled, fast, on one of them, driving her elbow into his windpipe, then turned her attention to the other. He had drawn a knife and was lunging at her with it. She stepped aside, swivelled round and grabbed his extended arm in a lever grip. She applied pressure. When his wrist snapped his howl of pain joined that of his colleague.

Jan stepped back and surveyed the three would-be rapists. The first one was now rolled into a tight ball; the second, his face going blue, was on his hands and knees and struggling to breathe; the third was still on his feet, holding his useless arm and staring at her with sullen wariness. She raised her hand and pointed to the entrance. "Out!" she commanded. The man with the broken arm made no attempt to move or help his companions, he just continued to stare at her. Then, out of the corner of her right eye, Jan caught a flicker of movement. She whirled round. A woman—she was sure it was one of the two she had seen at the fountain—was charging towards her. She was holding, in both hands, a large, Old Science frying pan. She must have been hiding in the rear of the shop, waiting for the men to complete their fun.

Jan barely had time to duck as the woman swung the frying pan at her head. It grazed the side of Jan's head in a glancing blow that was sufficient to cause a cloud of dancing lights to explode in front of Jan's eyes. Though dazed, Jan reacted quickly. Stepping forward before the woman had time to regain her balance she punched her on the nose. The woman staggered backwards and, to Jan's horror, stumbled over Robin's unconscious body and fell on him. Robin stirred and groaned. But before Jan could do anything for him she saw that the man with the broken arm was picking up his dropped knife with his good hand. This was a tough breed of people. She dashed over to the fallen woman, scooped up the heavy frying pan and turned in time to meet the man's lunging attack. She deflected the blade with the base of the pan and while the man prepared to get round her guard with a feint to the left before, she was sure, coming in low with a belly thrust, she flung the pan in his face. He was slammed back against a counter, blood streaming from his nose and forehead. She moved in and broke his other arm. Then she leaned against the counter and drew in deep breaths, trying to clear her cloudy vision.

"If this is an example of Minervan hospitality I hope we won't receive the same treatment." A man's voice.

Jan jerked her head up and spun round. The entrance was crowded with people. Jan stiffened. In the foreground was the young man, the Duke's son, whom Jan thought of as the Black Prince. Behind him was his loathsome one-eyed sister. She was staring at Robin. Behind them were five stolid-faced soldiers.

It was the Prince who had spoken. Jan glared at him and said, "They attacked me. They were going to rape me." She attempted to pull the sides of her ripped upper tunic together to cover herself but it was useless. She gave up trying. Let them look.

"Only the men, I trust," said the Prince, dryly. Then he gave an order to his men. "Get rid of this scum."

Four of the soldiers began picking up Jan's fallen attackers and carrying them outside. The fifth soldier remained behind the Prince and Princess, his eyes on Jan. The Princess moved closer to Robin and peered down at him. "He's still alive," she said flatly.

"Only just," snapped Jan. "Stay away from him. You've done enough."

The Princess turned and looked at Jan. "I loved him, you know. More than any other man I'd ever known."

"You have a curious way of displaying your affection," Jan told her bitterly.

"He used me. Pretending to love me. All the time he was laughing at me. He knew he had no intention of staying with me. Or the *Lord Mordred*. He was planning all along to join the Sky Woman, that bitch Jan Dorvin. *Your* former mistress."

Jan said nothing. The Princess moved closer to her, her one eye devouring Jan. "What is he to you, Minervan?"

"I love him."

"And, of course, he told you that he loves you too. I'm sure he sounded very sincere, as he did with me. Was he inside you at the time?" She gave a sharp, bitter laugh. "Girl, I've done you a favour, doing what I did to him."

"Forgive me if I don't thank you."

The Princess slapped her across the face. Though it stung Jan's cheek and caused the dancing lights in her head to flare up again it wasn't a hard blow, more of a gesture than a real blow. "Such insolence is not to be recommended, especially if you harbour hopes of joining us above."

"Above?" asked Jan, for the moment not understanding.

"Our Chief Tech, Lamont has been petitioning on your behalf with father. He wants to set up housekeeping with you. I presume it is with your assent?"

Understanding now, Jan said, "Yes . . . yes, it is. But only when Robin . . . when Robin. . . ."

"Father seems prepared to entertain the idea seriously; he likes Lamont. But my brother and I are not so sure, which is why we came down here tonight. And the demonstration of physical prowess that we just witnessed shows that you are indeed dangerous."

"Don't worry. I promise I won't murder you all in your beds."

"Yes, well, to put it bluntly," said her brother, "we don't trust you. So if father does agree to Lamont's request we warn you that we shall be watching you very closely. If you give us the slightest excuse we will contrive to have you put to death, one way or the other."

"I appreciate the warn—" Jan began, then stopped when she heard Robin groan. She quickly knelt down beside him. His eyes were open. He gazed into her face and she saw recognition in his eyes. She was gratified by this but when his lips began to form the beginning of her name she put her fingers lightly over his mouth. "Shush . . . don't try to talk. Save your strength."

But he kept trying. "J . . . a . . . n. . . ." It was a whisper, and she was sure that neither the Princess nor Prince heard. "Pain . . . so much pain. . . ." His voice was growing a little stronger. "What happened to me?"

"Don't ask," Jan told him with a grim smile.

His eyes widened as the Princess stepped into his field of vision. "Don't you remember what I did to you?" she enquired coldly.

"Stop it," Jan told her.

Robin frowned at the Princess. "Andrea . . . you're here as well? Are we on the . . . *Lord Mordred*?"

"The *Lord Mordred* doesn't exist any more—thanks to *you*!" she hissed at him.

Robin plainly couldn't comprehend what she was talking about. He looked to Jan again. "Jan . . ." he said hoarsely. "The ring . . . where is the ring I gave you?"

She held up her hand so that he could see she was still wearing it. She smiled sadly at him. "I thought for a time it might be more than a ring, but no. I tried it but nothing happened."

Robin, grimacing, reached up for her hand. "Jan . . . the ring . . . give. . . ."

She was abruptly hauled upright. The Prince stared fiercely at her. "He called you *Jan*."

Jan nodded resignedly. She knew they had overheard Robin's mention of her name.

"Jan Dorvin—the Sky Woman herself!" exclaimed Princess Andrea.

"Well, this will please father, though poor Lamont is going to be out of luck," said the Prince. He turned to his men. "Seize her. She's coming with us."

As two of the soldiers roughly took hold of her she cried, "Wait! What about Robin? You can't leave him alone down here. He'll die!"

"I'll cut his throat for you if you wish," said the Prince, drawing his dagger.

She quickly shook her head. "No . . . no. Don't."

232

The Prince smiled and sheathed his dagger. "Yes, let the pig die slowly. Come on."

The Duke looked surprised as they entered the store where he'd set up his base and living quarters. He was reclining on a mound of parachute silk. Nearby something was bubbling in a pot suspended over a small fire. Taking note of Jan's state of undress he raised an eyebrow and said to his son and daughter, "Oh dear. What mischief have you two been up to with her?"

Prince Darcy told his father of her true identity. The Duke then rose from his seat and stared at her with astonishment. "Well, well . . . I had my vague suspicions when I first met you but it seemed so unlikely. I saw the Sky Woman as someone more, well, *regal* I suppose."

"What are you going to do with her?" asked the Princess.

The Duke sighed. "Execute her, of course. Seems a waste though, a beauty like her. And Lamont is going to be very disappointed." He smiled ruefully at Jan. "Did you know I was on the verge of agreeing to his request concerning you? Such a pity."

In a display of fake bravado Jan said crisply, "If you're going to execute me hurry up and get it over with."

"Just *how* are we going to execute her, father?" asked the Prince.

"I think death by beheading would be appropriate, under the circumstances," answered the Duke, tugging on his beard.

"That's too quick," complained the Princess.

"And what do you suggest, my little kitten?" asked the Duke dryly. "Bury her up to her neck in an ants' nest? Impale her on a spit and roast her slowly over an open fire? We're not barbarians, you know. As our legitimate enemy she deserves an honourable death."

"Lucky me," said Jan.

The Princess looked at her and said, "All right, have her beheaded, but I still think she's getting off lightly."

"You have your dear, late mother's same depth of human compassion, my darling," said the Duke. To Jan he then said, "So that's that. It's all very unfortunate, my dear, but I must be bound by our traditions." He glanced at her exposed breasts then said, "If fate hadn't decreed us enemies I would have enjoyed getting to know you better."

"I'm sure you would have," Jan told him.

"Ah, well . . . Take her away and carry out the unfortunate deed. And mind the axe blade is *sharp*."

Jan felt her knees begin to tremble as she was escorted outside. Her brave façade was beginning to crumble. She didn't fancy the idea of having her head chopped off. She didn't fancy the idea of being executed, period, but being beheaded ranked high on her list of experiences she would rather forego. What would it feel like? How long would it take? And worst of all—what if she remained aware, even for a short time, after her head had been detached from her body? She began to feel very sick.

Outside they encountered Lamont, who first appeared very surprised to see her and then looked alarmed. Jan felt a brief surge of hope but then realised he wouldn't be able to help her.

"What's going on?" he demanded, blocking the leading soldier's path.

"Out of the way, sir. We're taking this woman outside to be executed. The Duke's orders."

"*Executed*? But why? I don't understand . . . what's her crime?" cried Lamont.

"Her crime," said the Prince who, with his sister, had followed the party out of the Duke's quarters, "is that the object of your desires is none other than Jan Dorvin, the Sky Woman herself."

Lamont looked stricken. He said to Jan, "Is this true?"

"Guilty. Sorry, Lamont . . . I don't. . . ." She stopped. Shots were being fired outside the building.

There was a long moment before anyone reacted, then the Prince cried, "To the main entrance, fast!" As one, the five soldiers began running up the walkway towards the entrance.

"What's happening?" It was the Duke. He was buckling on his sword belt as he emerged from his quarters. Jan's crossbow was strapped across his back.

"It's an attack, of course," snapped his son. "And by the sound of it, a large one."

"We'd better go and see," said the Duke, reluctantly. He looked at Jan. "What about her?"

"I'll guard her," said Lamont.

"No, *I'll* guard her," said Princess Andrea. She drew her dagger and smiled at Jan.

All his life the only thing that El Rashad feared was Allah. Until now. Now he feared Allah *and* the monster that was pursuing him. The monster that had consumed over two-thirds of his army and was now close behind him, crushing more of his men as they attempted to flee. It was a creature of Satan and it was after *him*, he knew it.

They had clear, flat land at last after the nightmare of struggling uphill through the blight with that thing pursuing them. El Rashad saw several men stationed in front of the structure's entrance; saw puffs of smoke from their rifles, heard bullets fizz past him, heard the bangs . . . and didn't even hesitate for a fraction of a second. More bullets were as nothing compared to that thing chasing them. "Charge!" he screamed at his men.

They needed no such urging, being as terrified as he was. To grapple with human opponents again could be a comfort. . . .

The black-robed warriors moved as a ragged wave over the ancient car park. Several of them fell, hit by bullets, but the wave swept on. The Duke's men started to fall back, still firing. Then, seeing that the situation was hopeless, they turned and ran.

A crude barricade had been erected across the entrance and the Duke's men took cover behind it, joined by reinforcements from inside the building. El Rashad's men, screaming, poured into the entrance tunnel. . . .

Just as the Duke and his son were approaching the entrance at a run they saw what was left of their small force being chased out of the tunnel by black-robed, sword-wielding warriors. Both men came to a halt. "El Rashad's men!" gasped the Duke, sagging inwardly.

"That damn glider that followed us," said the Prince. "It must have got back with the information. . . ."

Then the Duke saw El Rashad himself—the familiar, hawk-nosed profile easily marked him out. At that moment El Rashad turned in his direction and the Duke saw something in El Rashad's face that he had never seen before—stark fear.

El Rashad glanced over his shoulder, then started towards the Duke and his son. Both El Rashad's curving sword and his robes were splattered with blood. The Duke hastily reached for the crossbow; the Prince drew his sword. . . .

"Wait!" cried El Rashad. "Stay your hand! We must cease fighting amongst ourselves—a greater threat is close by. We must unite to fight it!"

"What trickery is this?" murmured the Prince, but the Duke saw the same look of fear on the faces of El Rashad's men as well. "Down your weapons, men of the *Lord Mordred*!" cried the Duke to his surviving men. They obeyed him, looking anxious and puzzled.

"The Hand of Satan is pursuing us!" cried El Rashad pointing at the entrance. "We must destroy it somehow! Build a fire to consume it . . . !"

To the Duke El Rashad looked quite demented, though

he didn't doubt that El Rashad was telling the truth about some dangerous creature being out there. But to call it the Hand of Satan was surely going a bit too far. *Superstitious fool*, he thought. It was probably one of the giant reptiles that Darcy had spotted from the air.

"Calm yourself," he told El Rashad. "We have weapons enough between us to deal with any beast. But your idea of fire is a good one. We will pile up every combustible material we can find in the entrance and perhaps the beast will be turned away by the very sight of the flames. How close behind you is the creature . . . ?"

His question was answered immediately and arrived in the form of one of El Rashad's men being ejected out of the mouth of the entrance with great force. He went sailing over the heads of the other men, screaming as he went, and crashed down on to the walkway. At the same time there was uproar as El Rashad's men tried to put as much distance between themselves and the entrance. The result was a tangle of struggling bodies. From inside the tunnel came the sound of things shattering—the remains of the barrier—and a steady *thud-thud*. The Duke felt the floor shake beneath his feet.

Then, out of the tunnel mouth, *it* emerged. "Jesus Christ," whispered the Duke, "it *is* a hand!" Seized by atavistic terror he turned and ran, dropping the crossbow as he did. Prince Darcy was already ahead of him. El Rashad followed close behind. . . .

It had gone quiet up above, which could mean anything. What Jan hoped it meant was that the attackers, whoever they were, had wiped out the Duke and his men. If so that didn't mean that her prospects of survival in the long-run would be any better, but it did mean she would escape an immediate beheading.

"What's going on up there?" muttered the Princess Andrea to no one in particular. She was standing close

237

behind Jan, the point of her dagger pricking Jan between the ribs.

Standing by the balcony, looking grim, Lamont simply shrugged. He had been silent since the Duke and Prince had gone. Jan continued to play idly with Robin's ring, pushing the stone in and out. She reflected again on Robin's concern for it. He had reached out for it, had clearly wanted it. Why? It didn't do anything. Not for her. . . .

No, not for *her*!

As the thought occurred to her she suddenly tensed, which caused the Princess to dig the point of the dagger into her even harder. "Careful!" she warned Jan, then gave a start herself when the noises of battle from above resumed. Shots, screams . . . then no shooting, just screaming.

Jan frowned. These were not men screaming in pain, these were screams of fear and terror. Then she heard the sounds of running feet on the walkway above. She sensed the Princess's distraction and whirled round. She grabbed her wrist, squeezed hard and was satisfied by both the girl's cry of pain and the sound the dagger made as it hit the floor. Then, as Lamont ran towards them, she flung the Princess at him. Both fell heavily.

Jan began to run. If she was right she had the means for both Robin and her to escape this dreadful place.

Chapter Twenty-Three:

Tyra lay face down on the bed, weeping. Milo stared at her as he pulled on his clothes. He felt a twinge of guilt. He shouldn't have lost his temper . . . shouldn't have been so impatient. It was his damned body's fault, with its pre-puberty sexual urge and no means of achieving a fulfilling release. The sooner he reached puberty the better. Surely it was only weeks away now.

He went out into the corridor and almost tripped over a spider-mech. "You're a disgusting person, Milo," said the mech in Ashley's amused voice, "What you did to that poor girl."

"Spying on me, as usual?" said Milo.

"What else is there to do?"

"Well, you dumped our passengers, not me." He moved swiftly on down the corridor. The mech scuttled after him.

"Where are you going?" asked Ashley.

Milo hesitated before answering. "Up top," he said at last. "Want to take a look at that flying machine again."

"You're always playing with that thing," Ashley said, sulkily. "But it's no good. You'll never get it to work."

"I know . . . I know, but it fascinates me all the same." And I live in hope, he added to himself.

It was warm on top and a hot wind was blowing strongly across the hull, even though Ashley had dropped the speed as requested. Gripping the safety line, Milo headed towards Robin's machine. Alongside lay the useless power cable that the mechs had laid out on Robin's instructions.

"Where are we?" Milo asked the mech that had continued to follow him, much to his annoyance.

"I dunno. I'll ask Carl . . . State of Tehuantepec, he says. Used to be part of Mexico before the break-up, if you're interested."

"Fascinated," he said, looking around. The rest of the fleet was strung out behind the Sky Angel, minus the *Lord Montcalm*. The Ashley controlling it had decided to go off on her own, along with her captive population.

The hatch on the flying machine had been left partly open. A mech controlled by Carl had succeeded in operating the lock but had no success in activating the machine itself. Or so he said, but he suspected Ashley had vetoed Carl from even trying.

Milo climbed into the machine and sat back in the comfortable couch. He gazed wistfully at the dark control panel and the blank screens. He sensed the tremendous power that the machine contained; power that lay dormant and beyond his ability to awaken. With a sigh, he ran his fingers over a row of buttons on the control panel. . . .

"You're wasting your time," said Ashley from the mech which had perched itself in the inner hatchway.

Milo tried to ignore her. He sat there playing with the control panel for over fifteen minutes, hoping he might chance across the correct combination that would activate the machine. But nothing happened.

"Out of the way," he finally told the mech. "I'm coming out."

Reluctantly, he followed the spider-mech out through the double hatch. Somehow he would find a way of bringing the machine to life. But first he would have to outwit Ashley. . . .

He looked dead.

Panting hard, Jan dropped to her knees beside him and placed her fingers against his throat. She felt a pulse and her

240

hopes lifted again. "Poor darling," she told him between gasps for breath. "We may still get out of this." She took his ring from her finger and slipped it on the middle finger of his left hand. Then, with a quick prayer to the Mother God, she pressed in the jewel. And kept it pressed in. This *had* to be the answer. The ring needed to be in direct contact with Robin in order for it to be activated. Maybe it recognised him by reading his genetic code. When Jan had tried it on her own hand it had 'read' her and, not recognising her as Robin, had refused to work. At least, Jan *hoped* that was the case. . . .

He was checking the wires that secured the machine to the outer hull when he became aware of a vibration. Yes, the wire he was touching was humming. *It was the machine!* Something was happening to it! He must have accidentally hit the right combination with the controls after all. He raced back to the hatchway. *Yes!* He could see the glow of the instrument panel through the hatch. As he made to climb in again the mech grabbed him by the back of his shirt and pulled him away.

"Don't get in there!" cried Ashley. "You're not going anywhere!"

He turned sharply, ripping his shirt, and kicked. The mech was heavy but the force of his kick was sufficient to lift it into the air and away from him. "Stupid, crazy bitch! I'm going to blow your hardware to bits!" he screamed. Even before the spider-mech had landed he was turning back to the hatchway. . . .

He was just in time to see the hatch slam shut. "No!" he cried. The humming sound coming from the machine deepened. Then restraining wires began to snap with loud *twangs*. "No!" he cried again. A snapping wire narrowly missed him as the machine rose from the hull. He backed away. The machine was rising faster now. He craned his neck back. "Come back . . ." he cried weakly. At a height above the hull of about two hundred feet it suddenly shot forward at tremendous speed. It was out of sight within thirty seconds.

Milo kept staring at the spot in the sky where the machine had dwindled away to nothingness. He was uncomfortably aware of the silent mech behind him. He thought he could hear Ashley's unspoken words: "You're going to be s-o-r-r-y. . . ."

"How touching . . . saying your last farewell."

Jan looked round. It was the Princess, dishevelled and with her chest heaving from the unusual exertion, for her, of running. She leaned her arm against a pillar for support. She had the dagger again. Lamont appeared behind her, also panting.

The Princess advanced, unsteadily, into the store. She raised the dagger. Jan let go of Robin's hand and stood to face her. Had she pressed the stone for a sufficient time? Perhaps the flying machine was too far away to pick up the signal from the ring. And perhaps she was just deluding herself after all and the ring was nothing but an ordinary ring.

"Princess . . . don't!" cried Lamont, following her into the store.

She turned on him. "My father has condemned her to death and I'm going to see that the sentence is carried out, now. And you're going to help me, or I'll see that you share her fate."

"Help you . . . ?"

"Overpower her. She's too strong for me. Grab her and hold her still while I despatch her."

Lamont looked helplessly at Jan.

"Do it, Lamont! It's a royal command!" cried the Princess.

Jan said calmly, "Lamont, you don't have to be subservient to her or her father any longer. They aren't royalty any more, they're just pathetic refugees like the rest of us. Their world has gone. Even the mini-kingdom they

242

attempted to set up here is over. Look. . . ." Jan pointed across the floor of the great structure. Men were pouring down the walkway. Most of them wore the black robes of El Rashad's men but some of the Duke's men were among them. They were all in the grip of a terrible panic.

Then Jan saw the reason for their panic. At first she thought it was a tremendous spider. . . .

"Mary Mother of God," gasped the Princess.

"It's a human hand," said Lamont, disbelievingly. "But it can't be! It's impossible."

As the hand overtook two running men and crushed them beneath its bulk Jan remembered Milo's tales of what rich men in control of the Gene Corporations, like himself, got up to on their private estates; the monsters they created for their amusement. They had been the source of, among other things, the giant reptiles. She had encountered many man-made horrors in the blight before but nothing as monstrous as this. . . .

Ryn drifted back up into the realm of consciousness again; back into the realm of pain and feverish sickness. He also felt incredibly thirsty. He opened his eyes and tried to speak. Nothing came out. He tried again. "Jan. . . ."

To his relief she appeared beside him, crouching low. He saw, to his surprise, that Andrea was nearby as well. And a man. They were crouching behind a counter. They both looked terrified. There was something about Andrea he was trying not to remember . . . but it came back to him anyway. What had she done to him? He groaned.

"Shhhh," said Jan, warningly, as she laid her cool palm upon his burning forehead. "Be quiet."

"Water . . . need drink . . ." he croaked.

"I'm sorry, darling. We don't have any."

Didn't she understand? He *had* to have water. He was dying of thirst. Dying. Yes, dying. He knew that. Nor did he really want to live, not after what Andrea had done to him. God, it had all gone so wrong, but *how*? He had been about to escape with Jan in the Toy and then . . . and then what? And how had he been going to summon the Toy? The answer was tantalisingly close. Something to do with a ring. He tried to concentrate but it was no use. . . .

He became aware of screams. Someone was screaming somewhere nearby. A man, by the sound of it. What is this place, he wondered? Then it occurred to him that he might be dead already and that this was hell. But no, it couldn't be hell because Jan was here with him. There wouldn't be any kind of comfort in hell. "Jan . . ." he said, and passed out again.

The Duke peered nervously over the top of the low wall. The creature was clearly sniffing the air . . . but with its forefinger. It was definitely seeking out any prey that it had missed. Then it suddenly moved forward and disappeared through a store front about fifty yards away. Screams followed from inside. The Duke glanced at El Rashad, who was crouching behind the wall next to him. El Rashad had his eyes closed and was mumbling the same prayer over and over again. Allah was being mentioned a lot. The Duke had been doing some silent praying of his own. He couldn't see a way out of this situation. They were trapped, and sooner or later the monster, whatever it was, would find them, kill them and later consume their bodies at its leisure.

"It's coming this way," moaned the Princess. Jan held her breath as the creature came to a halt by one of the fountains and turned in their direction, its forefinger raised so that it was pointing straight at them. Jan felt the skin over her spine go suddenly icy. She kept telling herself that the giant hand was nothing but a man-made abomination, but it was producing in her a feeling of profound supernatural dread.

The hand abruptly turned and then began to scuttle off away from them. Jan let her breath go. "I'm not staying here any longer," announced the Princess as the creature disappeared into another store. "I'm going to make a run for the walkway and go back upstairs."

"You'll never make it," Lamont told her. "That thing moves too fast."

But the Princess ignored him. She rose to her feet and went slowly out through the front of the shop; then she began to run. Jan alternated between watching the Princess and the store front which the creature had entered. Then something happened. Something marvellous.

A shadow fell across the floor. Jan looked up. An object was blocking the light from the gash in the ceiling. The object was slowly descending. Jan's heart leapt. It was Robin's flying machine.

Princess Andrea had seen it too. And recognised what it was. She came to a halt, staring upwards.

"The flying machine!" cried Lamont.

The machine turned as it descended then began to head towards them. Jan could now hear a powerful thrumming sound as it approached. She saw that the Princess, seeing where it would be landing, had started back across the floor. Jan also saw the Beast, attracted by the sounds, start to emerge from the store.

"I don't believe it—the traitor's machine, here!" gasped the Duke.

"But what's it doing here," asked his son.

"It's plain, you fool. It's come here for *him*! Come on, we've got to get to it!" The Duke sprang to his feet and ran out of the store. He glanced quickly back and saw that Darcy was following him. El Rashad remained cowering behind the wall.

The Beast came to a hesitant stop, probing the air with the tip of its forefinger. It was clearly confused by the presence, and sound of the flying machine. The Duke felt confident he would reach the machine before the thing could

245

catch him. Besides, Andrea was between him and the
Beast. . . .

The machine touched down gently in front of the store. It
had turned before landing so that the hatch was facing them.
Now it was beginning to open. Jan went to Robin and tried
to lift him by his shoulders. He groaned. With the machine
blocking the store front she had no idea how far away the
Beast was. She was sure it would be coming in their
direction, attracted by the arrival of the craft. She looked
desperately at Lamont. "Please!" she cried.

He came to her aid immediately, taking hold of Ryn's
ankles. Together they carried him towards the machine.

"Ryn? Ryn? Are you all right?" The voice emanated from
inside the machine. A woman's voice. Jan was momentarily
disconcerted by this but responded quickly. "Robin's been
hurt. He's unconscious." They had reached the side of the
machine now. While Lamont held Robin up Jan clambered
into the hatchway. Pushing her head and shoulders through
to the interior she saw that the craft was empty. Another
computer, she realised. She hoped this female-sounding
program proved more reasonable than Ashley.

"Robin needs urgent medical treatment," Jan told the
machine. "You must fly him to his home as fast as you can."

"Of course. Bring him in. His name, incidentally, is not
Robin but *Ryn*."

"Run, Andrea! *Run!*" screamed the Prince.

The Duke looked round. The Beast was closing in on his
daughter. Seeing her danger she abruptly veered sharply.
Good, he thought, now she was no longer running towards
the machine. But now Darcy was veering off as well, yelling
and waving his arm. *Good Lord*, thought the Duke. He was
actually trying to distract the monster away from his sister!
Such a display of self-sacrifice from Darcy, of all people!

246

How little we really know of our children, he mused as he concentrated on putting on more speed.

Kneeling on the couch, Jan pulled Robin in through the hatchway by his shoulders, assisted by Lamont outside. Then, with difficulty, she got Robin in a reclining position on the couch. It was a tight squeeze in the machine's small, one person cabin. Robin was muttering deliriously and she saw that the dressing between his legs was oozing blood. Then she heard a shout from outside. She looked up and saw the Duke's face through the hatchway. He was attempting to climb in but Lamont was holding him back.

"Let go of me, man! I've got to get in there!" cried the Duke.

"But sire, you can't! There's no room!"

"There will be, you fool! As soon as I drag that pair out!"

Jan said quickly, "Close the hatch, machine!"

Coolly, the woman's voice answered, "I will when you've removed your person from my interior. I cannot take you to Shangri La. It is not permitted."

This response didn't come as too much of a surprise to Jan. She realised she had been half expecting it. She looked towards the hatchway. Both the Duke and Lamont were out of sight now. There were sounds of a violent struggle. She sighed. If there was a chance that Robin could be saved she had no choice but to get out. Arguing with the damn computer would only take valuable time from his slim chances of survival. She prepared to pull herself out through the double hatch. . . .

Prince Darcy's screaming and arm-waving finally worked. The Beast halted and Andrea had time to reach the pillar she'd been running towards. If the Beast hadn't stopped it would have killed her by now. It swung round in Darcy's direction, then, apparently decided to attack the nearest prey first, turned again and continued on towards the pillar that Andrea was sheltering behind. Dropping its massive stump of a wrist to the floor it rose up on the heels of its palm. All five fingers came crashing down and the pillar shattered. Darcy heard his sister scream, but then she was drowned out by the sound of falling debris as a section of the balcony above disintegrated. Before a cloud of dust obscured his vision Darcy saw the Beast collapse under several large chunks of ancient masonry. Shouting Andrea's name and drawing his sword, he ran forward into the cloud of dust.

He'd hoped that the masonry had killed the monster, but no, though pinned down it was struggling furiously and would soon free itself. He couldn't see Andrea. He moved closer to the writhing monstrosity. As he did so he discovered it stank horribly. With an effort of will he got close enough to drive his sword into its side behind the little finger—itself the size of a small tree trunk. The blade penetrated only a couple of inches into the thick, grey skin. No, there was no hope of killing it. Calling Andrea's name he began frantically to search among the rubble in front of the Beast. Then he saw her, partially buried in debris.

Sheathing his sword, he pulled at her exposed, dust-covered arm with his one good arm and was rewarded by a moan. He clawed her free of the rubble that covered her, then hauled her upright. "Andrea!" he cried, straining to support her, "wake up! We must get away from here! Andrea . . . !" Behind him he could hear the Beast increasing its effort to free itself. It surely wouldn't be long now.

As Jan was about to clamber out through the outer hatch she hesitated. The Duke and Lamont were locked in a deadly struggle. Lamont lay on his back on the ground, the Duke on top of him, relentlessly driving his dagger down towards Lamont's chest. Lamont's strength was ebbing and Jan knew he would soon die unless she helped him. But just as she was about to jump down she heard a weak cry behind her. "Jan. . . ."

She twisted round and returned to the cabin. Robin was conscious again and, from the expression in his eyes, more lucid than ever before. "Jan . . . you brought the Toy," he said wonderingly.

"If that's what you call this thing, darling, yes, with your help. But I must go. It won't take you to safety until I leave."

"*No* . . ." he cried, and grimaced. He closed his eyes and Jan thought he'd lapsed back into unconsciousness but then he opened them and said firmly, "Toy, can you hear me?"

"Yes, Ryn. We really must get going. We have a long way to travel and, according to my sensors, you're very ill."

"Toy, since I altered your programming you must obey my every command, correct?"

"Yes, Ryn."

"Then I'm ordering you to obey the every command of this woman. Her name is Jan. Register her voice pattern. . . ." He paused. "Jan, say something to Toy."

"Er, hello Toy . . . I'm Jan."

"Name and voice pattern registered," said the computer briskly. "Ryn, they are not going to be pleased if you bring this person back to Shangri La."

Robin didn't answer. Jan saw that this time he had really lapsed back into unconsciousness. "Toy!" she cried as she wriggled all the way into the cabin, "Close the hatches, I command you."

"Whatever you say." The hatches simultaneously slammed shut.

Jan eased Robin as far as possible to one side on the couch and squeezed herself down beside him. It was an uncomfortable fit and she had to rest on her side. "Show me what's happening outside."

The monitor screens flared into brightness. One of them showed the Duke and Lamont. Lamont was lying still on the ground. There was blood on his chest and she was sure he was dead. The Duke was rising to his feet. He turned and, seeing that the hatch was now closed, ran forward, shouting silent words. He loomed in close-up then disappeared out of shot. Jan heard a dim thudding. He was obviously pounding on the hatch with his fists.

"Take us up, Toy, then hover."

Jan scanned the other monitors as the machine rose. She spotted the Beast on one of the monitors. It was following two people across the floor whom she recognised as the Prince and Princess. The former was supporting the latter. One of the Beast's fingers, the middle one, was held stiffly and appeared to be injured, which reduced the creature to a lumbering gait but even so it would soon catch up with the slowly moving couple.

She stared at the screen for a time then said, "Do you have weapons on board?"

"Yes."

"Then please destroy that creature down there."

"Which one? I can see three."

"The biggest of the three."

"Very well."

The nose of the Toy swung round then dipped. Jan felt a slight vibration and saw, on the screen, something hurtle down towards the Beast, leaving a trail of vapour. The Beast shuddered and skidded to a stop. It raised its forefinger questioningly, as if trying to discover where the thing that had struck it had come from. Then it blew to pieces, scattering great chunks of ancient, steaming flesh across the floor of the shopping mall.

The blast had knocked the Prince and Princess off their feet. Without waiting to see if they were unharmed, Jan ordered the Toy to rise up out through the hole in the roof.

She watched the building drop beneath them. What happened now to the Duke, his awful children and the other survivors, she cared nothing at all. To the Toy she said, "Take us to Shangri La."

250

Epilogue:

Milo woke with an unusually foul hangover. His head throbbed and there was a strange taste in his mouth. He was puzzled. He hadn't drunk much wine the previous night. Groaning, he reached for Tyra. At least she would keep his mind off his discomfort for a time.

His hand couldn't find her. He opened his sleep-encrusted eyes and saw that she wasn't in the bed. He sat up, annoyed. There was no sign of her. She knew she had to ask his permission to leave the room. "Tyra! Where are you?" he called. He would have to discipline her again—a thought that immediately cheered him.

He got out of bed and stood there holding his head while waiting for the alarming thudding to subside. "Tyra!" he called again, angrily. No answer. He went to the bathroom and threw the door open. Empty. So was the kitchen and sitting room. The bitch had dared to leave the suite! He would flay the skin from her bottom for this!

He marched towards the main door—and stopped. His mouth dropped open with his astonishment. The normal door—made, he guessed, of some lightweight plastic—was gone. In its place was a door made of metal. It had no handle.

Milo went to it and pushed. It didn't move, and felt very solid.

"Ashley!" he cried. "What the hell is going on here?"

Ashley didn't speak. He kept yelling her name, and Carl's, but there was no response. Then he began kicking at the metal door and beating on it with his fists.

He was taken by surprise when a slot suddenly opened in the door. The benign face of the Minervan man, Shan, smiled down on him through the slot. He was one of the few people allowed to remain on board the Sky Angel. "That won't do any good," he told Milo. "She's not going to let you out."

"What are you talking about? What's going on?" Milo demanded.

"You're being punished," said Shan. "Ashley doesn't like you any more. Not after you threatened to destroy her. You are to remain in here. I will be your only contact. She has had removed all audio and visual links from your suite. You are cut off from her and Carl. I will bring you food when the supplies in your kitchen run out."

Oh God, thought Milo. He should have expected something like this. But at least she hadn't killed him, or had him dumped on the ground. God, that stupid, crazy, electronic cow! She must have had Shan drug his wine last night and had the door replaced while he was unconscious. "Where's the girl?" asked Milo. "Where's Tyra? Can't I least have her in here for company?"

Shan shook his head. "Ashley has taken her from you and put her in my care. You have treated her very badly. It will take a long time for her to heal."

Milo stared at him in speechless fury. *His* woman being given to this placid Minervan wimp! How like Ashley to do this to him!

He fought to keep control of his temper. No use in making things even worse. As calmly as he could he said, "All right, so how long will this foolish business last? When am I going to be let out of here?"

"Never," said Shan and closed the slot.